ROMANCE ME, VISCOUNT

A Very Fine Muddle
Book One

Kate Archer

© Copyright 2023 by Kate Archer
Text by Kate Archer
Cover by Dar Albert

Dragonblade Publishing, Inc. is an imprint of Kathryn Le Veque Novels, Inc.
P.O. Box 23
Moreno Valley, CA 92556
ceo@dragonbladepublishing.com

Produced in the United States of America

First Edition June 2023
Print Edition

Reproduction of any kind except where it pertains to short quotes in relation to advertising or promotion is strictly prohibited.

All Rights Reserved.

The characters and events portrayed in this book are fictitious. Any similarity to real persons, living or dead, is purely coincidental and not intended by the author.

ARE YOU SIGNED UP FOR DRAGONBLADE'S BLOG?

You'll get the latest news and information on exclusive giveaways, exclusive excerpts, coming releases, sales, free books, cover reveals and more.

Check out our complete list of authors, too!

No spam, no junk. That's a promise!

Sign Up Here

www.dragonbladepublishing.com

Dearest Reader;

Thank you for your support of a small press. At Dragonblade Publishing, we strive to bring you the highest quality Historical Romance from some of the best authors in the business. Without your support, there is no 'us', so we sincerely hope you adore these stories and find some new favorite authors along the way.

Happy Reading!

CEO, Dragonblade Publishing

Additional Dragonblade books by Author Kate Archer

A Very Fine Muddle
Romance Me, Viscount (Book 1)

A Series of Worthy Young Ladies
The Meddler (Book 1)
The Sprinter (Book 2)
The Undaunted (Book 3)
The Champion (Book 4)
The Jilter (Book 5)
The Regal (Book 6)

The Dukes' Pact Series
The Viscount's Sinful Bargain (Book 1)
The Marquess' Daring Wager (Book 2)
The Lord's Desperate Pledge (Book 3)
The Baron's Dangerous Contract (Book 4)
The Peer's Roguish Word (Book 5)
The Earl's Iron Warrant (Book 6)

PROLOGUE

1802, in the vicinity of Taunton, Somerset

LADY MARGARET BENNINGTON, Countess of Westmont, had done her duty by producing an heir for her earl. The succeeding years, though, had brought a string of daughters in alarming rapidity, ending in the fifth who had ungraciously sent her mother to the great beyond. After the countess had departed the world, the natural question arose as to who would guide those five now motherless girls.

Governesses and tutors were all well and good, but there must be a gentlewoman, a blood relative or a new wife, to step in and act as mama.

Young ladies required more than manners drilled into them, or facts about history and literature crammed into their heads. Ladies must master more than the ability to bang out notes on the pianoforte or embroider one more pillow cover nobody knew what to do with.

A well-bred lady developed correct instincts that could be employed in any situation only by being brought up by a gentlewoman of the same station.

Had there been only one or two of those offspring requiring such a mentoring figure, there had been several relatives who might have stepped forward. Had there only been one or two, the earl might have convinced some lady to wed him. But *five* of them needing mothering?

Really, that was too much for anybody.

Anybody, that was, except Miss Eloise Mayton, third cousin, or perhaps fourth or fifth cousin, to the Earl of Westmont.

Miss Mayton had, at that precise moment in her history, found herself at loose ends, fading youth, and dwindling finances in Rome. Upon receipt of the earl's rather plaintive letter, Miss Mayton drank her last glass of Orvieto, ate her last maritozzo, waved ciao to her acquaintances, and decamped to the earl's estate in Somerset.

Ever since that time, she'd guided the earl's five daughters with her rather unsteady and fanciful hand. Though nobody was absolutely certain what sort of cousin she was, or for that matter what precisely she'd been doing on the continent for all those years, her five charges had settled comfortably into calling her Aunt.

Now, that whimsical creature was poised to guide the launch of the eldest daughter, Lady Beatrice. Trunks were packed, letters sent flying, and final preparations made—they were to depart for London on the morrow.

Chapter One

Beatrice surveyed her array of boxes and trunks and searched through drawers and under the bed for anything that might have been left behind during the packing.

Miss Mayton, a short and stout lady with a fondness for cakes, was not so bothered by the idea. She sat comfortably by the window with a cup of tea and a biscuit.

"Do not fret, Bea, if there is anything needed, we will purchase it in Town. I have already informed your father that we will be shopping as if it is our career. He shall not have a farthing to his name when we are through."

"I suppose he took that as well as could be expected," Beatrice said, laughing.

Her aunt delighted in telling her father that this or that thing would bring him to his knees, and then later pointing out that her excellent management had avoided the disaster.

"Our dear earl, he does not ruffle easily and so he took it quite stoically," Miss Mayton said complacently.

Beatrice's door flew open and a line of sisters rushed through it. Rosalind led the way, followed by Viola, Cordelia, and Juliet.

"Beatrice," Rosalind said, "you will just die to know it—"

"Terribly die," Viola confirmed.

"Instantly die," Cordelia added.

"If you do not die, you will be very put out!" Juliet, the youngest, said of her own assessment of the situation.

As Beatrice did not yet know what she must either die of or be put out to know, she said, "Well?"

"Father has been opportuned by, well, you will likely guess who," Rosalind said. "We heard it when we were passing by the library's door. Where we had stopped quite coincidentally. Our poor papa collapsed like a house of cards."

"We could not have avoided overhearing the exchange, naturally," Cordelia confirmed. "I do not believe those doors are as thick as they ought to be."

"Dinner," Viola said.

"Dinner tonight," Juliet said, to better confirm the time period in question.

"Is it Van Doren?" Beatrice asked. She could not imagine who else would invite themselves to dinner.

"Yes, *again*," Cordelia said.

Beatrice was not at all surprised. Matthew Lawson, known to the wider world as Viscount Van Doren, was their closest neighbor. They had known him all their lives and he spent a deal of time going back and forth between Faversham Hall and the Westmont estate.

He was her senior by two years and had been a rather irritating boy, requiring he be called Van Doren rather than Matthew by the time he was twelve years old. Now, he had grown to an exceedingly handsome gentleman with a very manly air about him—tall, dark-haired, and with a very strong and determined chin. His dark eyes were marvelous, too.

However, while his once chubby cheeks and his habits of pulling hair and hiding dolls may have long fled, he remained extremely irritating.

If Van Doren held an opinion, it must be recognized to be correct. He would take great pains to explain how that opinion was arrived at and how it was grounded in the practicalities and realities of life.

Practicalities and realities were his obsession, but where was the drama? The pathos? The hearts breaking to pieces or bursting with joy? Where were the dizzying highs and tragic lows of a passion-filled existence?

No, none of that was for Van Doren, which might have been all well and good had he not been determined to press his pedestrian ideas on everybody else.

He had drawn in her father, in particular, with these dull notions. Beatrice should have gone to Town two years since, but Van Doren had convinced the earl that she needed *time to mature*.

As if she had any intention of becoming a stick like him! She was irate about the delay, as were her sisters. Beatrice had just turned eighteen and could have been married by now, Rosalind too at seventeen, and then Viola was sixteen and ought to be coming out soon.

The only two sisters who were not trailing behind on time were Cordelia at fifteen and Juliet at thirteen. They would end behind though, as the earl thought bringing out more than one daughter at a time was not a good idea.

What if she did not marry this season and must come for another? At the rate they were going, one of them would be thirty by the time it was their turn.

Beatrice had grown tired of Van Doren's interference and endless instructions. Worse, his tedious sermons and meetings with her father had only increased in frequency as their departure for London approached.

"You are in for a dinner-scolding, Bea," Viola said, "though who knows what about this time."

"Indeed, *this* time," Rosalind said.

"He does have such a lot to say for himself," Juliet said.

"Such a lot," Cordelia said, nodding.

Miss Mayton clucked sympathetically and said, "Poor Lord Van

Doren, it is as if he came into the world with no heart at all. All facts and figures, which is a sad way to go on."

Cordelia, a natural actress, marched back and forth across the bedroom, rubbing her chin and looking serious. "Now, Beatrice, I cannot stress enough the rigors of a London dining table. Only the smallest sips of wine must be taken. The dinner will go on long and nobody wishes to see a lady stagger at the end of it. I only give you that hint."

Viola filled the room with peals of laughter. "Oh, that was last Wednesday's lecture we called 'Beatrice, do not get drunk!' Very well done, Cordy."

"I've a mind to get drunk this evening, just to point out to Lord I-know-everything that his advice washes over me like water off a duck's back," Beatrice said.

"I would encourage you to do it," Rosalind said, "but then you'd likely be sick in the carriage on the morrow."

"Oh, don't be sick, Bea," Juliet said. "Papa would be made unhappy, I'm sure."

Beatrice had really hoped it would just be the family to dine this evening. It was a momentous occasion. She was the eldest and would lead the way into London. She would be the first to float into ballrooms and find romance.

They were to set off first thing in the morning and of course she would not be so foolish as to over-indulge this evening just to make a point. It was only that she always did feel driven to make a point to Van Doren. There was so much to speculate on and dream of without the viscount frowning from every corner.

She was aware that he would go to Town too, and that he'd rented a house on their very street! Of all London, why did he need to put himself at Portland Place?

Her father viewed it a terrific idea. The earl claimed Van Doren would prove invaluable in squiring them around Town.

Beatrice did not see why he was needed. Her brother Darden lived permanently in their house on Portland Place and would know far more people than their scolding neighbor. She only hoped Van Doren was not planning to make himself a nuisance.

"Aunt," Viola said, "we will be subjected to Van Doren's dour ideas about romance this evening. Again."

"You mean, lack of *any* ideas about romance," Rosalind said.

"Oh, yes," Cordelia said, nodding vigorously. "Romance might tap him on the shoulder and announce itself and he'd say, *Who did that? I see nothing.*"

"Pathetic," Juliet murmured.

"Aunt, it does feel like a moment to hear of Count Tulerstein again," Viola said. "That would give us reinforcements in our hearts so we may stoically stand up against Van Doren's tiresome rants."

Though they had heard the story many times, the girls all nodded in agreement. Every so often a new detail regarding one of Miss Mayton's tragic European love affairs emerged, though they could never be certain when that delicious circumstance might occur.

Their dear aunt had been dreadfully loved by so many interesting gentlemen, but they had all been doomed in one way or another.

The sisters settled themselves comfortably, ranging themselves across Beatrice's bed.

"Poor dear Hans," Miss Mayton said, sitting her ample frame in a nearby chair. "It was a case of instant love, you see. I was attending a reception at the palace in Stockholm in a rather fetching gown of blue silk. Hans understood his heart was no longer his own the moment he clapped eyes on me. I ought not to have been surprised by it—instant love is terribly common if the love is true."

Beatrice nodded. She was rather counting on it being the case. She had resolved that in London she would look about her and wait to be instantly struck by her one true love. Once identified, all she need do was wait for him to prove his love by feats of passion and daring.

"From *my* side," Miss Mayton went on, "I liked Hans well enough. But did I really wish to live in a luxurious castle and have so many servants that they were always underfoot and so many dresses that I could not keep track of them all?"

"You did not have the true love in your heart for Hans, to be able to put up with it," Juliet said gravely.

"Just so," Miss Mayton said, nodding. "And, well, you know how it ended."

"But you must tell it," Viola said. "Describing it makes it more tragically romantic."

"Very well," Miss Mayton said, looking very encouraged. "After the reception, we were walking in a high meadow of the Alps for a picnic. It was quite beautiful—snowcapped mountains in the distance and cliffs that dropped hundreds of feet into rocky ravines."

Miss Mayton had a faraway look in her eyes, as if remembering the grandeur of the setting.

"As I was admiring the scenery and trying to stop Hans from holding my hand, he suddenly flung himself to the ground and begged me to become his wife. He did not kneel, you understand, but was prone on the wildflowers to better make his point of abject love."

"Flat-out prone," Viola said softly.

"Well, I had to regretfully decline because of the so many servants and the too many dresses and all the wealth and now the attempt at handholding. I only wish I had known…"

"What did he do next?" Cordelia asked, her voice no louder than a whisper.

Of course, they were all well aware of what Hans had done next. Still, it was always thrilling to hear it told.

"Hans was, naturally, entirely undone. That was to be expected. When a gentleman realizes that he is not to have his one and only true heart's desire, it cannot be stood up against. And so, he raced to the side of a cliff and threw himself to his death, crying, "My heart will live forever in these mountains—my dearest Eloise, I am eternally yours."

The girls all sighed in perfect satisfaction. Of all their aunt's many romantic interludes, poor Hans' tragic death was one of their favorites.

"Right over the edge in his dark green coat," Miss Mayton said wistfully.

"That is a new memory!" Cordelia said excitedly. "We did not know it was a *green* coat."

"Oh yes, I can see it in my mind's eye," Miss Mayton said. "The last I saw of him were his green coat flaps going over the side."

The sisters spent some few minutes considering the green coat flaps of Hans' final adieu.

Viola rolled off the bed and said, "Now we can go to dinner fortified with romance in our hearts. Good luck to Van Doren to get it out of us."

Yes, indeed, Beatrice thought. Good luck to Van Doren.

MATTHEW LAWSON, VISCOUNT Van Doren, rode down the wide and winding path that led through the oak wood dividing Faversham Hall and the Westmont estate. He had made the ride so often that he knew every tree and patch of wildflowers.

He did not see any of it at the moment. His thoughts were far too taken up with what was ahead of him in the coming months.

Matthew had successfully delayed Beatrice's come out for two seasons by making various arguments of sense to the earl. But that was all the success he'd had.

He'd been certain that time would bring with it some modicum of rationality. Surely Beatrice must see that her childish and rather fanciful notions must be put aside.

She was to engage herself in the business of life, and she was no more prepared than a newborn foal.

He laid the blame squarely on Miss Mayton's shoulders. And perhaps the earl's too, as he was far too indulgent of all five of his daughters' wild flights of fancy. And maybe Darden bore part of the blame as well. Their elder brother, the viscount, spent all his time in Town, when he ought to have been at home, straightening out his sisters.

The last time Darden had been home for one of his rare visits, Matthew had even broached the subject. Darden had laughed and said, "Bea *said* you were turning yourself into a stick."

Was he the only rational person in the vicinity?

What on earth would go on in London? It was one thing for Beatrice to advertise her bizarre ideas in what was a small, tight-knit, and rather forgiving neighborhood.

It was one thing for her to pronounce Mr. Wilton lacking in proper sentiment for failing to dive into a frigid pond to retrieve her handkerchief, though Matthew was all but certain she'd deliberately thrown it in.

It might be laughed off when Beatrice and her sisters all announced that they would never accept a proposal from a gentleman unless he was positively prone on the ground while he asked. Apparently, Hans from Sweden had done so before throwing himself off the side of a mountain.

It might be somewhat understandable that the sisters believed Miss Mayton's various lunacies over him and his superior judgement. The lady had, after all, acted as their mother, however ill-judged that idea had been in the first place.

But how many times must he inquire how Miss Mayton and Hans managed to get to an Alpine meadow when they had just been in the palace in Stockholm? If Hans was really a count and did a violence to himself, was there not an inquiry? And most of all, there was no such thing as instant love!

Beatrice could not carry on with such antics in Town. The *ton* would make short work of her if she went round telling the story of Hans, or Gregorio the Italian count, or Phillipe the French poet, or the mysterious duke from Transylvania. Or the plethora of other alleged dead loves from Miss Mayton's past, all of which he was certain were invented.

Why Miss Mayton made up all those stories, he could not be sure. He speculated that she'd been so disappointed by failing to marry that it had somehow dysregulated her mind.

As for why the earl put up with it, that he *really* could not fathom. Lord Westmont was only amused by it and did not seem to comprehend the danger of it.

Society's eligible gentlemen would not be interested in attempting to reach Beatrice's unattainable heights. They certainly would not be interested in throwing themselves off the side of an Alpine meadow or stabbing themselves or any of the other ways Miss Mayton's phantom lotharios had supposedly departed the world.

Oh, naturally, no end of fellows would be drawn to Beatrice. How could they not? She came with a sizable dowry and suitable background. And, if some gentleman were to hold looks above all else, he would not be disappointed there either.

Her hair was amber, the color of autumn honey, her pert little nose charming, and her eyes…those so very dark blue eyes. From afar, her eyes might almost be taken for brown, but when one approached closer one could see the depth of blue like the bottom of the ocean.

The entire situation filled him with irritation. And also, a certain type of dread. Men would flock to her, and then she would talk. She would tell them of her "requirements." It was then that he was very sure that Beatrice would receive a painful dose of reality.

For all her foibles, he did not wish to see her hurt.

As he did not see how it was to be avoided, he would do what he could to steer her right and then attempt to soften the blow when it came.

If there were anything to hope for, it was that Beatrice would quickly correct her notions and that her experience would serve as a clanging bell of sense to her younger sisters.

Beatrice's father, the Earl of Westmont, was the sort of gentleman she thought of as perennially content. Very little ruffled him one way or the other. His temperament could not have been more different than that of his daughters' own, who all felt things terribly deeply.

Of course, Beatrice presumed that the earl had at one time been helpless against violent feelings of love. It was hard to imagine, but it was even harder to imagine that her parents' love for one another had not been one for the ages.

That period of his life, though, was long over. Now, he was content to have the world do what it wished with him and he did not become discomposed unless the house was on fire. As it had only been on fire twice, he was very little out of sorts.

Now, the earl contentedly surveyed his family at table. And their interloping neighbor.

Van Doren was looking particularly well put together this evening. If he would not speak, or scold as he was wont to do, he might be very attractive.

Beatrice had sometimes looked at him as if he were a stranger and admitted that had he been somebody she passed on the road she would find him exceedingly interesting.

When she'd been younger and had not yet developed the sense to resent being scolded all day long, she had been quite bowled over by him.

Those days were long over and, alas, if there were one thing she had not the slightest hope for, it was that Van Doren would give up his scolding.

"Well, Bea, the moment has come," her father said. "You are to be introduced to society and we will see what sort of young gentleman you end up dragging into my library to say his piece."

"Papa," Beatrice said in an affectionate scolding tone she often used with him, "a gentleman I would have to drag in is not a gentleman I would accept."

"Naturally, she won't," Rosalind said. "We have had thorough discussions regarding what will be required from the successful suitor."

"Thorough," Viola confirmed.

"He must have the courage of Beowulf," Rosalind said.

"The strength of Hercules and derring-do of Robin Hood," Cordelia said.

"As gallant as Sir Gawain, with the depth of feelings of Shakespeare," Beatrice added.

"And Beatrice," Miss Mayton put in, "you were quite set on the gentleman having the stalwart heart of Henry the Fifth."

"This is ridiculous," Van Doren muttered.

The five girls round the table glared at him. Juliet said, "He must be all of that, *sir*, and he must be violently in love, tearing his hair out, and challenging other suitors to a duel. He might even threaten to do a violence to himself."

"I am a lord, not a sir, as you are aware, Juliet," Van Doren said. "As for this list of requirements, I would be interested to see the fellow who has torn all his hair out and is both attempting to kill another suitor and attempting to kill himself. Where is this bald lunatic?"

"I must point out," Beatrice said, "I would prefer only *threats* to do a violence to himself. I do not wish for anyone to be hurt. I am not unreasonable. I have said so several times."

"You are entirely unreasonable. If such a man exists," Van Doren said, "he *ought* to do a violence to himself."

"Come now, Van Doren," the earl said goodhumoredly, "allow

the girls to have their whimsies. Youth is a fleeting thing, after all, and should be enjoyed to the fullest before the dry practicalities of life creep in."

Beatrice watched, satisfied, as Van Doren put his attention on his beef. The only person in the room that he did not dare lecture was the earl.

"Though, Papa," Beatrice said, "my requirements cannot be considered a whimsy. If I am to accept a gentleman and be his lady forevermore, I must have requirements. It would be foolish not to have thought deeply on it."

"Yes, certainly, no harm in that," the earl said. "Though, I think you'll meet some young buck and then throw all your requirements out a window."

"Do you mean to say," Beatrice said slowly, "I could be struck by true love against my will? Against my very requirements?"

"Something like that, yes," the earl said.

Beatrice turned to Miss Mayton. "Can that happen?" she asked. "Could I fall in love against my will?"

"Oh, yes," Miss Mayton said confidently. "After all, I do not suppose that Hans preferred to leap to his death from unrequited love. He must have been against it all along."

"There is no Hans!" Van Doren practically shouted, gripping his fork as if he'd stab himself with it.

"Not anymore, sadly," Miss Mayton said, with the little sniff she often employed to signal to the viscount that she did not give a toss for his opinions.

"Again, I ask," Van Doren said, "how did you get from the palace in Stockholm to an Alpine meadow so fast? Assuming you got there on a flying carpet, as I do not know how else it could be accomplished, you were a single lady. Was there no chaperone? Did his family not wonder where he'd gone? Did you not seek help in case he was only injured? Did this tragic death never get reported in the newspapers?

And how did he manage to say so much as he was plummeting down a mountainside?"

"He wore a green coat, by the by," Juliet said.

"For the love of—"

"Poor Lord Van Doren…no heart at all," Miss Mayton murmured.

"I will caution you, Beatrice," the viscount said, "no gentleman of sense will tolerate these outrageous ideas. I only give you that hint."

Another of Van Doren's freely distributed hints. By gentleman of sense, Beatrice presumed he meant his own dull and dusty way of going about things.

"That is welcome news," she said, "as I would have no use for a gentleman of sense."

That had not been expressed precisely what she meant, but Beatrice was certain Van Doren understood her meaning.

The earl laughed, rich and deep. "Do not fret over that, Bea, so few young gentlemen are overburdened with sense. Van Doren is quite the outlier in that area."

And so the dinner went on as it always did when Van Doren was at table. He'd brought a proverbial bucket of water, determined to drown all their happy ideas.

He would not do it, though. They would set off for Town on the morrow and then he would see that there was no end of gallant gentlemen with romance in their hearts, willing to scale the heights of Beatrice Bennington's affections.

She must only be sure not to fall in love against her will.

Chapter Two

Matthew was atop his horse, going at a walk through the dark wood, the only lights coming from either end of the path. As he moved forward, they dimmed behind him from Westmont House and became brighter from Faversham Hall ahead.

If the trees had been interested in his feelings at that moment, or cared how he'd fared at dinner, they would have been quite distressed.

"Beowulf? Robinhood? As gallant as Sir Gawain?" he said, fuming at the night. "And then, the earl just laughed it all off, as if it were only an amusing bit of nonsense!"

That was the root of the problem. There was nobody to check those girls.

Falling in love against one's will? What did that mean? It was absurd.

When one wished to consider asking a lady the momentous question, one would carefully examine the lady's attributes and how they might complement one's own. Was there suitability on both sides? Was the lady temperate? Was she equipped to run a smooth household and preside over a table as a gracious hostess?

Only after careful consideration of these serious questions and so many more could one go forward with such a step. As for love, well, that would be expected to grow over time. Or if not love, then a friendship would take root if the couple was suited.

That was the reality of life, not Hans, the invention of Miss Mayton's bizarre imagination. Would he never be able to convince Beatrice that Hans-the-dead-Swedish-count had never existed? That *none* of those doomed lotharios had ever existed?

"I'd like to throw Hans over a cliff myself. This situation is intolerable," he said.

The oaks did not answer his threat against Hans, and so he went on. "We are all headed for disaster, and yet I am the only one that can see it."

As he assured himself that he viewed the situation clear-eyed, while the entire family, including the earl, did not…a niggling idea began itching to be looked at.

What if Beatrice were to find some close approximation to the hero of her imagination? Not that one actually existed, he was sure of that, but might not a gentleman pretend at it?

Beatrice's grandmother had amassed a fortune and passed it on to the girls. Her dowry was such, twenty thousand, he believed, that it might inspire a gentleman to deploy such a ruse.

That would be a far more serious disaster than Beatrice merely receiving her comeuppance and finding her ideas so far removed from reality.

She might wed such a man, and then discover later that she never knew him at all. She would be devastated and would have likely found herself in an unhappy marriage.

Who would be there to counsel against it? Miss Mayton would be just as taken in by such flummery, as would Beatrice's four sisters. The earl already expected a fool for a son-in-law, so he was not likely to intervene.

It must be him. He must interfere. None of them appreciated the care he took of them or how much he inconvenienced himself. It was an entirely thankless job, but he understood his duty as a friend to the house.

That rogue, that playactor, whoever he may turn out to be, must be stopped.

THE EARL'S BUTLER stretched his legs under the table and heard the familiar creak in his right knee. The final evening in Westmont House had been a long one. Finally, Lord Van Doren had been got on his way home and the family had retired.

Tattleton sat at the head of the servants' table and presided over their traditional biscuits and ale before sending the staff off to their own beds. He was of the opinion that a large glass of ale was helpful in encouraging sleep, and they would certainly all need it for the coming days.

Many of the servants had been sent off to ready the London house, led by the intrepid Mrs. Huffson. There was no telling what sort of discombobulation Lord Darden was living in. That young gentleman and his valet would camp in a tent and not notice the lack of comforts. The house must be put in order and readied to receive the earl.

Just now, he surveyed those staff who would travel with the family. Brown, the earl's valet. The lady's maids—Fleur, Maggie, and Lynette. Mr. James, the cook, and two of the footmen, Benny and Johnny.

"Miss Mayton says that Lord Van Doren was his usual wet rag at the dining table," Fleur said. "The viscount seems to despise Hans, though nobody can understand why. The poor count is dead at the foot of an Alpine mountain—adieu, bon monsieur."

"Adieu," Benny said in a rather scathing tone. "Everybody knows *you* would have married Hans if it had been *you* wandering round that Alpine meadow."

Benny said it in his usual irritated manner. Tattleton did not suppose Benny liked the dead count any better than Lord Van Doren did. He seemed to take umbrage with Fleur's admiration of the fellow.

Of course, Benny also took umbrage with Fleur throwing French phrases around, as everybody knew she'd been born in Pucklechurch, christened Flora, and there was not a drop of French blood in her. Rather, when she'd begun working for Miss Mayton, she'd learned some of the language from her mistress and suddenly insisted on being called Fleur.

Tattleton was just as irritated by it, though he never said so. As a butler, if he is to be of any use at all, he must carefully choose his battles. Flora/Fleur could rename herself Flambé next, with no complaint from him.

"And what if I would have married Hans?" Fleur asked defiantly. "I suppose I could have made Hans very happy. Had he lived."

"He *never* lived," Johnny said. "That's the real point. You won't get me to believe that some fellow flung himself off the side of a mountain for love of Miss Mayton. Not unless he was only trying to get away from her."

"She was younger, then," Fleur said. "She says she was quite beautiful."

"I bet she does," Johnny said with a snort.

Tattleton suppressed the urge to sigh—to sigh loudly. He agreed with Johnny that Hans had never lived. Nor had all the other unfortunate gentlemen who'd allegedly met bad ends simply by running into Miss Mayton in some foreign locale.

He had wondered for years why the lady went on with such stories. At first, when the earl's daughters had been very young, it had seemed to give them some comfort. Who could deny them comfort when they'd lost their mother? If they wished to believe in fairy tales, grim as they always seemed to end, then what harm done?

But Miss Mayton had kept on with it. Her stories had become something the young ladies measured the world by.

Tattleton had been certain they'd all grow out of it and quite naturally leave such nonsense behind.

He had been hoping Miss Mayton, herself, would grow out of it, as that lady must be forty by now. He had several times attempted to address her as *Mrs.* Mayton, as a sign of respect for her age, but she would have none of it.

He was certain she was secretly hopeful that she would meet some gentleman who would fall madly in love with her and, unlike all the dead gentlemen of her imagination, somehow stay alive.

That had not happened so far, and he had his doubts that it ever would. What *had* happened, though, was her young charges had developed an unwavering belief in a magical world of gentlemen as compelling as Greek gods. Those unrealistic ideas seemed very much cemented.

Where would it lead them? He had the rather uncomfortable feeling that Lady Beatrice was on the precipice of a grave disappointment.

―――

BEATRICE SURVEYED THE chaos on the drive as trunks were loaded. The lady's maids fluttered this way and that, scolding Benny and Johnny about this hatbox and that trunk, while Tattleton chased them away so the footmen could get on with it.

Were a gentleman traveling alone to change horses often, he might make the trip from Somerset to London in two days' time. Nobody in the Bennington household was so delusional as to imagine they could move one earl, one matron, five daughters, and the various servants accompanying them with such speed.

They were to attempt a more reasonable three days, stopping at The Lamb at Hindon, and then again at The Angel at Basingstoke. From there, they would proceed to Portland Place and discover what their brother, Viscount Darden, had been up to these many months.

A sudden clatter sought her attention. Beatrice turned and saw Van Doren cantering up the drive.

He reined in his horse. "Beatrice," he said, bowing as well as one could bow from a saddle.

"Van Doren," she said. "What do you do here?"

"I am to accompany you to Town. Did not your father say?"

Cordelia ran down the steps. "Van Doren. What do you do here?"

"I am here to—"

"Lord Van Doren. What do you do here?" Miss Mayton asked, coming out the door.

Rosalind was on the heels of Miss Mayton. She looked back over her shoulder and called into the house. "Juliet, you will just die to know it. Van Doren has turned up."

"Why?" came the faraway voice of their youngest sister.

"I am here because your father requested that I accompany this caravan of lunatics to London," Van Doren said through gritted teeth.

Rosalind shrugged and said, "It is no matter, Bea. He cannot scold us if we are in a carriage and he is on horseback. We will shut the windows if he tries it from atop his horse."

"I am only here to assist your father and your coachman in the event of a mishap. A broken wheel, or an encounter with any unsavory sorts."

"Well," Cordelia said, "if we are set upon by unsavory sorts, I hope you give them a rousing lecture that ends with *I only give you that hint.*"

"I presume those individuals would be better prepared to take my well-considered hints than any of you," Van Doren said.

Beatrice rolled her eyes, mostly because Van Doren could not abide it and had several times pronounced it coarse, unladylike, and suited to a fishwife.

While Van Doren was being questioned as to why he was there, Tattleton had somehow got all the trunks packed away in the luggage carriage, but for the jewelry cases that would travel with the earl.

Last evening, after Van Doren had finally taken himself off, they had agreed on how the carriages were to be arranged to everybody's satisfaction.

The five sisters and Miss Mayton were to ride together. It was to be a squeeze, but they'd rather that than be separated. There would be hours and hours of interesting conversation to be had and one never knew when their aunt would recall some new detail of one of her romantic interludes. Only yesterday, they'd discovered that Hans had been wearing a green coat.

Now that Beatrice was poised to step into her own romantic interlude, it was more important than ever to glean whatever bits of wisdom they could from their aunt's experiences.

The earl was perfectly amenable to the arrangements and would take a carriage for himself, Brown, and Tattleton. Her father was a very great reader of all sorts of literature and while some might have become sick from reading in a swaying carriage, it did not affect him at all. In his youth, he'd set off on a grand tour of the continent and had even read a book while crossing in choppy seas.

Tattleton could be counted on not to chatter, as their butler always seemed to have much on his mind. Brown was always silently brooding about the laundry or when the ironing would be done, and so would also not be a hindrance to the earl.

The lady's maids would travel in another carriage, Cook and the footmen in another, with Mr. James keeping a stern eye on those youthful fellows.

The whole thing would be capped off with a luggage carriage. As the earl only owned two carriages and employed one coachman, three carriages and four coachmen had to be hired to accomplish the moving of household.

It was to be quite the caravan.

And now, trailing behind them all, came Van Doren.

Beatrice had hoped he was not planning to make a nuisance of himself in Town, but she began to think he probably would. Why else would he insist on this ridiculous plan? Unsavory sorts, indeed. It was not as if they were setting off at midnight and risked highwaymen. In any case, they had five coachmen at their disposal, all well-armed.

Van Doren must have gone to some trouble to arrange it. He only brought panniers on his horse and had no doubt sent his other things ahead. He did not even have his valet with him.

It was silly, she thought. If he'd had sense, he would have set off on his own, in his own carriage. Or if he were determined to ride, he might have been in London in two days, rather than three.

That was Van Doren all over, though. He was certain he knew the correct way to proceed in every situation but, to Beatrice's mind, he was just as often wrong as right.

The earl came out of the house and surveyed the drive, nodding to Van Doren. "Well, I believe we might as well get this thing going."

Beatrice turned from Van Doren and scrambled into the carriage, taking her rightful place in a forward-facing window seat. Miss Mayton had the other.

It should have been Rosalind and Viola in the backward-facing window seats but Viola got sick traveling backward, so she was squeezed in the middle of the forward, while Juliet was sandwiched between Rosalind and Cordelia on the other side.

The doors were shut and the horses moved forward.

The moment had finally arrived. Beatrice Bennington was on her way to Town.

⇶⇷

MATTHEW SOMETIMES WONDERED if the earl were only absentminded, or whether he took some amusement in forgetting to relay some critical detail. He'd come to escort the Bennington caravan, at great inconvenience to himself, because the earl had asked him to.

Apparently, Lord Westmont had not seen fit to apprise anybody else of that fact.

The family's departure from the house was as eccentric as he'd thought it would be. All five sisters and Miss Mayton crammed into one carriage, the earl going with his butler and valet, the lady's maids tittering as they no doubt would the entire trip, and the footmen already with a pack of cards out while the cook stared at them grimly.

They'd not been a quarter mile down the road before Juliet was hanging out a carriage window and calling to her father that they must all go back. She'd forgotten her book.

"Van Doren," the earl said from his own carriage window, "you are the only one of us on horseback. Do go back and fetch it. Juliet will not rest easy if she does not have her book. The steward will still be in the library and can show you in."

Juliet blew a kiss to her papa, for his understanding of the importance of the matter.

Matthew nodded reluctantly, as he did not see how he was to refuse. "What is the book and where did you leave it?" he asked Juliet.

"It is my book of poetry and it is on my dressing table," Juliet replied. "Do not go snooping into my things!"

"I do not give a toss for your *things*. What is the name of the book?" Matthew asked. "I'd like to be sure of retrieving the correct one so that we do not have to repeat this adventure."

"There is no name, it is *my* book. My own book of poems I have composed."

"It is your commonplace book, then?"

"I suppose you might call it that, if you are determined. Though, as everybody including you knows full well, there is nothing at all commonplace about my poetry."

Matthew turned his horse and set off, rather than stay and argue the point. Though if he had wished, he certainly could have argued the point. Naming Juliet's poems *commonplace* would be the sort of high praise they had not come close to earning. Every single one of them that he'd been forced to hear had been dreadful.

He supposed he must only be grateful that they'd not got halfway to London before her book was remembered.

The steward, a hearty fellow named Lewis, let him in, looking rather surprised to see him back so fast.

"Lady Juliet has forgotten her commonplace book, which apparently she cannot live without," he said, by way of explanation.

Lewis, having served the family for above twenty years, nodded in sympathy.

"She says she left it on her dressing table," Matthew said. "Can you escort me there?"

Lewis glanced at the stairs. "Up there?" he asked. "I've only been up there the two times the house was on fire. To bring up more sand buckets, you see. I do not know which lady sleeps in which room, nor do I want to know. If I had ever an occasion to know, I have forgotten!"

Matthew was confounded. The earl might have told him where to go. Juliet might have told him where to go. But instead, they'd left it to poor Lewis who'd only twice brought up sand buckets and if he ever knew anything about it, he'd forced himself to forget.

"Very well," he said. "It is on her dressing table, at least so she says. Come up with me and we'll have a look."

Lewis shook his head violently. "You'll only see me up there when there's a fire, Lord Van Doren."

Matthew sighed. It was to be the usual Bennington family shambles. There was nothing for it, he dared not come back emptyhanded lest Juliet weep, then her sisters weep, and then the whole caravan would be turned round as the earl could not bear to see his daughters weeping.

He jogged up the stairs and began searching rooms. The earl's bedchamber was obvious enough, as it was the largest and very clearly a man's room, full of dark wood.

The rest of them were all in shades of pastel. He well knew when he'd stepped into Beatrice's room. For months last year, she'd waxed on about which design of paper-hanging she would choose, finally settling on a chinoiserie of pale blue dominated by pink peonies.

He did not know what sort of picture her descriptions had created in his mind, but the reality of it was jarring. For one thing, she'd not mentioned all the birds perched on branches or just how many oversized peonies were involved. It was rather like one had fallen into a giant garden of improbable flora.

Matthew could not imagine how she slept surrounded by such riotous images.

His eyes drifted toward the bed. There was something alarming about viewing where Beatrice laid her head.

He slowly backed out of the room.

Finally, he entered a bedchamber and saw an open book on a dressing table. He'd not been in every single room and, as the book was open, he thought he'd better at least glance at it to confirm it was Juliet's book of poetry.

Ode to the Orb
Wonderous orb, you did not forsake me
Instead you return to gently wake me.
Be of good cheer life-giving circle
That you are yellow and not tragically purple.

"This must be it," he muttered. "Heaven forbid we leave behind the ode to the wonderous yellow orb circle, otherwise known as the sun."

BEATRICE HAD WATCHED with interest when Van Doren was informed of the missing book of poetry. Those sorts of oversights drove him positively mad.

Whenever they all went on a picnic together, something was invariably forgotten. Van Doren would be sent for it, and then he would arrive back with mustard or rolls in hand and deliver his strongly worded lecture they'd long ago titled, *The Value of Making a List.*

Van Doren ought to have just thanked the stars that Juliet had discovered the oversight as early in the journey as she had. She was a poetess and could hardly be expected to proceed without her book of poems.

Though, Beatrice did not like the idea of Van Doren creeping round above stairs. And now that she thought about it, would Lewis be able to show him the way?

"Oh dear," she said, "I am wondering if Lewis knows where your bedchamber is, Juliet."

This gave all the ladies pause. Rosalind said, "You are right, Bea. I do not believe Lewis has ever been above stairs, save for the two times the house was on fire."

"Lewis will at least know my room," Cordelia said. "As that is where the sand buckets were going. Both times."

The girls all nodded. Cordelia had twice set her curtains afire, from twice setting a stage to act as Desdemona. The candles on the windowsill were meant to be the footlights, as she had already burned holes in her carpet from placing them there. Her acting was far too energetic to allow for candles at her feet.

Ever since the two fires in as many weeks, she'd been relegated to acting out her plays in the drawing room under close supervision.

They were quiet for some time, all reflecting on the two nights the house had been on fire.

Finally, their aunt put their minds at ease when she said, "The new curtains that replaced the ones that went up in that unfortunate fireball are so pretty, though."

They then moved on to other subjects, mainly having to do with the gowns and dresses that had been made for Beatrice's come out.

The sisters could not keep their minds on clothes indefinitely, however. Not while Van Doren was creeping round their rooms doing who knew what.

"I suppose he'll be wandering here and there, looking in doorways," Rosalind said.

"I hope he does not go snooping," Juliet said. "It would be just like Van Doren to snoop around."

Beatrice hoped he did no snooping, too. There was something uncomfortable about imagining Van Doren standing in her bedchamber and looking at her things.

But on the other hand, she *might* be interested to hear how bowled over he was to see the paper-hangings she'd specially chosen. The peonies were the height of grace and taste and had taken months to decide on.

"If he does snoop," Miss Mayton said, "it would only be to gather evidence against us to use in some later lecture. He cannot do it, though, without revealing he snooped. Let us see if he dares mention my rather extensive collection of romantic novels."

"He'd never dare," Juliet said.

"I do not suppose he would," Miss Mayton said contentedly.

"Aunt, you did bring some of those books with you?" Rosalind asked. "One wonders what we'll be able to scrape up in the Portland Place library. I expect it will be all old and dusty volumes. Darden would not have added to it, as he is not particularly a reader."

"Of course I brought some of my novels, my dear. This evening, when we are all snug after dinner, I will read to you from *The Terrible Goings-On of Montclair Castle*. I have already read it, several times, and I can assure you the goings-on are both terrible and romantic. A one-eyed duke is in love with gentle Marianna the governess, after losing both his wife and his eye in a terrible carriage accident. But how could she love him when he's only got the one eye?"

With that thrilling question hanging in the air, Beatrice heard the clip-clop of a horse. Van Doren was back and she crossed fingers that he had Juliet's book.

He appeared by the carriage window with the precious notebook and handed it to Juliet.

She took it and clutched it to her heart. "You did not go snooping, I hope," she said by way of thanks.

Van Doren looked just as irritated as Beatrice would imagine he would be.

"Very gracious, Juliet," he said. He turned his horse and said, "Let us be off before anybody remembers a forgotten ribbon."

CHAPTER THREE

MATTHEW SHIFTED IN his saddle. The sun was setting by the time they reached the outskirts of Hindon. He was beginning to wonder why he'd been so determined to ride, rather than go in his own carriage. He was also beginning to wonder how comfortable walking would be when he arose on the morrow.

Of course, when he'd made the decision to ride, he had been thinking of how it would be had he been traveling on his own, not with this menagerie of eccentrics.

How many times had they ground to a halt at Juliet's insistence to regard some interesting view? Her, hanging out the window and scribbling down various odes to farmhouses and cows. Beatrice, scolding him when he mentioned they'd better proceed on.

A poetess required inspiration, he was told. He'd held his tongue, though he would have really liked to point out that an ode to a wondrous orb circle that was not tragically purple could hardly be considered inspired.

Every time they stopped to change horses it could not be done speedily. No, of course not, because Cordelia would suggest tea, and then Rosalind would comment that if they would have tea they might as well have a plate of ham and rolls.

And then, Viola had somehow turned herself into the slowest eater in England. Matthew would stare at her to hint that she ought to speed up. She would stare back as she chewed one tiny bite at a time. How could one slice of ham take so long?

At any given posthouse, Beatrice was not interested in food, but only on the impression she might be making. She wished the door to their private dining room left open and placed herself in view of the doorway so she might be admired by passing gentlemen. This, of course, was only done so she might act shocked and demand the door be closed when she *was* admired.

How many times was a poor servant told, "Do leave the door open, we require air," only to be told minutes later, "Do shut that door, if you please. I despise impertinent gentlemen who peer in at me!"

And what did the earl think of all these ridiculous maneuvers? Did he go mad with frustration? Did he stamp his foot in a temper?

No, somehow he did not. He seemed to find the whole thing amusing.

Blessedly, The Lamb, with its comforting sturdy stone walls and clay roof tiles, came into view. Day one of this three-day adventure was finally stumbling to a close.

Or maybe he was being too optimistic in imagining they would actually arrive in London in a matter of three days. If this day was anything to go by, they might be traveling for the rest of their lives.

If Dante still lived, Matthew would fire off a letter to him noting that he forgot to mention the *tenth* circle of hell—the road from Taunton to London.

<hr />

BEATRICE LOOKED ROUND the tidy room in The Lamb that she would share with Rosalind and Viola. Three narrow beds lined up in a row, a dresser for their things, and a view of a charming garden.

On one side of the room, there was a connecting door to the room housing her aunt, Cordelia, and Juliet. On the other, a door led to the bedchamber housing their maids. It could not be more perfect.

The entire day had been perfect. What fun they'd had! They had stopped several times along the way to admire a particularly charming vista. Juliet had even been so inspired that she'd written three more odes.

The changing of horses had been no less engaging, as there were all sorts of people coming and going. All sorts of people Beatrice had never seen before, and who had not seen *her* before either.

It was very interesting to note what effect she might have on a gentleman stranger.

"Just think, Bea," Viola said, as Lynette fussed with Beatrice's hair, "your true love is out there somewhere. Now that we have left our own neighborhood, he might be anywhere at all. He might be walking into this very inn at this very moment, neither of you having any idea that you are about to be struck at the sight of one another."

"I know it," Beatrice said. "I kept my eyes open all day long in case he were to appear. A number of gentlemen in the posthouses tried to catch my eye, but I was not struck by any of them."

"Oh, do wait to be struck until we get to Town, Bea," Rosalind said. "I shouldn't like you to engage yourself before you've even been to a ball."

"That is true, of course," Beatrice said.

Before she could devise a practical way of meeting her true love and getting engaged while in Hindon, but still going on to London and balls, her aunt came through the connecting door, followed by Juliet and Cordelia.

"I am just finishing, Miss Mayton," Lynette said, adding a final pin to Beatrice's hair.

"Then we are ready to descend for dinner," Miss Mayton said.

"I do hope it is not ham," Cordelia said. "I have been eating ham all day long."

"I ate mine very slowly," Viola said, "to see if I could drive Van

Doren mad."

"Goodness, *that's* what you were doing," Miss Mayton said. "You should have said, my dear. I would have joined you in it."

"Let's all eat ham very slowly all day tomorrow and see what happens," Juliet said.

With that genial plan agreed on, the sisters made their way downstairs.

※

AFTER MAKING ARRANGEMENTS for the horses, Matthew had drunk a very large glass of ale. This had gone some way to softening his opinions of the day that had just transpired. After all, had he really expected anything else? Was it not his own fault that he had somehow deluded himself into imagining a straightforward and organized journey?

He should have known what he was getting himself into. The Benningtons would do nothing less than weave, double back, and hiccup their way to Town.

Now that he was perfectly aware that dawn would bring a new day that would go just as badly as this day had, he was a deal more sanguine.

They had all settled themselves to a dinner of roasted beef, potatoes, string beans, rolls, and salads. The food was very good, the claret perfectly acceptable and he found himself cheered by it. A good dinner always did restore him.

"What say you, Van Doren," the earl said from his place at the head of the table, "shall we have as pleasant a time on the morrow as we did today?"

There were times when Matthew really could not tell if the earl were serious or joking. "I imagine it will be similar," he said vaguely.

"I am glad I thought to bring several books with me," Lord Westmont said, "as I have nearly finished the one I was reading today. It is really very enjoyable to read a book in a carriage, I dozed off several times."

Matthew supposed it *would* be comfortable in a carriage, though he would not for the world admit it aloud.

"The ham at the posthouses was very good," Viola said, staring at him.

Matthew did not answer, though he certainly did notice that she'd dispatched her roasted beef a lot faster than she did any of the ham she'd eaten that day.

Two servants came in to clear the table and bring in a bottle of port and a tea service. Had they been at home, this would be the moment the ladies would retire to the drawing room to have their tea while Matthew and the earl would have some desultory conversation about their respective estates.

As there was no drawing room to retire to, the earl had said they would all stay together and entertain themselves as best they might.

Beatrice poured the tea and the earl poured the port. Lord Westmont said, "Juliet, I believe you mentioned you had composed an ode during our travels?"

"Several odes, Papa," Juliet said, taking up the precious book that had been in her lap.

"Do enrich us with your delightful phrasings, my dear," Miss Mayton said.

Juliet stood and opened her book. "I will read to you the one I consider the most inspired. It's called *Ode to the Bovine*."

Fine of form and gentle lowing
Round dark eyes full of knowing
I am a stranger that passes you by
Stay free good cow and do not die!

At the conclusion, Matthew watched Juliet's eyes drift toward her rather massacred plate of beef as a servant carried it out. He supposed she was not opposed to *some* cows dying.

There was enthusiastic clapping round the table and Juliet curtsied.

"Excellent, my girl," the earl said, "very original. Now, I believe Miss Mayton has said she will be so good as to read to us from her latest favored novel."

"Indeed I will," Miss Mayton said. "It is called *The Terrible Goings-On of Montclair Castle*. It is written by Richard Roydon, though I am certain that is a nom de plume. There is a woman's touch in the writing that cannot be ignored."

"Set the scene for us, Aunt," Cordelia said, "just as you did in the carriage."

"Very well," Miss Mayton said. "A one-eyed duke widower has fallen madly in love with Marianna, the gentle governess who is raising his children. *But*, can this lovely lady fall in love with a one-eyed man?"

Miss Mayton sat back looking very satisfied.

"That's it?" Matthew asked. "There must be more to the story. Is there a villain? Or an irate father? A haunting? A rival suitor? A plotting housekeeper? Something?"

Miss Mayton sniffed and said, "I am sorry that a duke who saw one of his own eyes roll across the road after a carriage accident does not seem to have a big enough problem for you, Lord Van Doren."

"Never mind," Matthew said, knowing it was futile to argue with Miss Mayton as he'd soon enough be arguing with the entire table who would leap to her defense over any and all matters. He downed his port. "By all means, proceed with this masterpiece."

Miss Mayton did proceed, and so proceeded one of the longest hours of his life. While the five sisters ranged round the table were held rapt by the tale, he could make nothing of it. In truth, he was surprised the earl allowed such drivel into the house, as it did not help to correct his daughters' outlandish notions about romance.

Beatrice, in particular, seemed deeply affected by the one-eyed duke. Did she not comprehend that she would never look upon a real man of flesh and blood in such a manner?

She was looking very charming just now, a curl escaped from her pins and falling on her forehead.

Miss Mayton ended the excruciating evening by reading:

Gentle Marianna laid her ear against the door. The duke raged within!

"How can gentle Marianna the governess truly love a one-eyed wretch like me!" His Grace cried.

Gentle Marianna the governess finally understood that the duke was desperately in love with her. Her mind raced with the question—could she love a one-eyed man?

There was only one way to find out, she must have a look under that patch.

Surrounded by feminine sighs, Matthew rose. "I am going to bed."

⊱⊰

BEATRICE HURRIED DOWN the stairs with Rosalind and Viola on her heels. By some miracle, they'd been up and dressed before dawn. Last evening, Van Doren had pointed out that they'd just made it to the inn as the sun was setting. It would be dangerous to lead such a caravan down dark and lonely roads.

He'd also mentioned that the hired coachmen were all threatening to quit and go home.

Beatrice had to privately admit all of that was true. It had been such great fun the day before, stopping where they liked and taking their time. They all wished to go on in the same manner, but none of them cared to take their chances with nighttime travel.

Or revisit the irate stares of the hired coachmen as the sun set lower and lower in the sky.

Therefore, the caravan must set off at dawn.

They had a hurried breakfast and were all got into their respective carriages with only a short delay as Juliet ran back inside to retrieve her book of poems from the dining room.

Even Van Doren seemed in relatively good spirits, though Beatrice was certain he walked with a slight limp.

That was what happened, she supposed, when a gentleman insisted on being on his horse all day. If he were crawling by the time they got to London he would have nobody to blame but himself.

Just before they set off, there had been an interesting-looking gentleman coming out of the inn, accompanied by his valet. He tipped his hat to Beatrice, but Van Doren steered his horse between them before she could decide how she would respond.

Beatrice certainly hoped he did not plan on any of those sorts of games in Town. If he got between her and her one true love, she'd knock him off his horse to get him out of the way.

The day that unfolded was thrilling, as every mile they traversed brought Beatrice closer to Portland Place.

It was also amusing, as when they stopped to change horses near noon, they all ordered ham and ate it as slowly as possible. Van Doren was left gripping his fork and Beatrice thought he was considering stabbing somebody with it. Later in the day, they did it again, but he just stayed in the yard and paced.

The Angel at Basingstoke was reached as the sun made its last appearance on the horizon. They might have arrived some hours before, but on top of the slow ham-eating, Viola had insisted on a salad, which she ate one leaf at a time to further enrage Van Doren.

Then, of course, Juliet was often struck by a vista.

As this was their second night at an inn, they proceeded to arrange themselves like veteran travelers and it was only a matter of an hour before they came down for dinner.

They had imagined that they would be led into a private dining room very similar to what The Lamb's had been. Instead, they found the innkeeper in distress, attempting to explain some matter to the earl.

"You see, my lord, it was a mistake. Somehow, the room was reserved twice, to two different parties."

Apparently, they were one of the parties, and the other party stood near the inn's front door and consisted of three ladies and one gentleman. The gentleman, a rather stern-looking figure, did not look amused by the mistake.

The innkeeper lowered his voice to whisper. "In any other case, I would say you must have the room, as you outrank Mr. Bigg-Wither, but he has an estate a few miles off and he is such a determined fellow!"

The man wrung his hands. His eyes darted this way and that.

"But tell me," the earl said, not appearing himself overwrought by the situation, "could we all of us together be fit in there? There are only four of them, after all."

"Yes! Yes, you could! I hadn't thought… You are all grace and generosity, my lord! One moment, if it please you," the innkeeper said, hurrying over to Mr. Bigg-Wither.

Beatrice watched Mr. Bigg-Wither hear the news while her father said, "That poor fellow will have an apoplectic fit if he does not calm down. It is only dinner, after all, and they appear to be respectable people."

Though the earl was perfectly sanguine, Mr. Bigg-Wither nodded in the affirmative but did not seem terribly enthusiastic upon hearing the solution.

The innkeeper led the other party to the earl. "Allow me the introductions," the man said, sweat running down his brow. "Mr. Bigg-Wither, Miss Bigg, Miss Catherine Bigg, and Miss Jane Austen, this is the Earl of Westmont and…and…"

The innkeeper had trailed off and Beatrice was certain he could not recall so many names.

The earl kindly stepped in. "The Ladies Beatrice, Rosalind, Viola, Cordelia, and Juliet. And this excellent lady is Miss Mayton. Ah, here comes Lord Van Doren."

Van Doren was, naturally, quite lost, though he executed an elegant bow to the strangers.

"These fine people are to join us for dinner, Van Doren," the earl said. "There was a slight mishap over reservations, but it's all been cleared up. Mr. Bigg-Wither, Miss Bigg, Miss Catherine Bigg, and Miss Austen."

"Glad to make your acquaintance, sir. Ladies, charmed," Van Doren said.

Beatrice eyed him. Charmed? Since when had Van Doren ever been charmed? There was something different in his tone with these strangers, and what was he doing now? He was smiling at Miss Austen. Why?

The innkeeper, who looked rather sick though his problem had been resolved, rushed toward the dining room door. "This way, gentlemen and ladies, if you please."

⸻

MATTHEW HAD, AT first, thought it deuced inconvenient that they were to be thrown together with another party. That had not lasted long, however.

While Mr. Bigg-Wither was a rather gruff sort of person, he seemed a man of good sense. Miss Bigg, Miss Catherine, and Miss Austen were very pleasant dining companions. It seemed Miss Austen was the sisters' particular friend and visited them, since they lived local to the area.

He would not be surprised if there were some thought of an engagement between the gentleman and Miss Austen in the works, though that might be a shame. Miss Austen was gracious and quick-witted, far more so than Mr. Bigg-Wither. It did not bode well for a lady to so decidedly outrun her husband's capacities.

If there had been anything unpleasant, it was to note how uncomfortably the Benningtons were shown in comparison to these three refined ladies.

Matthew realized that he'd got rather used to how eccentric they all were, though he'd also got used to continually pointing it out.

Now, a new realization came over him—it was something else altogether to regard the expressions of strangers and observe the family through their eyes, and the view was far worse.

It was likely the sort of reactions they could expect in Town.

Just now, Miss Mayton was relaying the story of poor, doomed Gregorio. As Miss Austen looked on in horrified fascination, Matthew had a great wish to whisper across the table. *Do not be concerned for Gregorio, he will die as they all do, and he is entirely an invention of her deranged mind.*

"And so you see," Miss Mayton said, "I accused him of being too proud but in the end I realized it was just my own prejudice."

"Do tell us the *very* end, though," Rosalind said.

"Goodness. There's more," Miss Austen said softly.

Sadly, there *is* more, Miss Austen, Matthew thought. So unfortunately much more.

"Well, if you must hear it," Miss Mayton said, appearing pleased. "Once I understood what a fool I'd been, I raced to his house. If only I had got there a minute or two sooner, we would even now be wed happily. As it was, I found Gregorio in the library, having just applied a deadly blow to himself with a sword."

Miss Mayton sighed contentedly.

Miss Austen laid down her fork, her eyebrows knitting together. Miss Bigg and Miss Catherine stared wide-eyed at one another.

Mr. Bigg-Wither said, "Why? What rational person stabs themselves?"

"That is just it, Mr. Bigg-Wither," Miss Mayton said, "there is nothing rational about true love. Once Gregorio became convinced that he could never have me, he could not go on."

"But he did not die right away, is that not so?" Viola asked.

"Oh no, he lingered on for at least a half hour, all the while professing his love for me. I stayed by his side and held his hand throughout."

"A half hour? Why didn't you go get help?" Mr. Bigg-Wither asked.

Yes, Matthew thought, the question of the hour. Why did not Miss Mayton ever make any attempts to save all her dead lotharios? As he knew them all to be fiction springing out of her unsteady mind, he must suppose she found something interesting about dead gentlemen.

Conveniently, Miss Mayton ignored that very practical question. Rather, she spent the next half hour regaling her confounded audience with various bits of nonsense Gregorio had allegedly murmured through his death rattles. *Having known you for one hour was worth a lifetime and I do not regret having met you and departing the world early* being perhaps the most preposterous.

"Well now," the earl said, "let us move the conversation on as there is nothing more to be done for Gregorio *now*."

The waiters had come in to clear the table and bring in dessert. Matthew would very much like a glass of port, but it somehow seemed wrong while these newly met ladies were at table. He settled for tea, though the presence of just introduced company did not stop Mr. Bigg-Wither or the earl from indulging.

"I know what you will ask, Papa," Juliet said suddenly.

"Do you? Have you taken to reading my mind now?" he asked goodhumoredly.

"You will wish that I recite one of my odes, to entertain during the dessert course."

"I hadn't thought of it, but you are very welcome if you wish, my dear."

Matthew suppressed a groan. Must they display every single one of their foibles to strangers?

Juliet stood and cleared her throat. "I composed this very nearby where we sit this evening, having viewed a very stirring vista. It is called *Ode to a Farmer's Fence*."

Sturdy wood, painted fence
Passed by not a moment's hence
It keeps you in or keeps me out
That is the thing I wonder about.

Upon speaking of her wonderment over a fence, Juliet got a faraway look in her eyes, as if she were remembering that remarkable encounter.

Matthew winced. He'd like to corral them all behind a fence just now. That piece of drivel was even worse than the ode to cows of last evening.

Juliet's sisters clapped with enthusiasm and it was apparent that Miss Bigg, Miss Catherine, and Miss Austen only took up the applause after they'd seemed to note that it was expected.

Miss Austen's lip trembled and Matthew was certain she was attempting to hold back her laughter.

Mr. Bigg-Wither stared as if he'd just heard something in a foreign language that he did not speak. Finally, he said, "It's about a fence, then?"

"Very elegantly put together, Juliet," Miss Mayton said. "Now, Miss Bigg, Miss Catherine, and Miss Austen, if you are prepared to linger an hour, I am going to read to everybody. We are just now hearing of the one-eyed duke who is in love with his gentle governess, but we do not yet know if she can love a one-eyed man."

Mr. Bigg-Wither said, "I really do not think—"

"Oh, let's do," Miss Austen said with a rather amused smile.

Matthew gripped his teacup. He motioned for the waiter to bring him a glass of port. Protocol be damned, it would be well to dull his senses just now.

The next hour found Matthew grateful for the glass of port, and the second one he drank. Apparently, the gentle governess was trying all sorts of gambits to see underneath the duke's eye patch and assess what she would be dealing with.

Did the fellow not notice when she tripped over an ottoman and grabbed at it? Was it not apparent when she tried to hook it with a fishing pole and ended up hooking his cheek instead?

He was considering a third glass of port when Mr. Bigg-Wither put an end to the evening by saying, "They both sound like idiots."

Chapter Four

BEATRICE SETTLED HERSELF in the carriage. This was the day. This was the moment her whole life had been leading to. When she laid her head down *this* night, it would be in London.

They waited to set off as Juliet had just run back into the inn to retrieve her notebook from wherever she'd left it. Van Doren had called out, "Ode to Who Is Surprised? Written by Lady Forgetfulness."

Beatrice had to admit it was rather amusing.

"Miss Bigg, Miss Catherine, and Miss Austen were so admiring of all of you," Miss Mayton said.

"I did offer to take up a correspondence with them," Beatrice said, "but unfortunately the Miss Biggs are shortly to travel to the Americas where they expect to live for several years and then Miss Austen recalled she is also to travel to America. She could not be certain when, but perhaps as soon as next week. They all seemed very cast down that our acquaintance must be so fleeting."

"I did note it, of course," Miss Mayton said, nodding. "They were very dejected over it. Especially when you offered to write them in America, but alas they do not know where they are to be settled in that vast land."

"I thought they must be going to Boston," Viola said, "but they all seemed certain that could not be it."

"To soothe their disappointment," Miss Mayton said, "I wrote out *The Terrible Goings-on of Montclair Castle* by Richard Roydon so they might purchase their own copies to read on the ship. And, of course, I could not help but notice how admiring they were of Juliet's ode so I copied that out too."

Beatrice rather thought it had been Van Doren who'd been the one doing the admiring last evening. He'd seemed to take great pains to see that Miss Austen, in particular, had everything she required.

Perhaps all her worry that Van Doren would make himself a nuisance in Town had been unnecessary. Perhaps he would be distracted from harassing her by other ladies who took his attention.

Of course, that must be right. He was of an age to marry and as he did everything that he deemed sensible, he was likely planning on looking for a wife.

And oh, what a paragon she must be! All seriousness and facts and figures, ready to take on the duties of the mistress of Faversham Hall.

Yet, Miss Austen had not been all seriousness. Beatrice had several times heard her say some bon mot that everybody had found witty.

Why had Van Doren thought *that* something to admire? He did not once ask the lady how she was at accounts or how she viewed managing a large staff or any of the other tedious matters he pestered Beatrice with.

"Beatrice," Viola said, as Juliet climbed back into the carriage with book in hand, "you are rather quiet this morning. Are you thinking about where your one true love is at this moment?"

"I was thinking, actually, that Van Doren paid much attention last evening to Miss Austen. That makes me think he comes to Town to find a wife."

"Van Doren married," Cordelia said softly. "It is rather hard to imagine."

"Somebody must marry him," Rosalind said. "He is a lord, after all. I am certain some lady will take him on…if she has no other choices."

"Poor lady," Juliet said. "Just think of it, lectured from morning 'til night for the rest of your life."

"She will have her work cut out for her," Miss Mayton said. "Or perhaps he will find a deaf lady who shouldn't mind at all."

"Or at least hard of hearing," Rosalind said. "That might work out very well. He is not terrible to look at, he is only terrible to listen to."

The carriage began to move. Van Doren urged his horse forward.

As he passed by their carriage, Juliet took that moment to lean out the window and shout at him, "Ode to a Scolder, written by Viscount Scoldy-Breeches."

And so, on that pleasant note, they were on their way.

※※※

MATTHEW WOULD BE very grateful for this journey to come to an end. His legs and other unmentioned regions were aching. He thought it very lucky that the Benningtons had not been charged with discovering the new world. It would have taken them years just to make it to an English coast.

They had been only an hour on the road when one of the earl's carriage horses had thrown a shoe. Everybody thought it very convenient that there was an inn nearby where they might seek out a farrier.

The earl, Mr. Tattleton, and Brown were speedily transferred into the carriage that carried Cook, while the two footmen were chased out of it to walk behind.

They were just now bringing the whole caravan into the inn yard and Cordelia was already calling out her window to the earl to get his opinion on ordering a plate of ham.

Matthew assumed if Viola and her tiny mouthfuls were to decide to partake, they would have time to have *all* the horses re-shod.

Just then, a lone horseman clattered into the yard. Matthew turned to see what sort of idiot came in so fast with no care for the dust he sent up.

He quietly groaned. It was as if the fates were all rubbing their hands together and thinking up new ideas to vex him.

It was Mr. Cahill, a friend of Darden's. On one of Darden's infrequent visits to Somerset, he'd brought the fellow along.

He was the type of gentleman Matthew did not care for—all fluff and no substance. The sort who took great pains with his neckcloth, but probably little care of his estate. Mr. Cahill fancied himself a wit and the visit had been full of jokes which Matthew had thought fell rather flat, but the ladies had found hilarious. The fellow played at being gallant, though his gallantry was flimsy at best.

What rational man would jump into the pond to retrieve Beatrice's handkerchief, even if it *was* August and blazing hot? Everybody had seen perfectly well that she'd purposefully thrown it in.

But no, he must go after it, and to do so bare-chested, leaving his coat and shirt behind! Matthew had been forced to cover Beatrice's eyes.

"Van Doren?" Cahill asked, appearing puzzled to see him there. Then, his puzzlement cleared, as he spotted first the earl, and then the carriageful of ladies the footmen were just now helping to the ground.

"Lord Westmont! Ladies, how wonderful to see you here," he called to the various carriages. "Darden told me that you were coming, though he did not say what day. I believe he said you would leave on the fifteenth and arrive either on the eighteenth or sometime next year."

"That scoundrel," the earl said, laughing as he descended to the ground. "We've lost a shoe and so stopped here. How do you do, Mr. Cahill."

"You are well met, my lord. What a happy accident! I am just come from seeing my mother and I change my horse here."

"I suggest we all go in and rest ourselves while the work is done," the earl said.

"We are going to order a plate of ham, Mr. Cahill," Beatrice said, "you must join us."

"I certainly could not resist an invitation for ham with five elegant ladies," Mr. Cahill said, bowing from his saddle.

Matthew pressed his lips together. Of all the nonsense...

He dismounted and led the way into the inn. There, he found an innkeeper delighted to hear that one of their horses had thrown a shoe.

The farrier would be sent for, but Matthew had no hopes of the thing being done speedily. Such had been the innkeeper's happiness to see them that he presumed that fellow would wish to give the party ample time to eat and drink as much as possible.

London was beginning to feel like a far-off dream. They were like Sisyphus, forever striving but never arriving.

"Van Doren," Mr. Cahill said, as they were being led into one of the private dining rooms, "Darden did not say you were escorting this charming caravan."

"The earl requested it," he answered, thinking Cahill would view it a deal less charming if he'd been a part of it these last two days.

"I doubt I mentioned Van Doren would be with us in my last letter," the earl said. "It seemed rather a given, of course he must come with us."

"Oh yes," Beatrice said, "Van Doren always seems to be about."

Matthew glared at her. It was rather rich that Beatrice sounded as if *she* were the one inconvenienced.

They had seated themselves round the table while two young men rolled in a cart laden with a tea service and cakes and biscuits.

"And we shall want a plate of ham, too," Cordelia said to them.

She'd said it as if she were a queen ordering about a page. Matthew supposed she was pretending to be Desdemona again. It was an odd obsession that had nearly burnt the house down twice.

At the mention of ham, Viola stared at Matthew as if she thought he might challenge the ordering of it. Which he would very much like to do.

Miss Mayton did the honors with the tea and soon enough everyone was supplied with what they wished for. And the inevitable slices of ham.

"It is a fine thing, Mr. Cahill," the earl said, "that you visit your mother. You ought to pass along the habit to my rascally son, as we do not see Darden nearly as often as we would wish."

"We always like to see Darden," Beatrice said.

"He is the finest of brothers," Juliet said.

"I do not suppose anybody has one finer," Rosalind said.

"Such a fine young lord," Miss Mayton said.

This tribute to the finest but always missing Darden was mercifully brought to a close by Mr. Cahill.

"I am certain he would wish to be among you more than he has been able," Mr. Cahill said. "But he is so taken up by the YBC these days."

"The YBC?" Beatrice asked.

"Ah, I am sure he will tell you all about it when you see him. Darden has founded a club. The Young Bucks Club, YBC for short."

"Very enterprising," the earl said. "And here I was, imagining he was gambling all night and sleeping all day."

"Well, there might be some of that," Mr. Cahill admitted. "Though in the general way of things, Darden is our leader and he does not like to be too idle. He keeps us all on the straight path. My mother admires him prodigiously."

Matthew attempted to keep his expression neutral. Darden was a decent enough fellow, though it seemed absurd to start a club that announced one considered oneself a young buck.

"Tell us more of the YBC," Beatrice said. "Darden will not mind it. He will be grateful, as he always says that when he is with us, he is drowning in our questions."

Mr. Cahill, looking very encouraged, said, "Well, we have rented a building on St. James and spruced it up, hired some staff—waiters, a cook, and some lads to clean the place. So far, we have eleven confirmed members. We will have more, of course. When a member puts somebody forward, they will be voted on. We are planning to be very exclusive, though."

Matthew suppressed a sigh. He supposed Darden would urge him to be put forward. He did not like the idea. Aside from the ludicrous name of the thing, those sorts of clubs always came with a hefty fee, and for what? So that one might gather in a building to play cards or drink claret or make childish bets? His money was best spent elsewhere.

"I wish ladies could have such clubs," Beatrice said wistfully.

"They do," Mr. Cahill said, laughing. "In truth, the ladies have far more than we do by way of Almack's and every drawing room in London."

"I suppose that is right," Beatrice said, looking very cheered.

"Oh father," Rosalind said, "you do think Beatrice will get a voucher from Almack's?"

"I imagine so," the earl said. "I wrote a note to Lady Jersey that we would come to Town, and she wrote me a veritable novel back and so I cannot think we would be snubbed."

Mr. Cahill laughed at this. "A novel, yes, she would do. She is not called 'Silence' for nothing."

"Do you go to Almack's, Mr. Cahill?" Rosalind asked.

"Indeed, yes," he said. "Of course, I take my invitation to be no high compliment. I like to dance and am thought rather good at it and that is always of interest to the Patronesses."

"Is the food really as dreadful as we have heard from Darden?" Viola asked, working her way through the now arrived ham slices. Matthew noticed she did not dally with it while Mr. Cahill was in attendance.

"The food is wretched," Mr. Cahill said. "And the drinks too. Everybody is well-advised to eat and drink before arriving. For all that, though, we at the YBC hold a great respect for our sister club and we close on Wednesdays on account of it. That was Darden's idea and he was clever about it. The Patronesses have taken it as a great compliment to themselves and there is nothing they like so much as a great compliment to themselves."

The earl roared with laughter. "That is my son—always knowing how to oil the cogs."

The innkeeper bustled into the room. "Mr. Cahill, your new horse is saddled."

Mr. Cahill rose and bowed to the ladies at table. "I would wish to stay and have this delightful company all the day long, but I cannot allow a saddled horse to stand about on account of my pleasant tarrying."

Matthew noted, to his annoyance, that all the Bennington ladies seemed very struck by the sentiment. As they would, Miss Mayton having filled their heads with nonsense. Pleasant tarrying, indeed.

Mr. Cahill departed and Matthew attempted to ignore the various sighs round the table.

"So genial," Miss Mayton said.

"Really so pleasant," Rosalind said.

"His words are always said in a very pleasing manner," Beatrice said, eyeing Matthew.

"Beatrice," Cordelia said, "did you find yourself struck by Mr. Cahill? It would be wonderful if you were to wed one of Darden's particular friends."

"I am afraid I have not been struck in that way," Beatrice said. "Miss Mayton has described true love as feeling as if one were both drowning and yet taking in more air than one has ever done."

"What?" Matthew asked incredulously. "How does one—"

"Also," Viola said, cutting him off, "one feels as if one's hair has been struck by lightning, and yet one is also filled with a sense of calm surety."

Matthew was not certain he would mind if Miss Mayton *was* actually struck by lightning or drowning.

"And do not forget how the heart changes its rhythm," Miss Mayton said. "It speeds up terrifically, and yet it does not feel ill."

"*I* feel ill," Matthew said.

"Such a stick," Beatrice muttered back.

>>><<<

BEATRICE SURVEYED THE drawing room of Portland Place. They had done it, they had arrived in London.

Good Mrs. Huffson had got the house in order and Beatrice was certain it had taken a Herculean effort. Darden, as dear as he was, made any place he resided in appear as if it had been struck by a violent windstorm.

Now, though, it was looking perfect. Beatrice had only vague memories of the house, as she had last been there when she'd been quite young. It was larger than she remembered, and the furniture was rather luxurious.

The velvet and brocade furniture coverings and silk pillows were very different from what they had at home. Her aunt had long advised the earl to choose fabrics that were not missed if they were ruined, due to how many things were spilled on them and the occasional fire from Cordelia's footlights.

As she waited for her family to join her, Beatrice considered all they'd experienced so far.

The last day of the journey was, not unexpectedly, peppered with several hiccups. One could hardly move so many people at once and not have hiccups, though apparently that fact was lost on Van Doren.

After saying adieu to Mr. Cahill, they had set off themselves not an hour later. Unfortunately, a quarter hour down the road they discovered that Juliet had left her book of poetry behind at the inn.

Matthew was sent to retrieve it and he was incredibly surly over it. Before turning round his horse, he'd stared at Juliet and said, "'Ode to Why Don't You Rope It to Your Wrist,' written by Lord Sick of Going Back for it."

Juliet had only raised a brow and said, "Scoldy-Breeches."

Some time later, Viola had got a stomachache, though she refused to say if it had been due to the large amount of ham she'd consumed. This necessitated a stop so that she might walk about in the fresh air.

While they were stopped, a young boy with a basket of four kittens trudged by Viola looking very dejected. She commanded him to stop and say what was the matter.

It turned out the boy's father told him to get rid of the kittens and he was very sure he was meant to kill them. He could not do it and had been walking for miles, looking for a farmer to take some of them for barn cats.

Over Van Doren's protestations that they would begin with four cats and end a year later with twenty, the poor little mites were speedily placed into the arms of the sisters.

Juliet had been delighted to inform Van Doren of his error—he should have guessed that all four kittens were female since they were all calico.

As Juliet gave Van Doren the what-for, the young boy sank to the ground and sobbed with relief. He was exhausted in both body and spirit from the trials of the day.

The earl very much doubted the little chap would have the strength to walk home, and so he was put in the carriage with Cook and the two footmen. They would further provide him with some ale to revive him.

A mile down the road, the caravan was stopped again, this time by Cook, who got out and had a conversation with the earl.

The boy's name was Charlie and it seemed his family were very poor and he was expected to find work but he could find none, being on the small side of things for eleven. Cook recommended they take him on as a boy of all work for his kitchens and of course the earl acquiesced, being so kindhearted.

Then, it was only a matter of locating Charlie's father, acquainting him with the scheme, and paying him money as he claimed the boy would someday grow very tall and he ought to keep him home in anticipation of it.

All the while, Van Doren complained and moaned and claimed they would never get to London. Really, his patience could be bested by a five-year-old.

Naturally, they did get to London. But even then, Van Doren did not seem happy about it. The last thing he said before proceeding to his own house across the street was, "And finally, the Bennington caravan limps its way into London."

Beatrice could not imagine why the earl had invited him to come to dinner. Had they not seen enough of Van Doren over the past three days?

And what did the fellow mean by renting a house right across the street? She'd been aware that he would be located on Portland Place, which was already too close, but a person with a strong arm might throw a rock from their door to his own!

She supposed she must only be grateful that Portland Place had a wide avenue, else Van Doren should be peering in their windows at night.

Well, she supposed it was no matter. The earl had sent a note to Darden at his new club to let him know that they'd arrived and he was expected to dine with his family. *That* was the thing to think about.

Her sisters had spent the past hour down in the kitchens, assisting in getting four kittens and one boy named Charlie settled into their respective places.

They would see Darden and he would tell them about the Young

Bucks Club and they could all ignore Van Doren huffing with manufactured outrage in a corner somewhere.

From the great hall, Beatrice heard the door bang open. Not a moment later, Darden bounded into the room.

"Bea, there you are," he said and grasped her hands. "Look at you, a full-grown lady come to Town."

"Dearest brother," Beatrice said, "we have all missed you so very terribly and have so many things to tell you."

Darden laughed and said, "Do not you always? How is it to be any other way when there are five of you?"

"That is very true. Now, the very first thing, guess who we met on the road?"

"You will say it was Cahill, I think. I just saw him at the club and he told me all about it. He said my sisters were charming, the earl gracious, and Van Doren a bit put out."

"Van Doren. Darden, you do not know what we have put up with from him. Juliet has taken to calling him Viscount Scoldy-Breeches."

Darden roared with laughter. "That is very good, very good, indeed."

"How many lectures can he compose? Beatrice, do not get drunk. Beatrice, do not say everything on your mind. Beatrice, you are to throw over all your ideas about romance. He would like to turn the whole world into a stick like him. It never really ends."

Darden chucked her chin and said, "Well, for all that, he is a decent fellow. He has always taken great pains to look after my sisters when I am not there and I cannot fault him for that. I suppose he will be a great success in Town—he has the dark looks and strong jaw the ladies seem to prefer."

That idea gave Beatrice some pause, though she could not pinpoint precisely why. She said, "He is very handsome, anybody can see it, though it is very hard to admire his countenance while he is talking."

Before Darden could answer, the drawing room was deluged by sisters.

"Darden!" Juliet cried, flinging herself at him. "We have brought four kittens and a boy!"

"Of course you have," he said, giving her a strong hug.

"We found them all on the road," Juliet said by way of further clarification.

"Where else?" Darden said, laughing.

The others surrounded him until the viscount was near to disappearing in yards of muslin.

"Dear Darden," Viola said.

"You are looking well, Darden," Rosalind said.

Cordelia kissed his hand. "Our brother Darden is with us again."

The earl entered the room and appeared charmed by the scene of familial felicity. "There you are, my boy. Drowning in a sea of sisters, as usual."

"Father," Darden said.

Behind the earl, Miss Mayton hurried in. "I heard the ruckus and was certain Lord Darden must be in the middle of it."

"Miss Mayton," Darden said, untangling himself from his sisters and bowing, "you are looking very well."

Miss Mayton blushed, as she always did when Darden paid her a compliment.

"This is really very pleasant," the earl said. "We will settle to dinner and hear all of Darden's news and he will hear ours. We only wait for Van Doren before going in."

There were various muttered "Van Dorens" heard at the mention of him, most in a grumbling sort of way. Juliet rounded out the comments with, "I believe you mean Viscount Scoldy-Breeches, Papa."

Chapter Five

Matthew had been near crippled by the time he reached his own house on Portland Place, and a deal crumpled too, as he'd not brought his valet on the journey.

Fortunately, that valet had been at the house for days and had been prepared for his arrival. Marcus had seen that buckets of water were simmering on a low heat in the kitchens so as to have a bath ready when it was wanted and he had clean and pressed clothes at the ready.

It had been rather blissful to be in the quiet order of his own house, sans one earl, one deranged matron, five unruly girls, a plethora of servants, one extra boy and four extra cats.

He'd really rather have taken a long hot soak, had a brandy, and repaired to bed to allow his legs to recover from all the riding. Excessive riding, too, as how many miles had he been put to in retrieving Juliet's awful book of poems or searching out Charlie's father's small farm, which had been miles off their route?

However, he'd told the earl he would come to dinner and so he must go. It would likely be his last opportunity to pound some sense into Beatrice's mind before she was let loose on the *ton*. He might even find a quiet moment to acquaint Darden with the landscape of his sister's delusions.

As he lay back in the tub, Marcus said, "I hope you had a pleasant journey, my lord."

This was said quite facetiously, as Marcus had grown up in the neighborhood and was well-versed on the idiosyncrasies and erratic nature of the Benningtons.

"Pleasant?" Matthew said. "Well, let's see. We stopped a thousand times for Juliet to regard the landscape and compose an ode—cows, fences, doorways, nothing was too small to be left out of the ode writing. You will know that though these odes were deemed remarkable, the book they were written in was left behind three times."

Marcus shook his head sadly.

"They proceeded to order ham absolutely everywhere we stopped and Viola, for reasons only known to herself, ate it as slowly as possible. This, I believe, was meant to annoy me and was entirely successful."

Marcus bit his lip.

"We were joined for dinner on the second evening by some very refined people, who were forced to endure *Ode to a Fence*, along with Miss Mayton's current literary obsession with a one-eyed duke and his governess. Oh, and of course, she had to tell of one of her invented love affairs again. Gregorio, the one who stabs himself."

"Poor Gregorio. It took him a full half-hour to die, if I recall rightly," Marcus said.

"And a full half-hour for her to *tell* of him dying. Apparently, he was quite the talker while bleeding to death. Then today, there was a thrown shoe, we met one of Darden's foppish friends, we had to stop to allow Viola to get out and walk because she ate too much ham, we encountered a boy with four kittens and quite naturally, we put the cats *and* the boy in a carriage and brought them with us. All in all, it was as expected."

Marcus, of all people, understood what he'd been through. As evidence of that fact, his valet sent a footman to fetch a glass of ale to begin to unwind his lord's mind from his recent travesty of a trip.

Now, Marcus had made him presentable in clean and newly

pressed clothes and he walked across the wide avenue to Westmont House.

No, he did not walk. He limped. Matthew had thought hot water and ale would ease his muscles, but he found that had only been a temporary relief.

He stepped gingerly lest his legs give up altogether and he end falling to the ground. It would be a humiliating way to end—run down by horse and carriage while trying to roll off the street.

He could see the family gathered in the drawing room as nobody had closed the curtains. They surrounded Darden, the finest but always missing brother.

Beatrice's hair shined in the candlelight. He had always noted the yellow gold glints amongst her amber locks when they caught the light of the sun or a candle.

Other gentlemen would notice too, no doubt. They would be as moths to a flame.

Until she announced her requirements, in which case they would flap away as soon as possible lest they be consumed by the fire of her delusions.

Though it was only a few steps up to the door, Matthew was only got there by gripping the railing. He was fortunate there *was* a railing, else he'd have to crawl his way up.

As he struck the knocker, he thought he would either wake up on the morrow improved or completely immobilized.

He straightened himself and attempted to appear uninjured as Tattleton opened the door and showed him in.

MATTHEW GAZED ROUND the dining table. His welcome had been less than enthusiastic. It was as if he were some kind of burden now that Darden was on the scene.

Darden himself had been very cordial, but when that fellow was in the room, the five sisters had eyes for nobody else. Beatrice had actually bumped into him as she followed her brother down the corridor to the dining room. It was as if he'd become invisible.

At least, invisible to most. Juliet had taken great pains to whisper *Scoldy-Breeches* as she maneuvered past him.

The earl was at the head of the table with Miss Mayton on his right, while Darden took the bottom and had Beatrice to his right. That left Matthew sandwiched between Rosalind and Cordelia, with Viola and Juliet making faces at him from across.

"Now, my boy," the earl said jovially to his son, "we met Mr. Cahill on the road and he has alerted us to the forming of a club. Tell us all about it."

Darden took a massive portion of roasted chicken from the footman's platter and said, "It is the Young Bucks Club, Father, we call it the YBC amongst ourselves. Mind you, White's and Brooks's are all well and good, and even Boodles for the country set, but they are rather staid these days. We wished to have somewhere younger and more full of life."

"What happens when you all grow older?" Matthew asked. "Will it be the Old Bucks Club?"

"It is the spirit of the thing," Darden said. "We are not looking so far ahead. We are young *now*."

"Yes, Van Doren," Beatrice said. "The spirit of the thing."

"Because they are young and carefree," Viola said with a grim stare.

"Anyway," Darden continued, "our motto is shenanigans, mayhem, and tomfoolery."

"Just ensure that none of the shenanigans, mayhem and tomfoolery ends up costing me a deal of money," the earl said.

Matthew thought the YBC sounded as ridiculous as he had imagined it would. He had firmly decided that he would decline an invitation to have his name put forward. About the last things he was interested in were shenanigans, mayhem, and tomfoolery.

"You will not be troubled for money, Father. I am very reliable about not asking for any increases to my allowance," Darden said. "When I come up short, I gamble to make up the difference."

"Very sensible," Miss Mayton said.

Was it? Of course, what would be sensible in Miss Mayton's mind could not be measured by anybody else's ideas of the notion.

"After dinner, I will stay with you in the drawing room," Darden said, "but then I must be off by ten o'clock. The members are meeting to discuss a ball we plan on hosting. It will be a masque and only the most ridiculous disguises will be admitted. At least, we will say that to be the case, as people always do like a little drama and excitement. Will they or won't they be admitted?"

"How creative, Darden!" Beatrice said. "I wonder if I might go as a man."

"That *would* be ridiculous," Matthew said.

"Shakespeare did not think so," Cordelia said. "Just ask Viola in *Twelfth Night* or Portia in *Merchant of Venice* or Rosalind in *As You Like it*."

"In Shakespeare's time, though, they were all men pretending to be women dressed as men," Matthew pointed out.

"Father?" Beatrice asked.

"Trousers would be, perhaps, skating a bit too close to the line. I am certain you can devise a costume that is both safe *and* ridiculous."

Matthew noted all five sisters turn their attention to their plate, always irritated when he gained his point.

"Never mind, Bea," Darden said, "I'll help you out. I've got piles of ideas and I'll get something for Van Doren and Father too."

"You are a very good sort of brother, Darden," Beatrice said.

"Do not make me *too* ridiculous, if you please," the earl said.

"Of course not, Father. Now, the more critical reason I'll have to be present at the YBC meeting tonight is to hear some names put forward. Some are easy enough, but I think we will have a discussion about at least one of the names. It is said the fellow once did not honor a debt and if that is true, we cannot admit him."

Matthew waited for the inevitable, *What say you, Van Doren? Shall I put your name forward?*

Rather, Rosalind said, "That would be very dishonorable, indeed. Who is the gentleman?"

"That I will not say, as I do not yet know if that story is true. I shouldn't like to pass on what might be only a groundless rumor."

"But Darden," Cordelia said, "what if this person becomes struck by Beatrice? What if he, or some other reprehensible person, approaches our sister?"

"Never fear," Darden said, "I shall give a thorough going over to any gentleman hanging about Beatrice."

Matthew was rather nonplussed by where the conversation was going. Why had Darden not pressed him to put his name forward for the club? He would refuse, naturally. But he had expected to be asked.

"Darden, we will tell you all about Beatrice's requirements over tea in the drawing room," Viola said. "You can use that as your yardstick against any hopefuls."

Darden nodded agreeably. Matthew wondered how agreeable he'd be when he actually heard the list.

"And if we don't run too late," Miss Mayton said, "you might even hear me read from a wonderful story we are in the middle of just now. A one-eyed duke widower is in love with the governess of his children but neither of them know whether she can love a one-eyed man. They are positively tortured over the question."

"That sounds suitably dreadful, Miss Mayton," Darden said good-humoredly.

"The governess is trying to see under the patch," Cordelia said.

"Of course she is," Darden said laughing, "what else would she be doing?"

"But she's having no luck with it," Rosalind said.

"No, I suppose she wouldn't," Darden said. "At least, not until somewhere near the end where she will discover she can bear it and all will end happily."

And so the dinner went on, from one nonsensical topic to the next.

<hr />

MISS MAYTON POURED the tea as her charges gathered round it. The earl, Darden and Van Doren had stayed behind to have their port in the dining room, though Beatrice did not think they'd stay long at it.

She was certain that Darden, though always so cordial to everybody he met, would not wish to hear too very much from Viscount Scoldy-Breeches.

As her aunt passed Beatrice her teacup, the lady said, "I could not help noticing that there was a quite natural moment in which Lord Darden might have invited Lord Van Doren to put himself forward for membership in the YBC."

"And he did not do it," Rosalind said. "Our good brother stood firm with the house against our meddling neighbor."

"Do you suppose that was why?" Juliet asked. "That he ignored the moment in solidarity with all that his sisters have put up with?"

"We ought to ask him, whenever we can pry Van Doren out of the house and we have a moment alone," Cordelia said.

"Very sensible," Miss Mayton said. "Now, while we wait for the gentlemen, we will not be without entertainment."

Miss Mayton reached into her sewing box and pulled out a stack of letters. "Tattleton handed these to the earl, who handed them off to me for perusal. They are all invitations, I believe."

Beatrice felt as if her breath almost caught in her throat. Of course, she had understood that she would be invited various places, but to see the evidence of it! It was positively thrilling.

The sisters all stared with wonder at the stack in Miss Mayton's hands.

"There it is, Beatrice," Rosalind said. "Your own future, held in our aunt's hands. Through one of those invitations, you will meet your true love. Fate will make it so."

Beatrice clasped her hands to stop them shaking. "Oh, let's do have a look."

Miss Mayton opened each missive, passing them one by one to Beatrice. There were all sorts of people hosting all sorts of entertainments. Balls, routs, musical evenings, theatricals, there were even several cards, one of which was Lady Jersey's.

That was very promising, Beatrice thought. She did not have a mama to escort her round to all her vast connections and Miss Mayton was, due to her history, not so very familiar with Town.

She would have to depend upon her father's and her brother's connections, which had already produced this pile of invitations, and the earl's cordiality with Lady Jersey, to expand her circle of acquaintance.

"Ah, here it is," Miss Mayton said, "our vouchers for Almack's. And here *we* are on a Monday, with Wednesday coming so soon."

"Tickets!" Beatrice cried. "If we are to go, we must have tickets too. Remember, Mr. Cahill did tell us of the tickets. Anybody might be turned away if they go without tickets."

"I am sure your father will arrange it," Miss Mayton said. "*We* might be better served to put our efforts to shopping on the morrow. For accessories and the like. I will hazard a guess that you will choose to wear the new violet silk for your first outing, but you are in dire need of a reticule that will complement it."

"Oh yes, a reticule to carry my voucher and my ticket," Beatrice said.

"Just so," Miss Mayton said.

"We might all go shopping together," Rosalind said. "A lady not yet out in society may still shop, may she not? Should we not all have new reticules?"

"Oh, yes, yes," Miss Mayton said. "Naturally, we will all go together. I am determined that you should all have as many entertainments as possible. In any case, I have warned your father that we shall spend all of his money in the shops, so he is well prepared for the bills."

The sisters happily contemplated the genial news that their father was fully prepared to be bankrupted by new reticules.

"Now that I think of it," Miss Mayton said, "these excursions round the town may serve a vital purpose for all of my girls. Rosalind is to come out next year and there is every possibility that her true love might spot her passing by and vow to wait for her return."

Rosalind appeared very gratified to hear it. Cordelia said, "Or any of us, really. After all, if a gentleman is in true love, he might vow to wait two or three years, or even five. What choice would he have?"

"I am going to keep my eyes wide open," Juliet said. "It would be quite something to see my true love and then dream about him for *years*."

"Nothing is impossible when it comes to true love," Miss Mayton affirmed.

These interesting considerations were interrupted by the gentlemen coming in.

Beatrice leapt up. "Papa, our vouchers have come, but we must be in all haste to secure tickets for Wednesday evening."

Rather than the earl positing some plan, Darden answered for him. "You did not think I would shirk my responsibilities to a sister? Tickets have been procured, Bea."

Beatrice threw her arms round her brother's neck. "Dear Darden, I should have known."

"Van Doren," Cordelia said, "I do not suppose our Beatrice will see you amongst the select guests at Almack's?"

"I imagine not," Van Doren said.

Darden led Beatrice back to the seat she had recently vacated, and the men took their places round the tea tray.

"I am certain Lady Jersey would have extended the invitation to you, Van Doren," Juliet said, "had she been aware of your existence."

"You see, Darden," the earl said, "how the girls like to tease our poor neighbor. He holds up against it remarkably well."

"Do I?" Van Doren said darkly.

"I might be able to fix it up for you, Van Doren," Darden said agreeably. "Lady Jersey is feeling particularly fond of me just now, as I have advertised far and wide that the YBC is closed on Wednesdays. Or, as I told her, what foolish gentleman would wish to be at his club when there is an Almack's assembly in the offing."

Van Doren took the teacup handed to him. "Well, I do not know—"

"He does not wish for the favor, Darden," Beatrice said, "as it is in his nature to be contrary."

"Of course he wishes it," Darden said jovially. "Van Doren is all sense and as he is also twenty-four and does things very by the book, I presume he's come to Town to look for a wife. No place on earth gathers together so many suitable young ladies coming along with handsome dowries than Almack's ballroom. You do look for a wife, Van Doren?"

"I…well I do not imagine I need proclaim what my plans might be," Van Doren said.

"*I* imagine that is rather a confirmation than otherwise," Darden said. "You will find yourself struck by some lady and we will soon enough have a new viscountess in the neighborhood."

"I do not believe Van Doren will ever be struck," Rosalind said, "he does not have the romance in his heart for it."

"Certainly not in the nonsensical manner you imagine," Van Doren said testily. "My choice, when I make it, will be grounded in sound principles. Is the lady of steady temperament and prepared to manage a household? Considerations of that nature."

"Full of good sense," the earl said. "Though one never knows how the thing will play out. Feelings are a funny thing, after all, and they sometimes have no respect at all for good sense."

"I'll speak to Lady Jersey," Darden said. "Now, Bea, what is this I hear of your requirements for the gentleman who will win your heart?"

The sisters, with the help of Miss Mayton, speedily apprised Darden of the qualities deemed absolutely necessary to Beatrice's happiness.

"So…he is to be Beowulf, Hercules, Robin Hood, Sir Gawain, and Henry the Fifth, all rolled together," Darden said, bemused. "That is quite the list."

"And he must be violently in love and might even tear out his hair," Rosalind said.

"Not too much hair, though," Viola qualified. "That would be unattractive."

"He will challenge any rival suitor to a duel, I'm afraid," Miss Mayton said, though she did not appear particularly averse to that violent outcome.

"And he will write Beatrice poems," Juliet said, "of which I will assess the depth of feeling."

"He may, in the course of things, threaten to do a violence to himself," Beatrice said. "Though I have repeatedly said I wish it to be only threats. I am not unreasonable."

"I am not convinced you will unearth such a fellow at Almack's," Darden said, laughing.

"She will not unearth such a fellow *anywhere*," Van Doren said. "As I have pointed out many times."

"As you can see, Darden," the earl said goodhumoredly, "your sisters have got rather carried away with ideas of romance. It shall all come out right, though. Beatrice will encounter some gentleman who may have some or none of the qualities on her list and he will be found very agreeable."

"You always do say so, Papa," Beatrice said, "and that I might fall in love against my will. But I vow I will not be prevailed upon to wed some person who is only concerned with my running of his household. I must be in receipt of finer feelings that soar above mundane practicalities."

"It is what makes life worth living," Cordelia confirmed.

"It is its very essence," Viola said.

"I will write an ode about it," Juliet said. "Ode to finer feelings."

"Very well, have it as you like it for now," the earl said indulgently. "Miss Mayton, you did promise to read to us again."

Miss Mayton nodded and pulled her book from her sewing box. Beatrice had often noticed that her aunt kept no end of things in her box, though very little actual sewing as she did not prefer the activity.

"As we know so far," Miss Mayton said, "the governess has been determined to see under the duke's eye patch. Will she recoil in horror and all is lost? Or will she see that she does not mind it, in which case all will end happily?"

Miss Mayton cleared her throat.

The governess had climbed to the roof and now hung herself over the side, determined to see the duke in his bath. Surely, he would take off the eye patch then!

She braced her feet between the stone crenellations and hung herself upside down.

She could see into his bedchamber!

But only the back of his head, as his bath was turned the wrong way!

Would this torture of not knowing plague her forever?

The duke stood and the governess was near blinded by a glimpse of nether regions she should not see!

Her shoes lost their grip and she plummeted down into a stand of bushes. She staggered to her feet.

"Wait a minute," Van Doren said, interrupting Miss Mayton. "She fell from the roof, but she's not dead? She just stands up like nothing happened?"

"She could hardly keep trying to see under the duke's eye patch if she was dead, could she?" Beatrice asked.

"I wish they were both dead," Van Doren muttered.

Chapter Six

Darden had been at his club the past hour and the members had made good progress. The question of Mr. Siddleton had been settled, regarding the possibility that he had not honored a debt. That had proved a fabrication of the first order and the gentleman was voted in. The gentleman who was presumed to have started the rumor would never be let in, which was fine with everybody, since nobody particularly liked him.

They had dispensed with that matter and then went on to confirm the details for what they would call The Tomfoolery Masque.

Now, they had rewarded their hard work with generous glasses of claret. As the other members joked and gossiped, Darden's mind kept drifting back to the recent scenes at Portland Place.

Beatrice was a dear of a girl, but he was not certain she'd be a married lady coming out of this season. Her requirements were such that no man could approach them.

Of course, his father might be right. In the end, she would meet some gentleman and throw over all her previous ideas.

It was too bad she would not choose Van Doren. Darden was convinced that fellow was hopelessly in love with Beatrice. Why else would the man spend half his life at Westmont House, abused by all five sisters? Further, he'd seen Van Doren looking at her when he did not think anybody observed.

Darden thought his neighbor might have been in love with Beatrice all his life. After all, when they were younger, it had always been *her* doll he hid and *her* hair he pulled.

Darden was certain that, when the fellow had turned twelve and informed everybody that he would from now on be called Van Doren, rather than Matthew, it had been to impress Beatrice.

She *had* been impressed. Then.

But as she'd grown, she'd taken Miss Mayton's stories more and more to heart. Van Doren could not possibly measure up against Hans or Gregorio or any of the other doomed lovers. Not if he planned to stay living, anyway.

If only Van Doren would not be scolding her all the time. Beatrice was much better managed with honey than vinegar. That did not make her particularly unique—most people were.

As a girl, she had been admiring of Van Doren's bossy nature, but as a woman, she would not tolerate it. The harder Van Doren tried to make her see sense, the harder she would cling to her delusions.

Or rather, Miss Mayton's delusions.

Miss Mayton, herself, had always been a bit of a mystery. Were any of her stories actually true? It did not seem as if they could be. But then, so often an invention had some grain of truth in it somewhere. Had there ever been a Hans? If so, where was he now? Dead at the bottom of a mountain or sitting comfortably in his club, thinking of a long ago meeting on an Alpine meadow?

At this point, Van Doren might be a bit too rational for Beatrice. It really was a shame. Van Doren might have too much of the seriousness about him, but he was a fine gentleman and would be careful of a wife. Beatrice would be in secure hands.

It really would be a very good match. Van Doren would be the anchor when Beatrice's ideas took flight and Beatrice would bring some lightness to Van Doren's often heavy step.

Darden paused in his thinking. Just because the two of them did not see that they were suited *now*, did that mean they would be blind to it forevermore?

What if they were helped along in some manner? And, if someone were to push things along for Beatrice, who better than a brother?

Those two people were both stubborn as mules in their own ways, but certainly it could be done. He would just require some help from the members of his club.

"Gentlemen," he said, "we have one more matter to discuss. This one will be filed under the auspices of one of our founding precepts—shenanigans."

MATTHEW HAD RISEN that morning, or at least tried to. His legs were leaden, each step a herculean effort. Never again would he ride on horseback three full days in a row. Not when a certain young miss's book of poetry must be constantly gone back for, adding unnecessary miles to the journey.

There was something excruciating about going forward three miles, only to have to go back three miles, and then retread the same three miles already traveled, all to find the initial three miles had become nine. It was even more excruciating that all those extra miles were to retrieve a book filled with wondrous yellow orb circles and gentle bovines.

He'd made it as far as the chair by his bedchamber window, where he'd been for some hours with a book. At least *his* book was a sight better than the one-eyed duke and his deranged governess. The lady fell from the roof and got up, indeed. What publisher read such a manuscript and thought, yes, I must purchase this and send it out into the world?

He supposed a publisher who was confident in there being enough deranged readers to make it a viable enterprise. Perhaps it provided a sad comment on the state of England's mental capacities.

Matthew watched out his window as the door to Westmont House flew open and Miss Mayton led all five sisters to a carriage.

Beatrice was looking charming in a simple muslin, only decorated with a yellow ribbon round her waist and topped with a velvet tippet and silk bonnet of the same color.

He could not hear what they said to one another, as his window was closed and the avenue too wide, but by the looks of it they were in high spirits.

Why wouldn't they be? Neither the earl nor Darden had bothered to check them last evening. He'd taken the opportunity of a private moment over port to bring it to their attention once more. It was apparent that both gentlemen viewed the sisters' bizarre ideas about love as simply an amusement, a phase that would not linger forever.

They did not comprehend the danger of it. No, instead, *he* was made to look like a stick for pointing it out.

And then Darden announcing that he must have come to Town to seek out a wife when he'd said no such thing. He would marry, of course. In due time. At the right time. In the fullness of time. Or sometime, anyway.

He supposed they would all think him very foolish to have come only to attempt to guide Beatrice.

The carriage clattered on its way and the Westmont ladies were off to terrorize London. Matthew rang his bell and ordered willow bark tea, as he did not know what else to do about his current condition.

Marcus brought his tea to him. "I've added a drop of laudanum. You'll never get anywhere with this," he said, pointing at Matthew's legs, "unless you walk it off. My father always said the more sore something is, the more you got to keep moving it. Excepting broken bones or a headache, of course."

Matthew nodded and took the cup, drinking it down.

"You'll need to be up on your feet and in fine fettle by the morrow," Marcus said. "Viscount Darden sent this over not a half hour ago."

Matthew was handed a small rectangle of cardboard and a bill for ten guineas, a ticket, and another bill for six shillings.

"Almack's," he said. "Darden claimed he would get me admitted, though I expressed no interest in it. Now I must pay or be forever blackballed by the Patronesses."

"It does seem like an ideal place to look for a wife, though," Marcus pointed out.

Matthew laid down the voucher and the ticket. "Why has everyone convinced themselves that I am here to look for a wife?"

Marcus appeared exceedingly puzzled. "Then, you come to Town for...for the entertainments?"

"Am I not to enjoy the entertainments of the season just as well as anybody else?"

Marcus only shrugged.

Good Lord. Perhaps he *was* becoming a stick—not even his valet could imagine him enjoying anything. He'd known Marcus as his valet since he'd been sixteen and Marcus not two years older. He'd known him from the neighborhood nearly all his life. He did not suppose there was anybody left alive who knew him better, but for the earl.

Did Marcus not think he enjoyed things? He could enjoy things if he wished to.

"Help me up," Matthew said, "we will take your father's cure and walk round the house. I must be able to dance by the morrow. Which I will enjoy. Because it is one of the entertainments of the season. That I have come to enjoy."

BEATRICE MARVELED AT the crowded London streets as they made their way to Pall Mall and the mythical Harding, Howell & Co, a destination that was said to sell everything worth having.

While it was indeed marvelous to see so many people and carriages going hither and thither, it did slow things up. At home, they would be trotting down country lanes at a brisk pace. There was no possibility of going at a trot here, however.

Beatrice had found some trouble in falling asleep the evening before and stifled a yawn. She did not know why it should have been so or why she'd kept thinking about Darden's claim that Van Doren came to Town for a wife.

It was just so odd, she supposed. Van Doren had been a fixture, always steady and always the same. It seemed impossible that he would do something to change what had always been. He scolded, she ignored. It had seemed the way of the world.

Well, it had not always been so, she admitted. There had been a time, when she'd been much younger and impressionable, that she'd looked up to Van Doren as the person who knew everything.

Of course, he'd been irritating by insisting on hiding her dolls and holding them for ransom or pulling her hair, but then it had always seemed somehow complimentary that he did so. He'd favored *her* dolls and *her* hair.

Beatrice smiled to herself as she recalled the day he announced he would only answer to Van Doren. They might call out for Matthew all they liked, he would not hear them. She'd been ten, and he twelve—she had been very struck by how manly it had sounded. She had even fancied herself in love with him.

As she grew older, though, his bossiness had grown tiresome and she had chafed under it. She had her own ideas and began to resist his attempts at correcting them. If anything, his opinions rather cemented her own. Since then, they'd been locked in their own strange battle.

She had imagined that in coming to Town, she would leave Van Doren just where he was, the fuming viscount sitting alone in the country. He would watch her go off to her new life, but *he* would not go anywhere. He would not change.

Beatrice could not imagine why she had thought so. Of course he would marry. Of course things would change.

A sudden galling idea came upon her. What if he married before she did? What if he were a success in Town and she a failure?

It would be too humiliating. She could not allow it.

"What do you think, Bea?" Juliet said, bringing her thoughts back to the present.

"I am sorry, Jules, think of what? My thoughts had quite drifted away from me."

"She is thinking of her true love," Cordelia said.

Though her mind had been far away from true love, Beatrice did not dispute it as she would not prefer to mention what she *had* been thinking of.

"I'll recite it again," Juliet said. "It is my ode to finer feelings."

Passion, thrills, heartbreaks, joy
These are the feelings I do employ
To fail to give these things their due
Would be death and I wave my final adieu

"That is very good indeed, sister," Beatrice said.

"Yes, I did think so," Juliet said. "At first I thought lack of finer feelings might be described as a sickness or a heaviness, but then I thought no, it must be death."

"Quite right, my dear," Miss Mayton said.

"Look, there it is," Rosalind said.

"That looks very grand," Viola said.

Beatrice peered out the window at Harding, Howell & Co. The building did indeed look grand, with its stone facing and large windows filled with interesting items of millinery and goods.

The grooms opened the doors, the sisters piled out, and Beatrice forgot all notion of Van Doren or any other gentleman. There were things to purchase, and it was time to purchase them.

TATTLETON ENTERED HIS quarters and slowly sat down on a chair. He had never had such an extraordinary conversation with one of the family since he'd begun serving the earl.

He'd gone into the library to inquire if Lord Darden needed anything, as he'd been in there for quite some time. As it happened, he did need something—more stationery.

The lord was down to a few sheets from what had been a generous supply. A stack of letters were piling up on the desk.

Tattleton had said, "My lord, I understood that you and the earl were still working on the guest list for the ball. Do the invitations go out today?"

"That is not what all this is, Tattleton. In fact, I might need your help in this particular matter, you'd better close the door and sit down."

"Sit down?" he'd asked, incredulous. A butler did not sit down in the library.

"Yes, just this once, if you please. I'd rather not crane my neck to have the conversation."

"Conversation?" Tattleton had asked, entirely nonplussed. Since when was he to go round the house having *conversations* with the family?

He had closed the door and then sat himself gingerly on the edge of the chair on the other side of the desk.

"I am sending letters to absolutely everybody I know in this town," Lord Darden said. "I wish to ensure that Lord Van Doren is invited everywhere. If Beatrice is there, I want Van Doren there too."

Tattleton nodded. He had long suspected that the earl and Lord Darden had charged Lord Van Doren with looking out for Lady Beatrice. How could he not have guessed at it? Lord Van Doren was always about the place and giving his hints to Lady Beatrice, no matter how much she did not like it.

"I am informing all London of this rare find that is Lord Van Doren—unmarried, a sizable estate, handsome, an excellent dancer, old family, exceedingly well-dressed, witty, and charming."

Witty and charming? Tattleton thought Lord Van Doren a fine gentleman, but apparently he'd been keeping his wit and charm under wraps.

"I intend for Beatrice to see how other ladies view his worth and, as Van Doren is devilishly handsome and comes with everything to recommend him, I have no doubt of the effectiveness of that strategy."

Now, Tattleton was entirely lost. What did Lady Beatrice viewing other ladies as they viewed Lord Van Doren have to do with looking after her?

"Now, here is where it gets a bit Machiavellian," Lord Darden said. "I am going to tell Beatrice of a ruse, but the telling of the ruse covers up another ruse!"

Machiavellian? Tattleton was beginning to think he was in the middle of a ruse himself.

"After the ball tomorrow night, I will tell her that a very fine gentleman was entirely struck by her. I will invent some tragic story about how he's vowed to never marry but now finds himself desperately in love and so is torn to pieces. He will need encouragement to come forward. Then, I will propose to Beatrice that my fellow YBC members pretend to also be desperately in love with her, thereby prompting this anonymous gentleman to step forward."

Tattleton gripped the arms of his chair. There began to seem every possibility that he had gone mad and was imagining this entire conversation.

"You see? She will be in on *that* part of the ruse, but Van Doren will not. He's the one I wish to step forward and he will be driven to distraction upon seeing all those gentlemen attempting to woo. He will come to his senses and declare himself. That is the *real* ruse that

Beatrice will not be apprised of. We're calling it Campaign Shenanigans. What do you think of that?"

Tattleton could not speak. What words were there in the world to attempt to untangle this unhinged scheme?

"I see you are confused, yes, it is a lot to take in. You see, Beatrice and Van Doren are very well suited, they just do not see it yet. We've got to shake them up!"

"We?" Tattleton said softly.

"I do not yet know what I might ask of you," Lord Darden went on happily. "Once we get things going, it will be a fluid situation. We must be ready to react at any moment."

"I see," Tattleton said. Though he *said* he saw, he did not really see at all. How on earth had Lord Darden come to the conclusion that Lady Beatrice and Lord Van Doren were suited? They were like oil and water. If he said up, she said down. If he said hot, she said cold.

"Now that you're apprised of the scheme, be ready for my directions should we need something done in the house. For example, when my friends come calling for Beatrice, make sure the curtains are wide open so Van Doren can see in from across the road."

"Curtains open," Tattleton repeated.

"Also, if the opportunity arises, give Beatrice any correspondence or flowers that's come for her when Van Doren is here."

"Correspondence and flowers," Tattleton said.

"And keep it all to yourself. Nobody must discover what we're up to."

What *we* are up to? How did he get himself involved in this? He'd only stepped into the library, and now he was embroiled in a deranged plot!

⋙⋘

THEY HAD ARRIVED at Almack's. Beatrice had been terrified as they'd shown their vouchers and handed in tickets. Though she knew they were perfectly welcome to be there, she had an irrational fear of being turned away at the door.

Miss Mayton had been equally shaken—she'd told Beatrice before they'd left that she was certain Darden had to press very hard to get her a voucher. After all, who was she? Had she married Hans the Swedish count, or Gregorio the Italian count, or the duke from Transylvania, she would be a titled lady, but they had all died tragically and left her as the same miss she'd started the world with.

The earl and Darden were a deal more sanguine—Darden knowing all the Patronesses well enough, and the earl not disposed to worry over any matter save for a house fire.

They were inside the doors and Beatrice tucked her voucher back into the charming, beaded silk reticule she'd purchased at Harding, Howell & Co.

The ballroom was awash in beautiful ladies in silks and dashing gentlemen in close-cut coats and tight knee breeches.

Beatrice found her confidence in her own looks a bit shaken. At home, she had only to compare herself to her sisters, if they looked well than she must look well too. Outside of that, there had only been Miss Braithwaite who was unfortunately short and Miss Columpine who had oddly round eyes that did not blink very often.

But here, there was so much beauty to behold. So much elegance, the sort that did not look too studied. She supposed she must take comfort in her dress, which was as elegant as any she saw.

The violet silk found its grace in its carefully composed cut, as had been explained to her by Mrs. Randower, the modiste who had made up her wardrobe. As the lady said, "Let other girls decorate themselves like overblown peonies, it will always be the simple construct of the lily that will catch the eye."

Beatrice had not mentioned that she favored peonies and Mrs. Randower had not remarked on the very large peonies surrounding them via her bedchamber's paper-hangings.

Her aunt nudged her and directed her eyes to a balcony overlooking the floor. There stood a group of seasoned ladies and Beatrice hardly needed to be told who they were—the Patronesses.

"Is Lady Jersey up there?" she whispered to Darden.

"Heavens, no. She likes to be down here talking. She is coming our way. If she stops, I will introduce you."

In a moment, Beatrice saw a very finely dressed lady bearing down upon them. "Darden, Lord Westmont, how very good to see you. I should scold you, Lord Westmont, for staying away from Town for so long."

"Ah, but Lady Jersey appears just as she did when last I met her," the earl said. "Has it been years, or only a moment?"

Lady Jersey shook her fan at him. "Still the master of his words, I see." She turned her attention to Beatrice.

"My lady," the earl said, "allow me to introduce my eldest daughter, Lady Beatrice Bennington, and Miss Mayton, my cousin."

Beatrice curtsied deeply. *Very* deeply, as she presumed Lady Jersey would be quite used to such obeisance.

"Charming," Lady Jersey said to Beatrice. "Miss Mayton. *Miss*, you did say?"

"Sadly, Lady Jersey," Miss Mayton said. "I have been unlucky in love."

Lady Jersey regarded Miss Mayton quizzically.

To her right, Beatrice felt a presence coming beside her. She rose from her curtsy. It was Van Doren.

His carriage had left Portland Place at the same time as their own, but they had left him behind when he got caught at the back of a slow-moving farmer's cart.

Of course, he would not have had that problem had he been on his horse, but Beatrice suspected he was a deal too sore to ride after insisting on riding all the way from Taunton.

Darden said, "Lady Jersey, this is Lord Van Doren, the gentleman I told you about."

"So this is the remarkable Van Doren," Lady Jersey said.

CHAPTER SEVEN

VAN DOREN BOWED to Lady Jersey, though he seemed rather surprised to be described as remarkable. As well he should be, Beatrice thought.

"Lady Jersey," he said, "I thank you for the kind invitation."

Lady Jersey looked well pleased. Why did Van Doren seem so different here? He was not at all like himself. Here, he seemed very genial.

"Well, Lady Beatrice, as you are at Almack's for your first ball," Lady Jersey said, "I will decide who may take a dance with you. Lord Van Doren, I give you leave to put yourself down for the lady's first. I think an old family friend will suit for the first dance out of the gate. Any further gentlemen requesting to enter their name on your card have been sanctioned by me, they all know the rules."

Beatrice could not be certain whether Lady Jersey thought she deserved thanks for the arrangement, though she did not feel particularly thankful.

The earl had nodded, and said, "Very thoughtful, my lady."

Lady Jersey nodded graciously and moved on.

"Do not think you will take all my firsts this season, Van Doren," Beatrice said, now that Lady Jersey was out of earshot.

"I did not have a say in the matter," Van Doren said, "as you well know."

Beatrice found herself unaccountably stung by that. She supposed

Van Doren would not have asked her at all, had he not been forced into it. There was something insulting in it.

"Lady Jersey pays you a compliment, Van Doren," Darden said. "She must have liked the look of you or she would have passed you over for Beatrice's card."

Why should Lady Jersey like the look of Van Doren?

Beatrice paused. Though she knew herself to have the unique ability to shape her thoughts in ways that were pleasing to her, even if the circumstances did not quite support them, she could not deny that Van Doren looked particularly well in dress clothes.

"Darden," the earl said, "I leave Beatrice in your hands. Miss Mayton and I will repair to the card room. She's promised me she will partner me in whist, and you know how skilled she is at distracting the other players with her interesting conversations. We shall trounce anybody coming near us."

Miss Mayton did not appear entirely enthusiastic to be going off to the card room and Beatrice supposed she would not have minded staying in the ballroom. Nevertheless, she graciously nodded, patted Beatrice's arm, and was led away by the earl.

A gentleman approached and, had Beatrice been impressed with the elegance of the attire found round the room, it was all rather put in the shade by the magnificence before her.

He was very tall, nearly a head over both Darden and Van Doren, his hair a dusky blond and his eyes hooded and deep blue. It was perhaps not so much his looks that struck, but there was something in his manner. It was as if he'd swept up all the confidence to be had in the world and put it in his pockets.

"Darden," the gentleman said, in a tone that Beatrice could only conclude was sophisticated and perhaps a little bored.

To her surprise, her brother appeared a bit flustered. "Your Grace," he said.

"Lady Jersey has extolled the virtues of Lady Beatrice and given me leave to claim a dance," the man said.

"Certainly!" Darden said, enthusiastically. "The Duke of Conbatten, may I present my sister, Lady Beatrice Bennington. And this is Viscount Van Doren."

The duke executed an elegant bow, stood, and seamlessly took Beatrice's card from her hands. He put himself down for a later dance, the one that would come before supper.

"Charmed," he said, and then drifted off into the crowd.

Beatrice looked at Darden, who appeared rather starstruck.

"Darden," she said, "do you know the duke well? You seemed rather awkward in his presence."

"He is not one of my intimates, nor is he anybody's as far as I know. Conbatten, well, he is Conbatten, after all. We've talked about asking him to join the YBC, but we find ourselves terrified that he would decline, and then more terrified that he would accept."

"Why?" Van Doren asked.

Beatrice would have liked to appear derisive over Van Doren's confusion, but she was rather confused herself.

"Did you not look at him? Or hear him?" Darden asked, seeming incredulous over their lack of comprehension. "He is, well there is an air about him. Nobody understands how he gets his neckcloth into such a knot. It is a popular sport to discover who his tailor is, as nobody knows how he gets his coats cut to such perfection. Even Brummel finds himself outclassed. It is said that Conbatten spends three hours at his toilette, must have his bath at precisely ninety-eight degrees, and ends with a glass of chilled champagne."

"That sounds ridiculous," Van Doren said.

"Perhaps for the likes of us," Darden said. "Though somehow, whatever Conbatten chooses to do, he makes it seem…well, very Conbatten. And, while he's going around looking like the magnificent Conbatten, he does everything he tries at expertly. He rides his own horses at Newmarket, he is a favorite sparring partner of Gentleman

Jackson's, and his dinner parties are unparalleled, if you can wrangle an invitation. While others pay great amounts to have a pineapple sitting on their table, Conbatten will send you home with your own."

"I shall not allow him to frighten me," Beatrice said, "no matter how long he spends in a bath or how many pineapples he's handed out."

Another gentleman approached. A certain Baron Farthington, who seemed a pleasant gentleman. Then another, and so on it went, Lady Jersey having composed her partners for the evening.

Darden had introduced both her and Van Doren to Lady Clara, a lady of similar age, and Beatrice was surprised to see both Darden and Van Doren put themselves on her card. And Van Doren be so pleasant to her, for that matter.

Just as he'd been at the inn while attending to Miss Austen, he seemed a different person when he spoke to ladies outside of the Bennington circle.

She did not know what she had supposed Van Doren would be doing all evening, if not dancing. Somehow, she'd had a vague idea of him standing at the edges of the floor while *she* danced.

"Now Darden," Lady Clara said, "I must steal your friend away. Everybody will wish to know Lord Van Doren and I am determined to take him round the room. I can see Lady Mary sending me meaningful glances already."

With that rather stunning development, Lady Clara led the smiling Van Doren away and into the crowd.

"How odd," Beatrice said.

"Lady Clara?" Darden asked.

"Van Doren," Beatrice said. "Why should the lady be so bold on his behalf?"

Darden laughed. "I think, Bea, you are too used to viewing Van Doren's countenance. To you, it is a familiar face. To the ladies in this room, however, he is the handsome lord just arrived and must be found quite interesting."

"Van Doren?" Beatrice said. Of course, she understood him to be handsome. Those times when she could ignore what he was saying and look at him as a stranger, he had always struck her as such. She just had not considered how other ladies might view him.

"Well, I imagine their interest will wane once they are in receipt of a lecture and a scolding," Beatrice said.

Darden smiled. "Have no fear on that score. As far as I can tell, he is only inclined to scold and lecture *you*."

"Perhaps that is so, but they will not find any romance in him. Not a single drop of it," Beatrice said, slightly embarrassed that she could hear what sounded an almost petulant tone in her voice.

"Not every lady looks for romance," Darden said. "Not in the sense that you do, anyway. Admiring his looks and his means may prove sufficient."

Beatrice stared at her brother. What an idea.

"Come," Darden said, taking her arm, "you must be introduced to any number of ladies while I put myself down on their cards. Van Doren cannot have all the fun tonight."

That was an even stranger idea. How on earth was it that Van Doren was the individual having fun? It was Lady Beatrice Bennington meant to be having all the fun while Van Doren watched scowling from the edges of the room.

She was very stung by the whole thing and felt herself very stupid for being so.

>>>><<<<

MATTHEW COULD NOT help but to have some sort of mixed feelings about the evening. Those feelings had begun before he'd even left Portland Place.

He'd arranged with the earl that their carriages would leave at the same time, and they had, but then his coachman had got them stuck behind a farmer's cart with no opportunity to pass.

He'd had time to consider what he'd witnessed before they'd set off.

Beatrice had looked magnificent. Surprisingly so. He realized he was so used to seeing her in a simple muslin day dress. She always looked well in such attire, but to see her descend the steps to the earl's carriage this evening!

Her hair had been swept up more formally, her dress was all elegance in a violet silk, a delicate diamond necklace sparkled at her throat, and a charming pelisse of dark blue velvet topped the whole thing off.

It was as if he viewed a different lady entirely. It really was a bit disconcerting.

Amidst the four younger sisters waving her off, Beatrice had got into her carriage with not even a glance across the avenue. He might have fallen dead where he stood and she would not have noticed.

Then, he'd finally got to Almack's and gained his admittance. Lady Jersey had been pleasant enough, though he had mixed feelings about dancing with Beatrice at such a moment.

Oh, he'd escorted her round the floor no end of times in their own neighborhood, at this or that house when somebody decided to roll up the carpets. But that was only for lack of partners and he'd felt he did a duty by it.

The prospect of this dance seemed very different. It was the setting, he supposed. And her dress and general mien this night.

On the other hand, Lady Clara had very helpfully introduced him to a number of other ladies and so he would not find himself standing awkwardly about. That, he found, was a very great relief. He knew one of his weaknesses was an abhorrence of appearing foolish, and so at least that flaw would not be tested. He was to dine with Lady Mary.

Now, the orchestra was tuning and people began to take their places. It was to be a Scotch Jubilee, a longways country dance, and apparently all the dances would be similar. Whatever the particular steps of this one, it would not be overly complicated and, as the most important lords and ladies were taking their place at the top, there would be ample time to view it.

Matthew noted Conbatten up near the top, as he supposed a duke would be. Three hours to get oneself dressed, what a notion. He hoped Beatrice did not see anything romantic in the idea, as it sounded very stupid.

He searched out Beatrice and found her still with her brother. He made his way over.

"Lady Beatrice," he said, holding out his arm.

She took it and he led her to the forming line.

"Why have you suddenly taken to calling me *Lady* Beatrice," she asked. "You never do so."

"Perhaps it is the environment," Matthew said. "Or perhaps I have just realized that all my guidance must now come to an end. You are a full-grown lady, out in society, and so must be the mistress of your own judgments. You must move from Beatrice to Lady Beatrice."

"Your guidance is come to an end?" she asked, seeming very surprised to hear it.

He supposed she would be, as he'd found himself a bit surprised to say it.

"Do you mean, then, the *I only give you that hint* lectures and scoldings are at an end?"

"However you prefer to characterize it," he said.

The idea had come upon him suddenly. In her silk splendor, she simply seemed too old to continue scolding. She did not seem the young girl anymore.

It was not that she could not use more guidance, as she'd taken so little advantage of any he'd given so far, but it would seem verging on the ridiculous as she appeared now.

As she had not listened to one iota of anything he'd counseled for or against, he must step back now and wait for the inevitable fall.

Matthew realized that seeing Beatrice as she was now had forced a revelation upon him. He had finally concluded that his words would never sway her. Experience in the world was the only thing likely to give her pause.

All he could do now was to be prepared to pick her up when she was felled by her own delusional ideas.

The music started and they waited their turn. Both of them watched closely as the first couples began the dance.

It was to be simple enough. The top couple would execute a simple allemande, then the top lady to the second gentleman, top gentleman to the second lady, top couple promenade halfway down, return, and take the second spot.

He noticed Beatrice watching the Duke of Conbatten execute his turn with some lady or other. It was elegantly done, and Matthew did not have much hope of besting it. Nor did he think any other gentleman nursed similar hopes.

The duke was to escort Beatrice into dinner. Matthew supposed his conversation would be all elegance too. Perhaps he would explain the various reasons for taking three hours to get dressed or why bathwater at ninety-eight degrees was superior to ninety-seven or ninety-nine.

Their turn approached closer. Finally, he led Beatrice.

Matthew thought her nerves must be taut, though she certainly did not show it. She looked for all the world as if she'd been dancing at Almack's under the hard stare of the Patronesses all of her life.

Beatrice Bennington might make no end of missteps in her thinking, but she never did misstep on a ballroom floor.

He took some pride in that, though he'd not had any hand in it.

So far, the evening had been extraordinary. Beatrice had danced with no end of pleasant gentlemen. Of course, it was apparent that her true love was not in attendance this night, as she had not been duly struck by any particular person.

Some gentlemen had been handsome, some amusing, but she did not feel as Miss Mayton had described—drowning but taking in more air, feeling as if one's hair had been struck by lightning, and one's heartbeat surging ahead of its natural rhythm.

Perhaps that was best. Perhaps it was well that on her very first outing she was not also bombarded with feelings of true love. It might have verged on overwhelming.

It was a shame the duke did not inspire those feelings. He was very handsome just now, leading her through the set.

He led her back to her place and he nodded to her as if to say *well done*.

Beatrice's mind kept drifting back to Van Doren. He was full of surprises this night when she had expected no surprises from him at all.

He danced with different ladies, looking very well pulled together in his dress clothes. He smiled an awful lot and Beatrice realized she'd almost forgot what his smile looked like, so little did he employ it at home. She presumed he said amusing things, if his dance partners' expressions were anything to go by. It was as if she were viewing a different person altogether.

The ladies in question all seemed very eager to have his attention.

And then, if all that were not enough, he'd called her *Lady* Beatrice and announced his scolding was at an end.

Could that be true, though? She could hardly imagine him resisting the urge to scold. It was what Van Doren did as a career.

What would they talk about if he were not scolding?

Perhaps they would not talk about anything. Perhaps he would be too busy talking to Lady Clara and her friends.

No matter. Van Doren could do as he pleased. Lady Beatrice Bennington had a true love to find.

The dance concluded and the duke put out his arm to lead her into the supper room.

"I do pray, Lady Beatrice," he said, "that you have consumed proper sustenance before arriving. The Patronesses' offerings are a special sort of torture."

"Darden did mention it, yes," Beatrice said. "He said the stale bread and butter might be turned away at a debtor's prison and the lemonade hints that it has never heard of sugar."

"Just so," the duke said. "I cannot mind it so much, though. It has the unique ability to prompt one to appreciate the bounty of one's own table, not the least of which is a good glass of claret."

The duke led her to a place. He raised his hand ever so slightly and a footman came running. Beatrice thought a gentleman placed as high as a duke never really had to seek out anybody's attention—he already had it as soon as he entered a room.

They were brought glasses of lemonade, and slices of dry cake. Tasting it, she said, "Well, it is not very good, but a deal better than stale buttered bread."

"This," the duke said, looking at his own slice of cake, "is the highlight of the menu and always in short supply. In a few moments, there will be some wild wavings at footmen to attempt to get it before it runs out."

The duke had been right, of course. There were some who seemed positively desperate to catch a footman's eye.

"Who is that interesting lady who keeps waving at you?" the duke asked.

Beatrice followed the duke's gaze and found her aunt smiling and giving her small waves. She smiled back.

"That is Miss Mayton, my aunt. Well, not really my aunt, but we call her so. She has been so kind to my father as to raise all five of his daughters."

"That is very kind indeed. Did she not wish to marry and have her own family?"

"Oh she wished it, very, very much," Beatrice said softly.

"Then it is even kinder still, that she has subsumed her own desires to care for you and your sisters."

"Our Miss Mayton has a terribly tragic past, I'm afraid. There were several times she might have married, but all of her love interests died before their time."

The duke nodded gravely. "In the war, I presume."

"Goodness, no. Count Tulerstein died going over the side of an Alpine meadow, the Italian count dealt a deadly blow to himself, and well, there were others. She really has had the worst luck, but she keeps her head up. She's helped me tremendously in developing my list of requirements for any gentleman wishing to approach me. I should have been completely lost on the whole thing had she not been my guide."

"You will own to making a list of requirements?" the duke said, appearing amused to hear it. "May one inquire into its contents?"

There was something in the duke's tone that made her not wish to inform him of her requirements. He seemed to find the idea amusing, though she could not see why.

"I suppose a title and money top the list?" the duke said, with a small smile.

"Indeed, they do not," Beatrice said. "Those sorts of worldly considerations are not on the list at all."

"I am surprised, Lady Beatrice," the duke said. "It has been my experience that those two items are generally at the forefront of a debutante's mind. Do tell me what other considerations must take precedence over those practicalities."

Though Beatrice had almost decided not to inform the duke of her requirements, she had felt a little insulted that he'd thought money and a title were to be of the utmost importance. And so, she did list out for him the qualities necessary to Beatrice Bennington's happiness.

The duke appeared ready to erupt in laughter. "Beowulf's courage, Hercules' strength, Robin Hood's daring, as gallant as Gawain, the stalwart heart of Henry the Fifth? Have I missed any?"

"The depth of feeling of Shakespeare," Beatrice said with a sniff.

The duke waved his hand at the long table. "In *this* town?"

"In this town, or wherever he may be. I am certain fate will bring us into the same sphere."

"Lady Beatrice," the duke said, clearly suppressing his laughter, "you will not find such a paragon anywhere on this earth and I pray you do not enumerate your requirements to anybody else. I say that kindly, as a gentle hint."

Beatrice was at once mortified and furious. Who was he to direct her behavior or dictate what her requirements could or could not be?

He sounded very much like Van Doren just now, and it was infuriating. What was it about these sorts of gentlemen, forever delivering their hints to unsuspecting people?

"It seems you are not of a romantic turn of mind, Duke," Beatrice said rather daringly. It was daring on two fronts, she knew. One, the very words. And two, he had not invited her to address him as Duke, rather than Your Grace.

"Perhaps I am not a romantic," the duke said, ignoring the liberty she'd taken. "Though I flatter myself that I understand the *ton*, and that I understand men. I say be cautious, Lady Beatrice, lest you end with a poet who will spin you stories until he's spent your dowry and left debts all over Town."

"I am sure I could never be taken in by one who would do such a thing," Beatrice said.

"No?" the duke said, looking highly amused. "All of your requirements would be things easily pretended at. That is, until the mask fell away, in which case it would be too late to do anything about it. Trust in what a man does, not in what he says. That is the true measure."

"I do suppose, though, that there are gentlemen of varying temperaments. One cannot simply assign a way to go about things to all of them. Some may be practical, and some of a more romantic turn of mind. Like a knight of old, for instance."

The duke nodded and Beatrice was a little appalled that his expression was one of indulgent condescension, as if she were a recalcitrant child.

"Chivalry is all well and good," he said. "Though, real chivalry is the quiet work of maintaining an estate and seeing that all in one's sphere are cared for. That sort of care is not the height of romance, it does not make a splash or find its way into poetry. Nevertheless, it is the bedrock of a man's worth. In truth, it is how a gentleman expresses both his character and his affection."

Beatrice had no answer to that, for of course she presumed her true love would be caring of all who depended upon him. He would simply be all of that, *and* poetic, romantic, stoic, wildly brave, madly in love, and passionate in his feelings.

She turned her attention to her dry cake and forced herself to sip at her very sour glass of lemonade.

"I see I have discomposed you," the duke said. "Terribly rude of me, I think. Let us move to more pleasant topics. Are you fond of novels, Lady Beatrice?"

Beatrice was rather relieved to be off the topic of her requirements, as the duke did not comprehend them at all. She said, "Goodness, yes. Just now, my sisters and I, along with Miss Mayton, are reading *The Terrible Goings-on of Montclair Castle*."

"That sounds suitably gothic," the duke said. "One hopes there is a ghost or at least a murderous servant creeping about the place?"

"Oh no, you see, the one-eyed duke is in love with his gentle governess but neither of them know if she can love a one-eyed man. She's been trying to see under the eye patch for ages and has just fallen off the roof while trying to peer through a window."

"I suppose there is no chance whatsoever that she will simply ask him to remove the patch," the duke said.

Beatrice wrinkled her brow. "I am beginning to think it may come to that, actually. She seems to be running out of ideas."

"I raise my glass to you, Lady Beatrice," the duke said. "You are a true original, and that is no small thing in this town."

Beatrice was inclined to believe that a compliment, though she could not be entirely sure.

In the end, she supposed it did not signify. Whatever the duke was, he was not her true love.

Chapter Eight

Matthew had just come awake at near eleven o'clock. Marcus had been considerate enough to keep the curtains closed tight and the maids from their work anywhere near his door, as he'd got home after three.

Now, he rang his bell, ravenous. His butler, Mr. Genroy, would order breakfast, and Marcus would bring it up. Perhaps not the most usual arrangement, but it was how they did things when he did not repair to the breakfast room.

He did not wait overlong, and Matthew assumed Cook had been at the ready and only needed to fry the eggs.

Marcus came in with the tray and said, "So this is to be the Town schedule, is it?"

"It was a ball, they always run late," Matthew said. "Though it was a ball with no wine at all served, and so my head is remarkably clear."

Marcus handed him a cup of coffee and picked up a pile of letters from the breakfast tray. "It is not to be the last ball, I do not think," he said, handing over the pile. "Various footmen with an invitation in hand have been arriving all morning like a migration of birds. Mr. Genroy finally put Roger on the front steps to waylay them, lest the door knocker wake you."

Matthew took the pile of letters. "This seems a somehow outsized response to one evening out. Lady Clara did mention a card party or something like it and Lady Mary spoke of a rout, but what is all this?"

"That I cannot know, other than to speculate you were quite the hit at Almack's," Marcus said, brushing a coat.

"Very odd," he said, flipping through the invitations, "I did not meet half these people last evening."

"May I inquire into how Lady Beatrice fared at Almack's?" Marcus asked.

"Oh, she looked very well. Like a proper lady. I informed her that my advice had come to an end."

"Why?" Marcus asked. Then, the valet seemed to comprehend that he might have gone a step far and said, "What I mean is, oh, I see."

"Yes, I know, you will wonder at it. It is just that, seeing her as she was last evening, it did make me comprehend several things. One, she is fully grown. Two, nothing I have ever said has made the slightest difference. I have tried, but Beatrice will have to learn through hard life experience."

"You mean, some gentleman will disabuse her of Miss Mayton's bizarre ideas."

"Yes, that is it. I can only hope it ends being quietly done, her recovery is swift, and her sisters learn a lesson from it so they need not repeat her mistakes."

"Did any gentleman seem eager to play the part of suitor at the ball?"

Matthew shrugged. "She dined with a duke. Conbatten is his name. Apparently, he is the epitome of sophistication and nobody is to match him. I shouldn't wonder if she were not building her fantasies of true love around that fellow this morning."

"Conbatten," Marcus said with a rueful smile. "Do you know he keeps several thermometers by his tub so it is ensured that the water is ninety-eight degrees?"

"I do know it," Matthew said. "The question is, how do *you* know it?"

"We valets talk from time to time," Marcus said. "Now, I suppose when you have done with your tray, you will like your own bath. In honor of the mighty Conbatten, I shall aim for ninety-eight degrees, though with no thermometer it's always a roll of the dice. Then, you'd better start answering all those invitations."

⇶⇷

THE BREAKFAST ROOM at Westmont House was lively indeed. Beatrice had been to a ball and she had four sisters who must hear of every moment of it.

"And so you did list all your requirements for the duke?" Viola said.

"I did," Beatrice said. "I really felt I must when he hinted that my list must only be money and title."

"Where do young men get such dry ideas?" Miss Mayton said, buttering yet another piece of toast.

"What did he say when he heard how honorable and good your requirements are?" Juliet said.

Beatrice shifted uncomfortably in her chair. "It appears he has not a romantic bone in his body, sadly. He said I should only concern myself with how a man treats his estate and his relatives. I am sure I expect my true love to do such very well, but that cannot be the end of it."

"Certainly not," Rosalind said. "Without the passion and romance, a well-run estate is not worth having."

"Well," Cordelia said, "the duke did not make you feel as if your hair had been struck by lightning and so that is that."

"A shame though," Rosalind said. "What a name he has. Conbatten. Your Grace, the Duchess of Conbatten, it sounds very good indeed."

"I suppose Van Doren was grimacing from every corner, as he always does," Juliet said.

Beatrice found herself rather flushed over the statement, as that had not been at all what Van Doren had been doing.

"Actually," she said, "he was on his best behavior. It seems he is only a frowning scolder with *us*. With other ladies he works to make himself pleasant and he danced all evening."

"Pleasant?" Juliet said, as if she could not comprehend such a notion.

"As well," Beatrice said, forging on, "he claimed he is done scolding and lecturing me. He called me *Lady* Beatrice and said I am old enough to be mistress of my own judgements."

This seemed to rather bowl over her sisters. Nobody had imagined that Van Doren's scolding would ever come to an end. Cordelia had once said that he'd be eighty and no longer able to ride to the house and would just shout from his window.

"He never did say the scolding was over," Viola said.

"He did," Beatrice said.

"Let us see, though," Cordelia said, "if he can keep to that vow. I think he'll have a terrible time sticking to it."

Beatrice was not so certain. "It may be that his attention will be pulled elsewhere. A certain Lady Clara seemed to take an interest in him."

"Is she mad?" Rosalind asked.

"Or hideous?" Juliet said.

"Or perhaps she is poor and getting very old and has developed the rheumatism," Viola added. "It is either Van Doren or wandering the streets aimlessly, hoping she isn't forced to become an aging governess for a pile of unruly children."

"She is none of those things," Beatrice said. "She is near my own age, is very pretty, and her father is a marquess. Darden says she comes with twenty thousand."

These facts struck all of the sisters very hard. That this lady who had nothing running against her might be interested in Van Doren upended everything they knew about him.

"It is as if the world has been turned on its head," Cordelia said.

"I feel as if my insides have been shaken up and settled in the wrong place," Juliet said.

"There is every chance it is only one of us dreaming, "Viola said. "We shall wake and see it for the improbable nonsense that it is."

Beatrice might have written it off as improbable nonsense too, had she not been a witness to it.

Darden came striding into the room. "I knew I should find you all together this morning. No doubt picking over the details of Beatrice's first ball like birds on a new-cut field."

"We've found out ever so much, Darden," Juliet said. "Conbatten is not a romantic and Van Doren knows how to make himself pleasant when he likes."

Darden laughed at Juliet's assessments, as he always did, they tending to leave out beginnings, ends, or supporting details.

"We are shocked to our toes to hear about Van Doren," Cordelia said.

"Can it be true that this Lady Clara both likes him and is not insane?" Viola asked.

"Lady Clara is as sane as you or I," Darden said, "and yes, I do believe she has a particular interest in Van Doren. Further, she is not alone. Lady Mary seemed particularly keen as well."

Juliet dropped her toast. Cordelia set down her teacup with a clatter. Rosalind went a shade paler. Viola merely stared, unblinking.

Beatrice did not know what to think. It was bad enough that Lady Clara…and now Lady Mary…

But why was it so bad? Why did it bother her anyway, other than it was a change in how they'd all always proceeded?

"He *is* a lord, after all," Miss Mayton said. "And these poor young ladies cannot know him like we do."

There was much nodding round the table, as certainly that must be the cause of this aberration so recently brought to their notice.

"Van Doren says he will not scold Beatrice anymore," Rosalind said. "We do not believe it, of course."

"Well," Darden said, "it seems he is at least prepared to make an effort at it. Now, I will repair to the library to look through some invitations and hope, Beatrice, you will accompany me. I have a particular matter from last evening that I wish to discuss."

"Oh, Darden," Juliet said, "we must all come and hear it. You know perfectly well that whatever you discuss, Beatrice will tell us all about it."

"That's very true, Lord Darden," Miss Mayton said, finishing off her sixth piece of buttered toast. "The girls are all so very close, you see."

Darden sighed and said, "Very well, but you are not to pepper me with questions as you are wont to do. This is a conversation between myself and Beatrice, not a family meeting."

Beatrice was rather taken aback. What mystery was this? Had she done something wrong the evening before, and Darden felt he must point it out?

It would be very crushing if it were so. Darden had never scolded or corrected her. He was the best brother in the world—always on her side.

"We will be quiet as church mice," Cordelia assured him.

"Even quieter," Juliet said, nodding.

"Deathly quiet," Viola said.

"Quiet as a churchyard," Rosalind said.

Darden folded his arms. "Even *approaching* quiet will be sufficient, though I find I must see it to believe it," he said good-naturedly.

They all speedily repaired to the library. Darden sat himself behind the desk and Beatrice in front of it, while Miss Mayton and Beatrice's sisters all squeezed together on a sofa on the far side of the room.

"I trust you had an enjoyable evening, sister?" Darden said.

"Indeed, I did," Beatrice said. "But Darden, you frighten me. Did I do something wrong?"

"Certainly not," Darden said, laughing. "No, this is a different matter entirely. I was at the YBC this morning."

"Yes, I did hear your horse going very early," Beatrice said.

"There were some matters to arrange regarding the painting of rooms and those fellows like to get started at dawn," Darden said. "In any case, while I was there, I was told something I think you ought to know."

Beatrice could almost feel her five sisters and Miss Mayton leaning forward. She faintly heard Juliet whisper, "What is it?"

"It seems there was a gentleman at Almack's who was entirely struck down by you. A case of instant love, I believe is the term Miss Mayton employs."

Beatrice felt her face flame. Who? Who could it possibly be? "Darden, I noted no such feelings on display."

"No, you would not have," Darden said. "He was so struck he made his excuses and left. I very much doubt you ever laid eyes on him."

Her sisters gasped behind her. "Left!" Cordelia whispered.

"But…why?" Beatrice asked. "If he were struck, one would imagine he would…"

"That he would stay and petition Lady Jersey for a spot on your card," Darden said. "Apparently, that could not be. My friend tells me that this gentleman has a rather tragic past—both his mother and his sister died in childbirth. So you see, the one thing he cannot do is *marry* his true love. He could not bear to lose her in that manner."

"But that means, if I am his true love, he may be mine," Beatrice said, "and I am doomed to never have him because of his care of me?"

"That would seem to be the situation," Darden said, nodding. "Though, I did have an idea."

"He's got an idea!" Rosalind said, behind Beatrice.

"What idea?" Beatrice asked.

"It seems to me that this gentleman might be pushed to get over his fears for his true love if he is forced to witness other gentlemen pursuing you. It would make him see that you will marry *somebody*, and who better to care for you than him?"

"That is true, I suppose," Beatrice said.

Darden leaned back in his chair and clasped his arms behind his head. "We must only speed things along. So, I talked to my YBC members and several of them will set out to woo Beatrice Bennington, very publicly and dramatically, so he cannot miss it. I really think he will not be able to bear it and will step forward."

"But who is he?" Beatrice said. "If we are to play at such a ruse, I would like to be able to judge the effect it has. I must also see if he makes my hair feel as if lightning has struck it. After all, it may be a case of unrequited love if I do not feel the same."

"I do not know who the man is," Darden admitted. "My friend who told me of it has been sworn to secrecy and, as a gentleman, he cannot break his word. All he would say is that he has long known him, he is handsome, titled, of a passionate nature, and the poor fellow was up all the night long cursing the fates. By dawn, he declared that he would be able to master himself should he encounter you, but would carry a heavy weight on his heart and soul forevermore."

"I imagine he even tore at his hair in the middle of it," Juliet said, rather loudly.

"I cannot confirm any tearing of hair," Darden said over Beatrice's shoulder, "but then, I cannot rule it out either. Now, what do you say? Are you willing to play along in an effort to draw him out from his misery?"

"I feel I have no choice in the matter," Beatrice said. "After all, it would be the tragedy of my life if he is my one true love and we never meet."

"Just as I thought," Darden said. "So, Mr. Cahill, who you already know, along with the lords Dunston and Jericho, and Sir William will be your pretend suitors. I suspect we will not have to play long at this game before our mystery gentleman steps forward and declares himself."

Beatrice's younger sisters, and Miss Mayton for that matter, could hold back no longer. They were upon their sister in a trice.

"A mystery gentleman tortured by tragedy," Miss Mayton said, sounding entirely satisfied with the circumstance.

"And you go to the theater this evening, Beatrice," Rosalind said. "He might very well be there!"

"I have been informed that he *will* be there," Darden said.

"It is so romantic—I feel almost faint over the idea!" Viola cried.

"Now," Darden said, interrupting them before Viola did actually hit the floor in a faint, "all of this is in the strictest confidence. Nobody but us must know of the ruse. Secrets have a way of becoming known. Not even Van Doren, family friend though he may be, can be let in on it."

"Certainly not Van Doren," Cordelia said. "He would try to stop it, to be sure. Whenever we have had an interesting plan in mind, what has he said?"

"You cannot do it because blab-blab-blah-blah-blab," Viola said.

"Precisely," Juliet said. "He would not comprehend the romance and the passion of it at all."

"Lord Van Doren does come to the theater with us this evening, though," Miss Mayton said. "We must be careful not to let on that anything is in the works."

"He will not be able to avoid noticing that Beatrice is pursued, as Mr. Cahill and Lord Dunston will be there, ready to set the ruse in motion," Darden said. "That is no matter, as long as he does not discover it to be a ruse."

"We shall tell Van Doren absolutely nothing," Beatrice confirmed. "But what about father?"

Darden hesitated just the least little bit, then he said, "I would not bother him with it. You know our father, he does not like to be troubled."

Everybody in the room nodded vigorously, this seeming a kind, considerate, and very convenient reason to not inquire into the earl's thoughts on the scheme.

⋙⋘

As his carriage barreled toward Covent Garden on the heels of the earl's carriage, Matthew was not at all looking forward to the evening. His carriage might be going at a good pace now, but as it neared their destination it would not be so. His conveyance would inevitably enter a long line of other theatergoers and sit there for ages.

That might turn out to be the most pleasant part of the evening.

It was not that he did not like plays. He did. He could happily attend Shakespeare's works every evening of the week, had they been on offer so often in Taunton. This, though, was not to be Shakespeare. It was a new play by a fellow named Thomas Holcroft called *A Tale of Mystery*.

That had not sounded so bad, until his valet had tried to explain the plot. Apparently, it was all the rage in Town and Marcus had gone to see it on his day off. It was what was called a melodrama and it was about some young girl with a hefty dowry who is poised to be married off to a powerful man's son, though she loves another. There is a poor fellow who has gone mute after having been almost murdered by who else but the powerful man?

Then at the end there was something about them all getting together in a cottage near a bridge with archers on their heels?

At least, he thought that was what Marcus had said. His mind had drifted off in the midst of the telling of the convoluted thing.

The play was unlikely to engage him. And then, there were other annoyances that were certain to present themselves.

Beatrice very much enjoyed noting who was looking at her and that habit must reach new heights in a London theater box. Any misguided gentleman making the mistake of even vaguely glancing in her direction would be pronounced terribly in love with her.

He had watched her come out of the house in a rather smashing yellow gown, though as fast as he'd admired it, he'd also thought she'd chosen it to stand out in the dim lights of the theater.

Miss Mayton had made the rather interesting choice of a dark purple taffeta, her head sprouting a green ostrich feather. As she was short and rather well-padded, she looked like nothing so much as a turnip just pulled from the ground.

As his carriage slowed and now inched forward in the inevitable crush of a line, he considered where his own eyes would be traveling this night. He planned to keep them firmly on the stage, no matter how dreadful the performance was. Both Lady Mary, who he'd dined with at Almack's, and Lady Clara, who he'd danced with, had pried into his schedule.

As it happened, both of those ladies' families had a box at the theater and they would attend too. Lady Clara had already seen the play and was wild for it, so she and her mama would come again. Lady Mary had only heard tell of it and was much looking forward to it.

Those two ladies, and several others he'd danced with at Almack's, made him uncomfortable in some manner. They were all exceedingly pleasant, but he got the feeling of being stalked through a wood like a stag. There was something in their manner that said they meant business, and that business might be him and his estate.

He should not be surprised to note it. After all, marriage was what they had come for. It was what Beatrice had come for. It was what he, himself, would come for, some season.

Just not this season, he did not think.

As lovely and pleasant as the ladies were, it was impossible to imagine them gracing his table. He could not know how prepared they were to manage a household, and for all he knew they would do it brilliantly. But there was something else…not quite right.

Finally, his carriage came to the doors of the theater. Beatrice was already bounding up the steps while Miss Mayton attempted to keep up with her and the earl followed leisurely behind.

Beatrice glanced this way and that. She was not even inside yet and was looking about to see if anybody was struck by her.

Let the melodrama begin.

Chapter Nine

TATTLETON FELT SURROUNDED from all sides. First, there was Lord Darden's deranged plan of throwing false suitors in front of Lady Beatrice, all to force Lord Van Doren to claim feelings that Tattleton was certain he did not have.

Then, both the footmen and the lady's maids had gone wild over some duke named Conbatten. From what he could gather, this fellow did everything spectacularly well.

As always happened in Town, the servants had made quick work of becoming acquainted with the other servants in the neighborhood. *That* was how they suddenly knew so much about this fellow Conbatten. He was the talk of London, or so everybody said.

Since when was a butler to entertain entreaties from footmen that they had need of a thermometer to ensure their bath was ninety-eight degrees? They only took a bath once a week and it was in the same water, with just more of the hot dumped in, for all of them. Mrs. Huffson was of the opinion that he ought to let them have one, it being a small price to pay for peace.

But what next, then? Apparently this Conbatten ended his ablutions with a glass of chilled champagne. Were they to ask for that next? What right did a footman have in attempting to live as a duke?

It was hardly less ludicrous than how the maids had been carrying on. Once Miss Mayton had delivered a detailed description of this Conbatten's person to Fleur, they all seemed as if they had plans to marry the duke. Fleur had even had the temerity to say, "Stranger things have happened."

No, Fleur, a stranger thing has *never* happened!

On top of all that, Lady Beatrice's sisters had been devastated that they must be left behind when the carriage left for the theater.

Though they had cheerfully bid Lady Beatrice farewell, that had not held up long. The lamentations when the carriage turned a corner and was out of sight had been such that one might have thought somebody died.

Lady Juliet, in particular, found offense in it. As she was to become a lauded poetess, and possibly even a lady playwright, she felt she had the God-given authority to attend any theater she liked.

To cheer everybody up, Lady Cordelia had put on her own play. It was the same play as always—Desdemona weeping about something or other. But how many times had he requested that she not require footlights for her performances?

He'd had to move a chair to cover the new burn hole in the carpet.

The young ladies had consoled themselves over the third fire this year with tea and biscuits.

"Well, Mr. Tattleton," Mrs. Huffson said, sipping her tea with contentment, "things have settled above stairs and I think once you deliver the footmen a thermometer, peace shall reign once more."

"I see," he said, "and am I to deliver the Duke of Conbatten to your maids to satisfy them as well? I fear that whatever is to reign over this house in the coming days, it will not be peace!"

⁂

BEATRICE HAD BEEN doing her best to be discreet, and yet still look everywhere. Darden had it on good authority that the mysterious gentleman who was hopelessly in love with her would attend the performance this evening.

Who was he? Where was he?

Darden said the YBC was determined to drive him out from his covey of despair and that Mr. Cahill and Lord Dunston were prepared to begin the ruse to do so.

Flowers would be sent, stares would be evident, bows would be made, and raised glasses would be held in her direction—it was all to be as obvious as the sun rising in the morning sky. The mysterious gentleman could not help but to perceive it.

The poor gentleman had vowed to never marry, but certainly when he considered her future belonging to another, he would relent.

They had passed through the crowded entrance hall, a crush of people milling about, and climbed the carpeted stairs to their box. It was heaven! They had nothing like it in the environs of Taunton. At home, they sometimes had a play put on in the assembly rooms by a traveling troupe, but there was no proper theater house.

Here, they had a quite commodious box with well-padded seating for all of them and a marvelous view of both the stage and the other theatergoers.

She'd sat herself down and glanced surreptitiously at the boxes that could be viewed.

The earl said, "I am not quite certain what it is we will see this evening. Some sort of mystery, I believe."

"My valet tried to explain it to me," Van Doren said, sitting just behind Beatrice, "but I could not make heads or tails of it."

"That is because it is a melodrama mystery," Beatrice said. "One must view it to understand it."

"That makes sense," Miss Mayton said, her green ostrich feather waving cheerfully as she spoke.

"Does it?" Van Doren said.

"Oh look," Miss Mayton said, "there is Mr. Cahill in the pit. He is trying to catch your eye, dear."

"I see him," Beatrice said, thrilling at the notion that the ruse had well and truly begun. Even now, her tortured suitor might be viewing the goings-on.

The earl nodded genially to Mr. Cahill. "Now who is that fellow with him? Another friend of Darden's I suppose."

"I believe that is Lord Dunston," Beatrice said, of course knowing that was who it must be from dear Darden. "He was pointed out to me at Almack's."

Both gentlemen raised their glasses to Beatrice, and she pretended at modesty and looked away.

Had her tortured gentleman seen it?

"Dunston seems as foppish as Cahill invariably does," Van Doren said.

Beatrice ignored the comment, as naturally Van Doren did not have the first idea of the game that was actually afoot. True love might very well be at her doorstep and whether Mr. Cahill or Lord Dunston were foppish was quite beside the point.

"That young lady is staring in this direction," Miss Mayton said. "Just across the way."

Beatrice followed Miss Mayton's gaze and noted Lady Clara, the same who had been determined to introduce Van Doren around at Almack's.

Lady Clara inclined her head at seeing that she'd been noted. Beatrice did the same, though she did not give a toss for Lady Clara.

The earl chuckled and said, "I believe the lady is making eyes at Van Doren."

"Certainly not," Van Doren said.

Certainly not was just what Beatrice thought. Why should Lady Clara make eyes at Van Doren at the theater?

"Well, never mind," the earl said, "I suppose you will have more than one lady attempting to catch your eye this season, eh, Van Doren?"

"I hardly think—"

"Now, do not protest the idea," the earl went on. "It has occurred to me that we are all so used to seeing you that we have failed to notice the effect you have on other ladies outside of our sphere. I believe you are found to be devilishly handsome."

Beatrice looked at her father in some amazement. Then she looked back at Lady Clara, who was just now prettily fanning herself.

"I suppose if she is not particularly romantic, she would make a very fine viscountess," Miss Mayton said.

A very fine viscountess? As in, Van Doren's viscountess? Why did everybody seem to wish to marry him off so quick?

Why was everybody thinking of who Van Doren ought to marry, rather than who she ought to marry? There was a man out there somewhere who loved her!

The acrobats had been flinging themselves round the stage for a good quarter hour. Now, the orchestra began to tune. The melodrama mystery was set to begin.

There was a soft knock on the door. Van Doren rose and opened it to a footman holding two small bunches of violets.

"This is not at all appropriate," Van Doren said, giving the footman a coin and taking the flowers.

The earl shrugged. "Violets. A message of modesty. And look there, Mr. Cahill and his friend have surely sent them. They bow to me as if to excuse their boldness. Ah, what it is to be a young man."

Beatrice grabbed the bunches from Van Doren's hands and held them high enough to be seen over the balustrade, in case her tortured gentleman was watching.

Mr. Cahill and Lord Dunston were acting their part terrifically by bowing and smiling in her direction.

"You'd better give them over to me," the earl said, "lest they cause talk, as innocent as they are."

"What are those two thinking?" Van Doren said.

"They are thinking with their hearts, Lord Van Doren," Miss Mayton said. "A thing you might try out some day."

Beatrice suppressed the urge to laugh. It was just the sort of comment that would make steam come out of Van Doren's ears.

She could not think of him for long, though. The play was starting and Darden's plan had come off terrifically. If her tormented gentleman were in the theater, he could not have failed to perceive that there were two gentlemen in the pit who were fascinated by Beatrice Bennington.

Be brave, good sir, and make yourself known.

MATTHEW DID HIS best to keep his attention on the play, and what a play it was. Nobody in it seemed to have any sense at all. Most particularly Señor Bonamo, who appeared to believe whoever he'd spoken to last. That fellow had been better off to listen to his servant, as the lady seemed to be the only rational creature on the stage.

Though he had sternly forbidden his eyes to go anywhere but for the stage, they kept drifting to the now wilting bunches of violets the earl had laid on an empty chair.

What he had feared had begun. He was certain Mr. Cahill had no real interest in Beatrice aside from her dowry. They had met more than once, and Matthew had detected no particular regard coming from that quarter.

No, Cahill had unexpectedly met them at the posting house and then proceeded to give the matter some thought. Or rather, to give Beatrice's dowry some thought. He'd come out of that consultation with himself deciding that he admired her dowry very well indeed.

Worse, he had been exposed to the Benningtons enough to understand how to make headway in his suit. He'd heard their ideas about romance, he understood that Beatrice would look for grand, romantic gestures.

Matthew knew that Cahill, though he might pretend at it, was absolutely not what Beatrice looked for. She thought she looked for a paragon among men, but Matthew was convinced that she'd be disabused of those ideas and settle for a gentleman steady enough to indulge her and make her feel admired.

Cahill was not the man for the job. He was a falsely gay sort and seemed very much the man about Town. He was probably the type to keep a mistress, which would destroy Beatrice.

Cahill would try to keep that liaison, or perhaps many such disgraces, a secret. But those things always became known one way or the other. His father had once told him that when it came to wives, they had senses no less keen than the wolves of old. Make a misstep, and they would somehow sniff it out.

And who was this other fellow? This Lord Dunston? He seemed very chummy with Cahill, so that was not in his favor. Dunston would not know Beatrice's proclivities, but he seemed to be following Cahill's lead.

In any case, how long would it be before all the *ton* understood Beatrice's idiosyncrasies? She was not shy about advertising them, after all. When that happened, every fortune hunter in England would be sending her wilting violets.

Should he warn Darden of what was developing? The earl did not seem to perceive the danger of the situation at all.

As he mulled over what he ought to do, especially in light of the fact that he'd told Beatrice he would no longer scold, the play dragged on.

Finally, the villain, Romaldi, was dead. Though, for all the running around that was done and the archers having him in their sights several times, it was a bit of a letdown that he died by slipping on a rock. At least, he thought that was what happened. Or perhaps he was not dead at all. The curtains had been pulled closed, so they might never know.

As he did not care whether Romaldi was dead or alive, he would not feel deprived to go through life without that information. He was of the opinion that Juliet Bennington could have written something better, and that was really saying something. *Ode to the Bovine* had, at least, not gone on as long.

BEATRICE HAD PRACTICALLY floated into her bedchamber after arriving home from the theater. She was not at all surprised to find her sisters there, though they should have been abed.

"Now," she said, "before I tell you all about the play and everything that went on, how did you occupy yourselves while we were out? I see you did not burn down the house, which is a very promising start."

"Oh no," Cordelia said, shaking her head, "Tattleton extinguished the tipped candle on the carpet before it could really catch fire."

"Footlights again," Juliet said.

"Only a few charred bits, which Tattleton very helpfully covered up with a chair," Cordelia said.

"We did not have much choice but to insist on Cordelia acting out Desdemona," Rosalind said. "It was the only thing that could distract us from being left behind."

"That is true," Viola said. "We spent a terrific amount of time complaining about the injustice, and then we thought we better have Desdemona to cheer us up."

"And then Juliet wrote a smashing ode to describe our misery, which did cheer us too."

Juliet nodded and stood. "Ode to Missing Out."

The carriage rolls, we are left behind
It must be done, though so unkind
When I am king, or queen, or Prime Minister

I shall pronounce the habit totally sinister

"Well done, Jules!" Beatrice said. "And of course I was sorry that we could not all go together."

"But tell us, Bea," Rosalind said, "did Darden's plan begin?"

"Oh yes," Beatrice said, nodding. "Mr. Cahill and Lord Dunston located themselves in the pit and did a terrific amount of raising their glasses and bowing and smiling up at me. Then, as the final touch, they sent two bunches of violets to me and I made sure to hold them high enough so that my gentleman might perceive it."

"Do you have any clue at all who it might be?" Rosalind asked. "Did any gentleman appear to give himself away?"

"No, I noted nothing unusual in any of the gentlemen in the various boxes. But, though I did not discover him, I must imagine he is pacing and raging over the violets just now."

Juliet suddenly laughed. "He ought to be friends with Van Doren. I suppose he was raging against the violets too."

"Naturally, Van Doren said it was not at all appropriate and then Papa took them so we would not cause talk. That part was quite right, as a lady cannot stop a gentleman from sending flowers, she can only refuse them when they arrive. In any case, the violets were only part of the ruse."

"Poor Van Doren," Viola said, though there did not seem to be much actual pity in her voice, "he has not a clue what is going on. In the dark, as always."

Beatrice nodded, though she noticed that she did not tell her sisters that Lady Clara had been there, trying to get Van Doren's attention. Nor did she mention her father's notion of him being thought devilishly handsome.

After all, it was her season, not Van Doren's. Why should anybody make a fuss over him? And what if he did go off and marry the likes of Lady Clara? It was nothing to her—she had her true love out there somewhere, just now raging over the violets. He might even be tearing at his hair over it.

Though Beatrice was not so very fond of self-reflection when it caused her discomfort, she could not avoid some of it now. It occurred to her that she was irked by Van Doren's sudden popularity because his attention had always been on *her*.

She did not need or want the attention, of course, but she supposed she'd got used to it. It seemed very strange that his eyes and his thoughts were poised to go elsewhere.

"Well, Bea," Cordelia said, "we will see what sort of gentlemen callers turn up on the morrow. Perhaps *he* will come."

"And you will know him as soon as you set eyes on him," Juliet said. "I shall write an ode about it—Ode to the Mysterious Gentleman. Once I have perfected it, I will write it out in calligraphy, have it framed, and give it to you as a wedding present."

"Capital idea, Juliet," Viola said.

Beatrice was thoughtful for a moment, then she said, "I do not think we will see *him* on the morrow. As we know from Darden, he has been tortured by tragedy. I expect we will have to escalate our plan over time to drive him to it."

"Tortured by tragedy," Cordelia said with the slightest of sighs. "Now that's something to think about."

"Darden says my false suitors from the YBC will call on the house on the morrow. I did ask what the purpose could be and he said he has every suspicion that my tortured gentleman will be lured to the neighborhood and watching carefully who goes in and who goes out."

"So tortured," Viola said wistfully.

"I only hope," Beatrice said, "the poor gentleman is able to get some sleep tonight. I would not wish to know that he had tossed and turned and never felt rest. I would not want his health to suffer over me."

"You would not?" Juliet asked, apparently surprised to hear it.

"Well, not terribly, anyway," Beatrice said.

MATTHEW HAD NOT got much sleep the night before. He found himself tossing and turning and reviewing what he'd witnessed at the theater. The hunt for Beatrice's dowry had begun. He was certain he ought to stop it, he just did not know how.

Now, he found himself hurrying across the street to call on the Benningtons in all haste. He would not have thought of it, had not Marcus alerted him to the arrivals to that house. According to Marcus, a stream of gentlemen on horseback had just made a terrible ruckus in arriving and going in.

He had the feeling of the Benningtons coming under siege, as certainly that was the case. A stream of men, all looking to line their pockets with Beatrice's dowry, were headed toward Portland Place. And she, innocent and misguided Beatrice, would perceive none of their real intentions.

Tattleton showed him into the Benningtons' drawing room and what he viewed was precisely what he had feared.

Beatrice held court on the sofa, surrounded by a slew of ersatz admirers. She wore a charming muslin with a blue ribbon round the waist.

She nodded to acknowledge him but did not stop her talking.

"I really decided I must include the stalwart nature of Henry the Fifth because he just refused to give up," she said.

"And you find that quality attractive," Mr. Cahill asked, as a statement, more than a question.

"Indeed, so I must," Beatrice said. "I would wonder at the lady who did not."

Some gentleman unknown to Matthew dramatically threw his chest out. "I am exceedingly stalwart, Lady Beatrice," he said. "Once I decide on a thing, it is decided. Unless, of course, my lady was to object. Then I would naturally move heaven and earth to satisfy her wishes. But other than that, once I am decided I am stalwartly decided!"

Stalwartly decided?

Beatrice nodded graciously. "I find the exception to your rule to be very well thought out, sir. One must always put one's lady's wishes ahead of all else."

"Here is Van Doren come among us," Mr. Cahill said. "Van Doren, this is Lord Jericho, and there is Sir William, and that fellow over there is Lord Dunston."

Matthew bowed, though he'd really rather show them all the door. Further, he now knew that it was Sir William who found himself stalwartly decided.

"Lady Beatrice," Matthew said, glancing round at the interlopers into her drawing room, "does Darden not attend you?"

"He's gone off to the YBC," Beatrice said.

"It was quite the emergency that took him away," Mr. Cahill said. "Darden asked the painters for green walls. We were thinking a very dark green to give it a sort of hunting lodge effect. Well, they heard *gold* and now the place looks like the Palace of Versailles. We simply cannot live with it."

Matthew nodded, though he was not certain he required such a detailed explanation.

"Lady Beatrice was just telling us of her requirements," Sir William said, as if Matthew might be unaware of why she'd been talking about Henry the Fifth's stalwartness.

Matthew suddenly noted Beatrice's other sisters, and Miss Mayton, all squeezed together on a sofa at the far end of the room. The curtains on those windows were closed, casting it in shadow. He supposed Miss Mayton was meant to be chaperoning this farce.

"Do you enjoy poetry, Lady Beatrice?" Lord Dunston asked.

"I adore poetry, my lord," Beatrice said. She paused, as if she had in some way puzzled herself. "Perhaps I ought to make a love of poetry one of my requirements," she said.

"Wordsworth has come out with a terrific poem," Lord Dunston said. "It's called *Composed on Westminster Bridge.*"

"I should very much like to hear it, my lord, if you have committed it to memory."

Lord Dunston stood and cleared his throat. "Earth has not anything to show more fair: dull would he be of soul who could pass by a sight so touching in its majesty…"

Dunston droned on about splendor and majesty, smokeless air, and who knew what else as Matthew looked on. Finally, the fellow wrapped it up with a notion of a mighty heart lying still.

The party politely clapped. Beatrice said, "Very well done, Lord Dunston. But goodness, it is very long, is it not? My sister Juliet is a poetess and she has a particular knack for expressing a moving idea with far fewer words."

"That's me," came a shout from the other side of the room.

Juliet helpfully waved, in case there be any confusion about who it was that could so handily best Wordsworth.

"A challenger to Wordsworth!" Mr. Cahill said with what Matthew was certain was a false enthusiasm. "Certainly, Lady Juliet, we must hear something from you."

Before Matthew could even give Miss Mayton a warning glance, though it probably wouldn't have signified, Juliet was up on her feet and practically running toward them.

One might have thought a girl her age would be shy in front of all these gentlemen strangers. Alas, shyness had entirely skipped the Bennington line.

"As you know, Mr. Cahill," Juliet said, "our neighbor Van Doren accompanied us on our trip to Town. This is an ode to *him.*"

Matthew pressed his lips together. The little minx. Whatever was to come next, he was assured it would not be flattering.

CHAPTER TEN

JULIET CLEARED HER throat to prepare for reading her latest ode while Matthew glared at her. "It is called *Ode to Scolding*," she said.

Rant and rave and complain all day
What's the point? I cannot say
No end in sight, it never ceases
For one as taciturn as Scoldy-Breeches.

Juliet concluded her sophomoric effort and curtsied, amidst the roars of laughter from the gentlemen.

"Very funny, Juliet," Matthew said. "Now perhaps Miss Mayton ought to escort you back to the schoolroom."

"Oh no, Lord Van Doren," Miss Mayton said from across the room, "I do not conduct school while we are in Town."

"Truth be told, you have not conducted much school *anywhere*," Matthew replied.

"You see the teasing relationship of old family friends," Mr. Cahill said. "It is quite amusing."

"Is it?" Matthew said.

"Well, Lady Juliet," Mr. Cahill said, "you are not to fear. You will not have Lord Van Doren scolding you much longer. Not while he is pursued by so many interesting ladies."

"Is that so, Lord Van Doren?" Lord Jericho asked.

"Certainly not," Matthew said.

"So says the man of the hour always," Sir William said. "Does not Conbatten do just the same? He pretends he does not see the ladies everywhere who have set their cap on him."

Mr. Cahill nodded to confirm the idea.

Juliet said, "We have heard it said that Van Doren has got popular. We just have a hard time believing it. But then, Miss Mayton says all these ladies do not know him as we do."

"Does she say that," Matthew muttered.

"Mark me," Mr. Cahill said, "the name Van Doren is just now on feminine lips all over Town."

"I believe you have convinced me, gentlemen," Beatrice suddenly put in. "I must add a love of poetry to my list of requirements."

"Ah, Lady Beatrice," Lord Dunston said, turning to her, "we have not even thoroughly examined the list—tell us of Robin Hood's derring-do that you seek."

And so the conversation went on in the stupidest manner possible. Each time Beatrice described one of her requirements, the gentlemen all made speeches about how it was as if she described him down to his shoes.

Sir William even went as far as to outline his derring-do in the face of losing both his valet and his housekeeper in the same month. Apparently, it was quite the trial of bravery and courage.

Matthew sat through all of it, until the four idiot gentlemen were forced to leave for the sake of propriety. Once he'd seen them all safely on their horses, he marched back to his house across the street.

He felt as if all the world had agreed to a collective madness but had chosen to leave him out of it.

⇢⇢⇢⇠⇠⇠

AS LYNETTE HELPED her into her dress, Beatrice thought about the scenes that had transpired in the drawing room earlier in the day.

There was so little she kept from her sisters or her aunt, but she had not wished to discuss it in any detail.

Van Doren had come crashing in as usual, just when she was enjoying listing her requirements and wondering if her tortured gentleman was even then watching the house from afar.

It was bad enough that he'd pushed in, but then to hear Mr. Cahill speak of him! Van Doren was to rival Conbatten. His name was to be on feminine lips everywhere.

Could it really be so?

She had a great need to unburden herself, and Lynette had been her and Rosalind's maid for years.

"Lynette," she said, as her maid fussed with the hem of the dress, "Mr. Cahill says that there are many ladies in Town who are wild for Van Doren. What do you think of that?"

Beatrice noticed, a little uncomfortably, that she was hoping Lynette would pronounce it utterly impossible.

"Hmm," Lynette said, "of course, he is no Conbatten. We're all terribly in love with the duke below stairs. Fleur even says it would not be impossible for him to wed a lady's maid. She says stranger things have happened, though Mr. Tattleton says a stranger thing has certainly never happened."

"But what of Van Doren?" Beatrice asked. "Certainly, there cannot be ladies wild over him."

Lynette began to work on her hair. "It's funny, I saw him getting on his horse the other day and for a moment I did not recognize him. I did think, now there is a dashing gentleman. But then, I realized who it was."

That summed up Beatrice's feelings fairly succinctly. There was something unsettling about taking a step back and viewing Van Doren as a stranger. He *was* dashing then. She was so used to viewing him otherwise, though.

These other ladies, these feminine lips that Mr. Cahill had spoken of, they were viewing him as she did herself sometimes. When she stepped back.

"I wonder if he will ever love a lady," Beatrice murmured.

"Oh, I expect so," Lynette said. "He seems all practicality now, but some lady or other will drive him to distraction."

Beatrice noticed she felt rather sick at the idea. Van Doren. Driven to distraction. Might he even tear at his hair?

Lynette put the final touches to her own hair and added a thin gold chain to go round her neck.

Beatrice ought to be caught up with the divine dress she wore, a seafoam green silk, or how well Lynette had composed her hair, or what sort of people she might encounter at Lady Worsted's rout. Rather, she was caught up with imagining Van Doren driven to distraction.

It seemed very out of character for him. And a little fascinating.

⫸⫷

DARDEN HAD CALLED a meeting of *Campaign Shenanigans* at the YBC. He had gathered Cahill, Dunston, Jericho, and Sir William in one of the smaller coffee rooms.

"Well, gentlemen, our plan is underway and going at a fast clip. It seems both my sister and Van Doren were entirely uncomfortable with the proceedings today—exactly how we want them."

"Van Doren looked vexed as anything to find us in your drawing room," Lord Jericho said. "Splendid idea to make our arrival so boisterous—he could not have missed it."

"I saw his valet poke his head out the door over the ruckus as I was leaving," Darden said. "Naturally, he would have gone running to his master to alert him to it."

"He was clearly aggravated to find you had left your sister alone with a heap of gentlemen," Lord Dunston said.

"Oh yes, I knew he would be," Darden said.

"Darden, you missed a very nice touch. We said feminine lips all over Town are just now whispering the name Van Doren," Sir William said, laughing.

"Excellent. We assault them from both sides," Darden said. "Van Doren is led to believe that Beatrice has a slew of admirers and Beatrice is now convinced that ladies everywhere have set their cap on Van Doren."

"And then Lady Juliet put the final touches on it by poking Van Doren about his scolding," Cahill said. "She recited a poem naming him Scoldy-Breeches. He was rather raw over it."

"Poor Van Doren," Darden said. "He is such a good and reliable fellow, but he is often rather raw over something."

"What next?" Lord Jericho asked. "What is our next move?"

"Tonight," Darden said. "They both attend Lady Worsted's rout. We continue on with the campaign. We point out to Beatrice all the ladies we suspect of having set their cap on Van Doren. Some of them are actually true, I suspect. Lady Clara and Lady Mary in particular."

The gentlemen nodded as if they had just received military orders.

"Then, you are all to sing Lady Beatrice's praises to Van Doren," Darden continued. "And perhaps hint you are not alone in the admiration—there are others interested in her too. Perhaps we even hint Conbatten has his eye on her?"

"Conbatten," several of the gentlemen murmured, as if they had just heard the word of God.

"I suppose we still have not resolved whether to invite him to join the club?" Lord Jericho asked.

"Well…he might say no," Darden said.

"Or more worrying," Sir William said, "he might say yes."

They were all silent for some minutes, none of them knowing what to do about Conbatten. It would be a feather in their club's cap were the duke to join, but then what to say to the man if he turned up for a coffee or cards?

When it came to Conbatten, Darden found himself both intimidated, which he would never admit, and a little annoyed that he felt so.

"We'll table the Conbatten question for now," he said. "Let us gird ourselves for *Campaign Shenanigans*. A new sortie commences this evening at Lady Worsted's rout. I am determined that my sister be suitably married to a gentleman I can trust with her happiness. She may have *her* list of requirements, but that is *my* requirement."

※※※

MATTHEW HAD ACCEPTED the invitation to Lady Worsted's rout, though he had not initially had any intention of doing so. Routs were the stupidest of affairs—neither this thing nor that. Just a houseful of people expected to entertain themselves with whatever was laying about. Perhaps a lady ran into a musical instrument and would play, or a gentleman might spot a pack of cards and deal, or if one were extremely lucky, one might stagger into a refreshments room. All the while, everybody was pushed and shoved and pardon me'd to death.

But then, the earl told him that he would take Beatrice and Miss Mayton and that Darden had said all his friends from the YBC would attend. That had swayed him. The YBC, which he still had not been asked to join though he would refuse, was chock full of suspicious gentlemen.

He could not ignore what he knew to be Cahill's designs and would ensure that rogue did not take those designs any further than he had already. Then there was Lord Jericho, Sir William, and Lord Dunston. Cahill was the most worrying, in Matthew's view. The family knew Cahill far better than the others and, worse, Cahill knew the family far better.

Violets, indeed. And then that ridiculous scene in the Benningtons' drawing room with those rogues all gathered round her.

Once he'd said he would go to the rout, the earl had pressed him to join them in his carriage. There was no point to taking out two carriages when only one was needed and Darden would go straight from his club.

That would be convenient, as he would not risk becoming stuck behind a farmer's cart while unsuspecting Beatrice was worked on by the scoundrels after her dowry.

He'd paused his thinking then, as it occurred to him that perhaps he was being a bit narrowminded to think that it was *only* her dowry those idiots were after.

She was striking looking, that could not be denied. Further, though her conversation regarding her requirements was silly, Beatrice was in general a very good conversationalist. She had a certain wit that must be admired. And then, her family was respected—the earl was master of a large estate with a long history, and he was liked everywhere he went.

Yes, that was the real truth of it. Beatrice Bennington did not come with even one strike against her, other than her fanciful notions of romance. How easy it would be for a gentleman to overlook that proclivity. Or even to indulge it for a short period of time.

"There really is nothing against her," he said softly.

Marcus was knotting his neckcloth and said, "My lord?"

"Lady Beatrice," he answered. "I can see why all these swine are circling round as if a farmer has come out with the bucket of feed."

"I always have wondered, my lord," Marcus said slowly, "if there were not a match for Lady Beatrice somewhat…closer to home."

Matthew was startled at the statement, and he knew perfectly well what his valet hinted at. He, a match for Beatrice?

No, it could not be so.

He might have thought it, from time to time, years ago. But that was when she had only ever looked up at him with admiring eyes.

Those days had long passed.

He could never consider her as she was now. A wife, at the very least, must admire a husband's judgment. As for *his* judgment, she was less than admiring of it.

"I only say," Marcus pressed on, "it would be a rather wonderful match."

"Don't be ridiculous," Matthew said sharply. "I'll thank you to refrain from such opinions in future."

Marcus said softly, "Understood, my lord."

Now Matthew felt foolish. He never spoke to his servants in such a manner. He'd sounded very like a petulant and spoiled king.

"Never mind, Marcus," he said. "I only find myself out of sorts this evening. Have some of my good brandy and forget I ever said anything."

"Indeed, my lord," Marcus said, looking remarkably cheered.

As Matthew supposed he would be. The last time he'd made such an offer, Marcus had managed to down half the bottle. He'd likely be undressing himself when he got home, his valet snoring in a chair.

Still, he'd rather make amends with a good amount of brandy than go on uncomfortably with his valet. Despite how outrageous the man's opinions were.

Now, the earl's carriage trotted along at a good clip. Beatrice was looking very well in a pale blue-green silk, a thin gold chain calling attention to her slender neck.

Miss Mayton said, "It was so very good of Darden's friends to call today. Earl, you are to know they were all exceedingly admiring of Beatrice."

"Yes, of course they would be," the earl said in a satisfied tone.

"Indeed, they were all most anxious to prove they met her requirements."

"Did they now?" the earl said laughing.

"Oh yes," Miss Mayton confirmed. "When it came to Robin

Hood's derring-do, Sir William relayed a very stirring account of himself."

"He told of losing his valet and housekeeper in the same month," Matthew said. "Hardly going toe-to-toe with the Sheriff of Nottingham."

"Nevertheless," Miss Mayton said with a sniff, "it was a very trying situation."

"What say you about all these gentlemen, Beatrice?" the earl asked goodhumoredly.

"It is far too early to conclude anything, Papa," Beatrice said. "They all still have much to prove."

"They are not going to prove anything, and if they do, it is just playacting," Matthew said.

"Do you say that none of them can be bothered to meet my list of requirements?" Beatrice said, looking more than a little put out.

"I say, as I have said several times, that no man has the *ability* to meet your list of requirements. Unless you consider Robin Hood's derring-do to be losing a few servants. In which case, you are well on your way to locating your prince."

"Perhaps Lady Clara and Lady Mary and some others have their own list of requirements," Beatrice said. "What then?"

"Nothing then," Matthew said. "Though, if they have gone so far as to make such a list, I pray for their sakes that it is something sensible and there is not a whiff of Beowulf or Gawain or anybody else on it."

"Ah here we are," the earl said. "Now you two sparrers can go in and be admired by everyone you encounter, and we will see in the end who meets your requirements. I fully expect to see requirements flying out of windows sometime in the near future."

Oh, Papa, you always do say so."

"So I do, my dear."

BEATRICE COULD NOT be at all satisfied with the conversation in the carriage. Though Van Doren had scolded and scolded about her requirements before they'd come to London, why did he go on with it now?

For one thing, he'd said he would stop scolding. For another, he'd been in her drawing room today. He'd witnessed how eager the gentlemen were to satisfy her requirements.

Of course, it was only Darden's friends and a ruse to drive her tortured gentleman from his lonely despair. But Van Doren did not know that!

Why had not he been struck by it?

To add further irritation to Beatrice's already prickly feelings, who did she suppose was wandering round so near the front doors? None other than Lady Clara, who proceeded to pretend it was entirely happenstance though Beatrice was certain she'd been cruising those waters like a shark looking for her fish.

The fish in question did not seem to at all perceive it. Van Doren appeared pleased to see the lady.

This prompted Beatrice to catch Conbatten's eye when he passed by. He stopped. "Lady Beatrice, Miss Mayton," he said, as Lady Clara cast her net round Van Doren and told him some stupid story about the carriage traffic earlier in the day.

"Father," Beatrice said, "this is the Duke of Conbatten. This is my father, the Earl of Westmont."

"Your Grace," the earl said, "very pleasant to know you."

"Do address me as Duke," Conbatten said, "Lady Beatrice already does so."

"Does she now?" the earl said, laughing.

Conbatten nodded his head and looked to move off, but Miss Mayton stopped him by saying, "Your Grace, you are to know that you are all the rage in our servants' quarters. The maids are quite besotted."

This gave everybody a deal of pause. Even the earl was looking rather wide-eyed, though so little ever ruffled his feathers.

"I do not believe I am acquainted with any of those ladies," Conbatten said drily.

"Well, it is just a bit of silliness," Miss Mayton said. "Though we feel it sometimes. Earlier today, I could hardly find Lynette to dress Beatrice as they were all in the kitchens gossiping and here we had so many members of the YBC coming to see Beatrice—Mr. Cahill, Lord Dunston, Sir William, and Lord Jericho."

Though Beatrice adored her aunt's rather forward way of communicating, she began to think Miss Mayton told the duke a bit too much about the activities of their household.

"Lady Beatrice," the duke said, "perhaps I might escort you to the refreshment room, if it please the earl. Lady Worsted is rather renowned for her wine cellar."

The earl nodded, and Beatrice thought her father did so rather gratefully.

Conbatten bowed and led her through the crowd of people, Beatrice said, "Please do not mind my aunt, her thoughts are often spoken as she has them."

They had made their way into the refreshment room, which was a large space and not as crowded as the other rooms. Conbatten led her to a chair and motioned for a footman. "I suggest the Canary, it is quite good."

Beatrice nodded, as she did indeed like a good Canary.

The footman hurried off and Conbatten said, "I was not at all alarmed by your aunt's phrasings, Lady Beatrice. Every family has an old aunt who will say discomfiting things. Though, I have not the slightest intention of becoming acquainted with any of your maids."

"Certainly not," Beatrice said. "For their sake as well as yours. It is one thing to gossip in the kitchens, but were they to encounter you, I suspect they'd fall over in a faint. In any case, you must not be too flattered—last year they were all wild for a vicar who visited the neighborhood."

This caused Conbatten to laugh. "So it is myself and the vicar keeping company."

The footman returned with the glasses of Canary on a silver tray.

Conbatten handed her a glass. "No, Lady Beatrice, I wished to speak to you on another matter. Your aunt seemed determined to have all know that half the members of your brother's club attended you this day. This is perhaps ill-advised."

"Ill-advised?" Beatrice asked, not having the first idea of what the duke meant by it.

"All four gentlemen named by Miss Mayton are perfectly acceptable fellows, but everybody knows that both Lord Dunston and Mr. Cahill do not have any intention of marrying so soon. Sir William is under the thumb of his mother, who is set on another lady. And then, Lord Jericho is biding his time until a lady from his neighborhood makes her debut next season."

"Whatever their circumstances may be," Beatrice said, "there can be no scandal associated with their call to my father's house."

"Certainly not," Conbatten said. "It is all very proper. However, you have informed me of your list of requirements and therefore I must presume you wish to marry. I only say that having those fellows trail you about might keep another more likely gentleman away. There are those who are not as loud and chattering as those YBC fellows. I can think of several offhand and none very likely to push through such a throng."

Beatrice did everything to stop herself from laughing. Little did Conbatten know that it was all just a performance, and it was to drive somebody in, not out.

Then she paused. Perhaps she should not be so quick to dismiss the duke's caution. After all, might not her tortured gentleman be among these fellows who were hanging back?

"Duke, these gentlemen you think of, do any of them have a tragic past? What I mean is, have any of them lost both a mother and sister to childbirth?"

"What a question, and no, I do not believe so."

Alas, none of them were her tortured gentleman.

In a grave tone, she said, "I will take all of your thoughts under advisement, duke."

"By the by," the duke said, "you really ought to address me as Your Grace until I give you leave to call me duke."

"Do you give me leave?"

"Well, it's a little late now. You'd best just carry on as you have been."

The duke was an odd sort of creature, though Beatrice began to like him very well. Despite the interested glances of all who entered the refreshment room, there was not the slightest bit of romance or flirtation between them. They were, however, becoming friends, she thought.

The poor fellow had gone out of his way to give her a hint. Somehow, his handing out of hints just now did not make her cross, as Van Doren's so often did.

That it was a hint not at all required, he need never know.

Chapter Eleven

Matthew had slipped away from Lady Clara when the opportunity came. She'd turned to greet a friend and he disappeared into the crowd.

It was not that he did not like the lady, she was very pleasant. However, there was something uncomfortable in her mien. Her eyes glittered, she laughed too easily and perhaps too long, her color was high. Her nerves seemed at a fever pitch, and he was very afraid he knew why. He'd been singled out.

He did not wish to be singled out by her or any other lady. Not this season. Not yet.

A sudden slap on the back woke him from his thoughts.

"Van Doren," a hale and hearty voice said from behind him.

"Cahill," he said, turning. As if one of the YBC would not be enough, Lord Dunston was with him.

"We find ourselves entirely dejected just now," Lord Dunston said.

Matthew did not think they looked at all dejected. In any case, while a rout was not the most pleasant thing to attend, it could hardly engender such strong feelings.

"I see you did not note it," Cahill said. "The great Conbatten has whisked off our Lady Beatrice."

Matthew attempted to parse the various outrages in the statement. *Our* Lady Beatrice? Since when was she to be *their* anything? And what was this about Conbatten?

"Whisked?" he said.

"Oh yes, he swooped in like a falcon and now they are heads together in the refreshment room," Lord Dunston said.

"I do not suppose we have ever seen Conbatten take such an interest. Perhaps the great man is finally to be caught," Mr. Cahill said.

"That must be well received by you, Van Doren—your neighbor will become a duchess," Lord Dunston said. "Though we must be crushed by this turn of events."

Mr. Cahill sighed very dramatically. "I suppose he will have no trouble at all fulfilling Lady Beatrice's list of requirements. Conbatten never has any trouble with *anything*."

"Her list of requirements is a lot of nonsense," Matthew said, "as I believe you are all fully aware."

"Nonsense?" Lord Dunston said, appearing very aggrieved. "But certainly, Van Doren, a lady such as that has every right to define her requirements."

"Yes, yes," Matthew said, "but her list is…well, the derring-do of Robin Hood? The depth of feeling of Shakespeare? The stalwartness of Henry the Fifth?"

"But Van Doren," Mr. Cahill said, "it is Lady Beatrice we speak of. Perhaps no other lady might have such expectations, but Lady Beatrice has every right!"

Matthew narrowed his eyes. "You may praise her to the skies, but I am confident of my understanding of the real case of things. I believe I understand her *real* attraction."

"Clarify yourself, my lord," Lord Dunston demanded, looking exceedingly affronted.

"I will not, as I do not believe you have need of it," Matthew said. He turned on his heel and pushed his way through the crowd.

Ahead, he spotted Lady Clara. Taking a sharp right, he saw Lady Mary. Both of the ladies were closing in.

He was a hunted stag and the people milling about were the trees he attempted to hide behind. He did an about face and dodged and weaved away.

This was speedily becoming one of the most irritating nights of his life.

>>><<<

BEATRICE HAD LONG since left the company of Conbatten and had various conversations, some with people she had met at Almack's and some she was newly introduced to.

All the while, she took surreptitious glances round the room. Was there a gentleman here somewhere, watching her. Tortured by her? Wishing to approach but holding himself back on account of his love of her?

The only gentleman who could be positively identified as watching her was Van Doren, as he was so predisposed to do.

She supposed Van Doren would agree with Conbatten regarding the unsuitability of the YBC members, both of those gentlemen entirely in the dark as to what was really going on.

Now, Lord Jericho and Sir William made a great show of paying her attention.

"Oh, look there," Lord Jericho said, laughing. "Lady Clara follows Van Doren in a most determined manner."

Beatrice followed his eyes and indeed it was so. Lady Clara practically elbowed people out of the way to find herself near her quarry.

"She will find she has some stiff competition," Sir William said. "All I have heard this night is Lord Van Doren this and Lord Van Doren that."

"Certainly not?" Beatrice asked, glancing at Van Doren again.

"Oh yes," Lord Jericho said, "the rest of us poor gentlemen have seemed to have become the paper-hangings in the background."

"Even his name is said to be dashing," Sir William said. "I heard one lady, who I shall kindly leave unnamed, say that it spoke of a romance of old."

"And there is something in his serious disposition that makes them all swoon," Lord Jericho added.

"They imagine it would be something indeed, to bring a fellow like that to his knees," Sir William said.

Beatrice experienced another moment of a step back in viewing Van Doren. And what did she see when she viewed him thus?

A tall and well-built gentleman with a sweep of dark hair and a strong, determined chin, his dark eyes smoldering. His neckcloth was perfection, his clothes cut precisely. His general air of seriousness giving him perhaps a more outsized presence than a viscount had a right to.

There was a confidence about Van Doren, though not like Conbatten's brand of certainty. It was a quiet confidence, not built for show.

Lynette's words fairly rang in her ears—a lady would someday drive Van Doren to distraction. It seemed he was driving various ladies to distraction, but someday it would be he who would find himself so.

No wonder his name was on everybody's lips. No wonder he was compared to Conbatten. These ladies wished to conquer the unconquerable Van Doren.

Beatrice had noticed that these moments of a step back in viewing had begun to come more often in Town. It was as if Van Doren were somehow transforming in front of her.

How was he doing it? Was it only that now other ladies were noticing him, she must notice him too? Now she must see him as the rest of the world saw him?

What did he think when he viewed *her*? Did he step back and see her differently than he had at home? Did he step back and see what he imagined other gentlemen saw?

He had taken to calling her *Lady* Beatrice, after all. At least, sometimes he did, though he often slipped up out of habit.

Beatrice chased away whatever feelings were circling round her. She could not even say what the feelings were. She was certain she was only becoming distracted because she still had not identified the tortured gentleman who was besotted by her.

These games they played to draw the gentleman out were all well and good, but she must know him. Then, all thought of any other gentleman, and certainly all thought of Van Doren, would fly out of her head.

"I wonder if the gentleman we seek is here this evening," Beatrice said, a little surprised at the sulk that had crept into her tone.

"I would think so," Lord Jericho said, "but dash it, I wish I knew who he was."

"I too, Lord Jericho," Beatrice said softly. "I too."

<hr />

MARCUS TOOK MATTHEW'S coat and said, "How did Lady Worsted's rout come off?"

His valet slightly weaved as he took the coat away and Matthew assumed much had been made of his earlier offer of brandy.

"It was the usual crush of people all aimlessly milling about," he said.

"I suppose the great Conbatten ruled over them all," Marcus said. "I have had several encounters with his valet—a French fellow named Henri who is insufferable. Apparently, the duke's bath is closely timed. At precisely twenty-six minutes, a bell is rung below stairs. This sets the butler racing to the wine cellar for chilled champagne in an equally chilled glass, where it flies up the stairs and into Conbatten's hand. Why twenty-six minutes? Why not twenty-five or twenty-seven? I *asked* him. The insufferable Henri claimed he could not reveal the reason. Insufferable."

Matthew suppressed a smile. He was certain Marcus was drunk, or he would not be hearing in detail of his disdain for someone else's valet.

"Conbatten is rather insufferable too, I think," Matthew said. "Some of those YBC fellows think he's got designs on Lady Beatrice. What do you think of that—Beatrice to become a duchess?"

Marcus appeared rather staggered by the idea. Truth be told, Matthew was rather staggered by the idea himself.

Conbatten was not at all right for Beatrice. She required a certain level of attention, and that fellow was too wrapped up in his bathing habits to be any use.

"You must tell her of Henri!" Marcus fairly cried out. "Our poor Lady Beatrice cannot live in the same household with such a scoundrel, rotter, insufferable rogue!"

Matthew nodded, but did not answer, as he had no intention of informing Beatrice that Conbatten's valet was deemed insufferable by his own.

"And *you* must go to bed, I think," Matthew said. "I can undress myself."

Marcus nodded sadly and looked to be transforming from outrage to maudlin. "I did perhaps indulge in some brandy," he said.

"Some?" Matthew asked.

"Much. I will admit it. I began to reflect on my conversations with that insufferable Henri and it occurred to me that he was attempting to put himself above me in some way and it did aggravate my nerves to such a degree! And then, you did say…"

With that, his valet weaved from the room, closing the door rather harder than was strictly necessary.

Matthew blew out the candles in the room, but for one lone that he took with him to sit by the window.

There was a single lighted window across the street. Beatrice's no doubt. Her sisters would have waited up for her to return and relay every detail of the evening.

Would she speak of Conbatten? Was there really something there?

It would turn his ideas upside down. The YBC members were one thing—all jockeying for Beatrice's dowry.

But Conbatten would have no need of it.

Perhaps he found her wrong-headed ideas charming? Perhaps Conbatten had found himself bored by all the usual ways of a London lady. Then, along had come Beatrice, with her particularly original ideas.

It would be disastrous. The man was too self-involved to put Beatrice first. What sort of man made his butler run to the wine cellar twenty-six minutes into a bath? What sort of man lounged around in a tub for that long anyway? And then started drinking champagne before he was even out of it?

If he had any designs on Beatrice, they must be stopped.

But then, how on earth to stop it? It would be the most brilliant match of the season. What was he to say? *Now, Beatrice, I must regretfully inform you that the duke will care more about his bath than his wife.*

It was all such a muddle.

The light across the way went out. Beatrice would be laying her head down to sleep.

Would she dream of Conbatten?

※

IT WAS SUNDAY and the earl had directed that Sundays in Town were to be no different than Sundays at home.

Beatrice did not mind it. Sundays were for family—church in the morning, then all together in the drawing room, playing cards and games, and then a cozy family dinner.

The only outsider who was ever allowed to cross the threshold on a Sunday was Van Doren.

The earl did not like that his neighbor lived alone with nobody to dine with, so he must come for dinner every Sunday.

This Sunday was to be no different, apparently.

What *was* a difference though, was that they had Darden with them now.

Darden and the earl were closeted in the library, taking care of some estate business, but they would not stay away long. As they waited for their father and brother, her sisters and Miss Mayton occupied themselves in the drawing room.

Beatrice leaned back against the sofa and craned her neck to casually look out the window at the darkening street. For all she knew, the mysterious and tortured gentleman might be haunting her neighborhood. Darden had said he might do it, and when better than a lonely Sunday?

If he were, he would see Van Doren coming into the house. That might be just as helpful as Darden's friends hanging about. After all, her poor gentleman could not know that Van Doren was only a neighbor from home. He might be taken as a suitor too.

The idea gave Beatrice some sort of uncomfortable feeling. Van Doren. As a suitor…

Juliet stood with a paper in hand. "I have just finished a new ode," she said.

"Do read it to us, dear," Miss Mayton said.

Juliet cleared her throat. "Ode to the Person Who Always Seems to be Coming for Dinner."

Why is he here, does anybody know?
He comes and comes when we'd rather he go.
They say he is popular, but can that be true?
If it be so, it is certainly new.

"Well done, Jules," Cordelia said. "You've captured Van Doren perfectly."

"I'd like to see Wordsworth set the scene so economically," Rosalind said.

Though Beatrice had always found great amusement in Juliet's various odes against Van Doren, somehow this one did not move her so.

The earl and Darden came into the room, having concluded whatever business they had been attending to.

"Van Doren will be here shortly," the earl said, "he knows we dine early on a Sunday."

"He is always here," Viola said. "It almost seems he ought to have a room above stairs. It would save him the walk."

"Now, there girl," the earl said. "One day, I think you will all appreciate the worth of our neighbor. He has been a stalwart friend to this family."

Though their father never scolded, all of the sisters understood when he meant them to correct their course on some matter. It was gentle, but it was hard to miss.

"He is a fine gentleman," Darden said, "if you would only step back and see it."

Step back. Beatrice fairly shivered at the phrase. It was what she had named those instances when she did not look upon Van Doren as their scolding neighbor.

When she looked upon him as only a gentleman recently met.

"I suppose we could have a worse neighbor," Rosalind said grudgingly.

"I will go so far as to admit it," Juliet said, much to Beatrice's surprise. "Imagine if our neighbor was Mr. Graydell, always threatening to shoot a person he thinks is eyeing his coveys?"

"Or Miss Fairweather?" Cordelia said, laughing. "Never was a lady less aptly named. She'd have been better named Miss Stormy-Weather."

"Now, that poor lady does suffer from the rheumatism, which can make a person less than genial," the earl reminded them.

"Oh Papa," Viola said, "we were only working to rein in our disdain for Van Doren, do not scold us about Miss Fairweather too."

"I only say," the earl said, "you must learn to take people as you find them. It is a far more pleasant way to go on."

"If I must discover a compliment somewhere," Cordelia said, "and I only look for one to please you, Papa—it does at least seem as if Van Doren is turning himself into a usual gentleman upon his arrival to Town."

"Yes, we have heard he makes himself pleasant and is ever so popular," Rosalind said.

"Perhaps one of these ladies he meets will start his heart beating and he will discover some romance in there somewhere," Miss Mayton said. "Anything is possible, after all."

"Beatrice?" Darden asked. "What say you regarding our worthy neighbor?"

All eyes turned to Beatrice. In truth, she did not know what to say. It felt as if the world was very much upside down just now.

Tattleton opened the drawing room doors. "Lord Van Doren," he announced.

Van Doren came in as he always did and looked as he always looked. Yet, somehow different.

"Van Doren," the earl said jovially, "we were all just singing your praises."

Van Doren looked entirely skeptical to hear it. "Really. All of you?" he asked, eyeing Juliet in particular.

"Papa pointed out you were not so bad as a neighbor," Juliet said, shrugging at the improbability of it.

"I admitted you could be worse," Rosalind said.

"And I said, our neighbor might be Mr. Graydell, which would be worse," Juliet said.

"Or Miss Fairweather," Cordelia said.

"I could write some odes about *them*," Juliet said.

"But then, Papa reminded us that Miss Fairweather suffers from the rheumatism, though no excuse was posited for Mr. Graydell. He is just daft," Rosalind said.

"Then, we were waiting to see what Bea would say," Cordelia said.

Again, all eyes turned to Beatrice, with the addition of Van Doren's eyes.

"I must agree with the consensus, I suppose—it might be worse," Beatrice said.

It was just the type of comment Van Doren would expect from her. The sort she'd said a thousand times before. Somehow, though, she could not be quite satisfied with it.

"I have often thought just the same," Van Doren said.

This seemed to strike the sisters quite hard. It struck Beatrice fairly hard. She was certain that it had never occurred to any of them, including herself, that he would consider them as *might be worse*.

Though he scolded all the time, Beatrice had assumed they were all held in very high regard. They were the Benningtons after all. And he was, well, he was Van Doren.

Had Van Doren really looked upon them and thought, well, it might be worse?

It was an uncomfortable idea.

Chapter Twelve

Matthew could not be certain what he'd walked into when he'd arrived at the Benningtons' drawing room.

Apparently, he'd been the subject of some discussion, concluding that they might have had a worse neighbor than he.

Another gentleman might have taken umbrage to such an assessment, but it was the highest praise he could recall receiving from the five sisters in recent years.

He'd been further surprised by how taken aback they'd all looked when he'd mentioned he'd often thought they could be worse too. They'd appeared to not have the faintest inkling of what trouble they all were. Only the earl and Darden had not seemed surprised to hear that opinion.

The dinner had been odd, to say the least. There had been no faces made at him from across the table, no jabs thrown, no insulting odes recited. Juliet had even asked him a very civil question about his favored horse.

What was happening?

They all seemed more sensible or reasonable or…not like themselves.

It began to dawn on Matthew that since he'd reined in his scolding, they had improved.

It was positively diabolical. His scolding was meant to prod them toward improvement, and yet they only improved when he stopped?

But perhaps it was only Darden's presence. They did worship him, and perhaps they wished to please him.

Beatrice had been very quiet throughout dinner, which was not at all like her. He'd even tried to draw her out on two occasions, but she'd blushed and given short answers.

That was concerning. What was taking up all her thoughts?

If he knew Beatrice as he thought he did, there could only be one thing taking up her thoughts—romance.

Had Cahill made a move he was unaware of? Or worse, had Conbatten?

They had since repaired to the drawing room. Cordelia was consulting with Miss Mayton and Darden on how they would manage footlights and not burn anything at the same time.

This was considered from every angle, as everybody knew the earl would be unhappy if something were to catch fire. Not to mention Tattleton, who would have smoke coming from his ears were they to start a fire so soon on the heels of the last one.

Matthew sat next to Beatrice, waiting for Cordelia's inevitable overwrought account of Desdemona to proceed. Cordelia liked to recite the end of Othello, removing everybody else's lines but Desdemona's. It made absolutely no sense, but they were all so used to it that it had somehow begun to make sense.

"I must ask, Beatrice," he began. "That is, I mean, *Lady* Beatrice," he said, correcting himself, "you seem very quiet and out of spirits this night. Are you well?"

She seemed surprised to be asked, or to even find him beside her, as if her thoughts had been very far away indeed.

"I am perfectly well."

He did not think that was at all true.

"I only wondered if something had occurred to put you out of sorts," he said.

"What on earth could put me out of sorts?" she asked.

If he knew that, he would not be asking. He was silent for some moments, then he said, "All of this, coming to Town and receiving invitations, will be so new to you. Then, of course, those YBC gentlemen hanging about, and their mentioning that Conbatten took an interest…I just wondered if something…had been said. If you…consider something."

Matthew watched her closely to see her reaction. She did have a reaction, but he was at a loss to interpret it.

"I consider a lot of things, just now," Beatrice said.

"I will only say," he said quietly so as not to be overheard, "about Conbatten, it's all well and good that he's a duke, but he takes entirely too much time on his person and I cannot imagine that would suit you. As for those YBC fellows, they may be friends of Darden's, but they do not seem…"

He'd trailed off, and as well he should. What on earth was he doing? He was in the earl's own house, talking down his son's friends? And then a duke, for good measure?

"If I have any thoughts about any gentleman," Beatrice said, "then they are my thoughts alone. I see no reason to speak of them just now."

So it was a gentleman. The question was, who?

It must be Conbatten.

"I see," he said stiffly.

"I very much doubt you do."

What did *that* mean?

Cordelia interrupted his thoughts. "I think we have it suitably arranged," she said.

Cordelia, Darden, and Miss Mayton had taken a low table, turned it lengthwise, and lined it with candles for Cordelia's footlights. Desdemona's dying was set to commence.

Cordelia curtsied and said gravely, "Desdemona's final adieu."

The family clapped, which Van Doren knew perfectly well was de rigueur at such a moment.

She draped herself across the mantel and cried, "Alas! He is betrayed and I undone. O, banish me, my lord, but kill me not. Kill me tomorrow, let me live tonight. But half an hour. But while I say one prayer."

Now they would come to the pivotal moment when Cordelia would dramatically run across the room. This was generally when a candle got knocked over and a fire was started.

Matthew noted the earl paying close attention to the candles and Tattleton glancing at a sand bucket near the hearth. He was certain they were both less concerned with Desdemona's fate than they were the risk of flames.

Cordelia twirled and raced to the window. Naturally, one of her legs bumped the table and the candle on the far end wobbled. Viola was able to grab at it before it hit the rug.

The earl sat back looking relieved. Tattleton steadied himself on the doorframe.

In front of the window, Cordelia cried, "O, falsely, falsely murdered! A guiltless death die I. Nobody, I myself. Farewell! Commend me to my kind lord. O, farewell!"

There was another round of clapping.

"Well done, Cordelia," the earl said.

"Very moving," Darden said, though Matthew was certain he found the whole thing as ridiculous as he did himself.

Beatrice had clapped, though she did not commend her sister aloud.

"It simply gets better each time you recite it," Miss Mayton said.

Cordelia took all of these compliments in stride. Matthew was certain she silently complimented herself in far more lofty terms. If it were at all a possibility for a lady to tread the boards, Cordelia would be hotfooting it toward Covent Garden just now to share her Desdemona with the world.

"Now I wonder," Miss Mayton said, "whether there is any interest in discovering what the one-eyed duke and his gentle governess are up to?"

All the sisters were enthusiastically interested in it. All, except Beatrice. She smiled and said that she was, but it lacked the feeling he would have expected. On the other hand, the *earl's* enthusiasm was far more than he would have expected.

As for Matthew's own feelings, they always seemed beside the point.

Miss Mayton, having fully expected to be encouraged to it, had already the volume in her hand.

"We are just getting to the duke seeing all the scratches on his governess," Miss Mayton said. "You will recall, she fell off the roof in an attempt to view the duke in the bath without his eye patch on and landed in a stand of bushes."

All eyes drifted toward Matthew. He supposed they wished to discover if he would once again challenge how the lady fell off the roof and then just hopped up and dusted herself off with only a few scratches.

He sipped his tea. There was no reasoning against the preposterousness of the one-eyed duke and his governess.

"Excellent," Miss Mayton said, and began to read.

"Governess!" the duke raged, "These scratches on your hands and face! You have been attacked! I must know who has done this to you! I will have vengeance for this outrage!"

"Oh no, Duke," the governess said, "nobody has attacked me."

"Tell me you did not attack yourself! I will not have my gentle governess attacking herself!"

"I accidentally fell off the roof, you see."

"Nobody accidently falls off a roof!" the duke cried.

No, they do not, Matthew thought. At least, not while hanging upside down while trying to get a look at a duke in a bath.

He leaned his head back. He would like to doze off just now, but it was impossible with Miss Mayton practically shouting the duke's and the governess' ludicrous conversations. He had begun to notice that this particular duke said everything with an exclamation point.

He imagined that might be uncomfortable to live with for his gentle governess. *Good morning! It's raining! Shall you want eggs!*

As the hour droned on, the one-eyed duke refused to believe that the governess had fallen off the roof and was convinced she'd been attacked. He mounted his horse and rode to the village to discover the culprit.

First, he encountered a butcher who had blood on his apron, indicating a recent struggle. Naturally, he must be slain.

Then, the duke realized his mistake when he encountered a woodsman with scratches on his arm, so he must die.

But then, the duke was not so sure he got the right man, or two men at this point, as he'd just seen another man with a scratch on his face.

It seemed everybody was scratched, they all must die, and the bodies were piling up.

Miss Mayton laid down the book with a sigh. "I expect our governess is going to be very moved when she finds her duke is a murderer three times over for love of her."

"I don't suppose a magistrate will bother to inquire why there are now three dead bodies in the village," Matthew said.

Darden laughed and said, "I doubt it, that would be very inconvenient to the burgeoning love affair between those two. They need all the help they can get."

"Don't they just," Matthew said.

"Well," the earl said, "it is only a story, after all. Let us hope the road to marital felicity runs smoother for our Beatrice."

"Perhaps that road will run straight into a duchy," Darden said.

"People are saying that Conbatten takes an unusual interest."

"Beatrice a duchess?" the earl said. "That would be pleasant, I dare say."

Matthew noted the glances and small smiles made between all the sisters at the mention of Conbatten. And Miss Mayton, for that matter. They knew something. They knew a secret they kept between themselves. They often did so, they were rather like a cabal when they held a secret.

"Father, she would be duchess to not just *any* duke," Darden said. "We are talking about Conbatten. He is…well, he is Conbatten."

Rather than comment on the idea that Conbatten was Conbatten, Beatrice stood and said, "I find I am very tired this evening. I think I will go up early."

Matthew watched her kiss her father good night.

It *was* Conbatten. She had become discomposed to hear the duke spoken of. Something had been said. If not an outright proposal, then a hint that one was in the offing.

Could she really consider it, though? Beatrice had never been swayed by rank or money and what else did the fellow have?

He might be tall, confident, highly placed, the owner of vast estates, dressed superbly, and worshipped by the *ton*. But that was really all he had going for him.

Conbatten must be stopped. For Beatrice's sake.

※

BEATRICE HAD BEEN asked if she were out of sorts and she'd denied it. The truth was, she was very out of sorts. Of all the things she imagined might happen to her in London, suddenly failing to understand her own feelings had not presented itself as a possibility. There was a heaviness she could not name, and though she sought out the cause it would not make itself known.

Lynette had come when she rang the bell and she was swift enough into her nightclothes. She dismissed her maid, wrapped her shoulders in a blanket, and sat by the window overlooking the wide avenue of Portland Place.

The street was dark but for the soft glow of the oil lamps and the occasional carriage returning home. Portland Place was such a haven of peace, it not being open to the through traffic of carts, hackneys, and drovers.

At least, she *had* felt its peace. She was not certain why she did not feel it now.

A soft knock on the door stole her attention from the window. "Come," she said, assuming Lynette had forgotten something.

Rather, it was her aunt.

"My dear," Miss Mayton said, bustling in, "I thought to pop up and check on you. You were so very quiet this evening, I fear you have developed a headache or a stomachache."

"Neither of those," Beatrice said, "though I cannot even explain what ails me."

Miss Mayton came across the room and sat in the oversize chair next to her. "It is nerves, I think. I did wonder when they might catch up to you."

"Is that what it is?" Beatrice asked, having not considered the possibility. She had never known herself to be a nervous person.

"I imagine so," Miss Mayton said. "Just think, all your life you've been comfortably going along in Somerset. Everybody and everything was known. Now, here you are in this tremendous town with strangers everywhere and people coming and going to who knows where. As if that is not enough to jangle the nerves, you've come to find your true love. I should wonder about you if you were not shaken by the experience."

"Perhaps that is what it is," Beatrice said. "Nothing seems as it was. Not even Van Doren. He seems so different than he has always been."

"Ah, it sounds very like when I returned to Transylvania and encountered the duke on the Borgo Pass, where we were both taking the air. He was so changed!"

Miss Mayton sighed. "It was ever so disconcerting. Though, how was I to know he'd been wasting away for me all those years and would eventually throw himself off the highest point of Bran Castle and be impaled by one of his own flagpoles?"

"You could not have known it, Aunt," Beatrice said. "Sometimes, when I look at Van Doren now, he seems a different person altogether, just like your Transylvanian duke did. Though, he is not wasting away. He is going in the opposite direction, he is becoming more. Somehow."

Miss Mayton nodded. "I must admit, Lord Van Doren is turning out to be a deal more popular than I had imagined he would be. Lord Darden says that there are at least two ladies who have very determinedly set their cap in his direction."

Beatrice felt a little sick at the thought. Though she could not list all the facts against it, Van Doren should not marry. At least, not anytime soon.

"Lady Clara and Lady Mary," she said. "At first, I could not understand it. What did they see in Van Doren?"

"Precisely my thoughts too."

"But now, I think I can," Beatrice said slowly. "Being in Town has given me some…distance, I suppose. I almost look at him as I had done, years ago."

"Oh goodness, you did trail him around back in those days," Miss Mayton said. "I still remember when he announced he would no longer answer to Matthew. Your sisters were so teasing over the idea, but you backed him on it and insisted it must be Van Doren. You were ever so impressed with it."

"Of course, those days are long past," Beatrice said softly.

Her aunt patted her hand. "He is a handsome devil, I'll give him that. But, he will only be suited to a lady that does not require any passionate feelings. I hope Lady Mary and Lady Clara know it. As for you, there is a tortured gentleman out there somewhere."

"Yes, but when will I discover who he is?" Beatrice asked. "I hope I am not to end the season still wondering about it."

"I cannot imagine he will hold out that long. In the meantime, Lord Darden's plan goes along swimmingly. He's putting it about that Conbatten is included in your line of admirers. The girls and I were so very amused when he mentioned it this evening."

"Hmm," Beatrice said, "I wonder if Conbatten would be amused by it, though. There really is not the slightest spark between us."

"Of course there is not," Miss Mayton said. "He is not your tortured gentleman."

"No, that particular duke is not tortured at all," Beatrice said, laughing for the first time all day.

"Sleep, my dear," Miss Mayton said. "Tomorrow will be sunnier for you. Do not forget, we have the Bloomingtons' masque on the morrow. I am told it is one of the events of the season. I am certain your gentleman will be there and I was also thinking—might he dare to be closer to you while masked?"

"He might well do," Beatrice said, intrigued by the possibility. "Darden has arranged my costume—I am to go as Beatrice from *Much Ado about Nothing*. Darden says it is so clever to go as a character named the same as myself and he has been told the tortured gentleman is both an admirer of wit *and* a devotee of Shakespeare. He thinks it might very well prove too tempting and prompt my gentleman to speak. I am to see if someone as yet unknown to me, and likely dressed as a Shakespearian character too, requests an introduction."

"It is a thrilling idea. Perhaps all will be revealed on the morrow."

Her aunt kissed her forehead and left her to dream of the tortured gentleman standing nearby Shakespeare's Beatrice, preparing to speak.

Tattleton drank his ale and sent his staff to bed. Then he poured himself a generous glass of brandy from his own private stock. Sundays used to be so regular and calm.

Of course, that was before he'd been dragged into Lord Darden's lunatic plot.

Where did the lord think it was going? He could not be certain, though he could be certain that it was ongoing—the talk of Conbatten this night had been all for Lord Van Doren's benefit.

Had Lord Van Doren seemed the least affected by it? He thought not. As far as he could see, Lord Van Doren's interest had only been piqued when Lady Cordelia had acted out Desdemona. That, he was fairly sure, had been interest in whether or not she'd start another fire.

Tattleton had been on tenterhooks himself, ready to race for a sand bucket.

Lord Darden had approached him after the family had retired and let him in on a new scheme. Not that he wished to be apprised of it!

Apparently, Lady Beatrice was to present herself as *Much Ado About Nothing's* Beatrice at Lady Bloomington's masque. Lord Van Doren was to go as Benedict, her lover and sparring partner. Neither knew of the other's costume.

Lord Van Doren had told Darden he did not know where to even rent a costume for a masque and Lord Darden said he'd take care of it.

Lord Darden believed this might prompt them both to see what Shakespeare's Benedict and Beatrice had eventually discovered—for all their bickering, they were meant for each other.

It was preposterous.

As far as he could understand it, Lady Beatrice had fallen in love with a phantom gentleman who did not exist and Lord Van Doren went on as he always did—stifling yawns while Miss Mayton read from *The Terrible Goings-on of Montclair Castle*.

The goings-on in question grew more and more bizarre. Now the one-eyed duke was randomly killing villagers. Somehow, the Bennington ladies all found the murders highly romantic.

Tattleton was certain that other fine families did not carry on in such a manner.

He was certain of it, but there was not much he could do about it.

"There is nothing for it," he said with great determination to the now empty servants' hall. "I must only hold on tight while this out-of-control sleigh of bizarre plans and wrong-headed ideas flies down its mountain of absurdity to eventually crash at the bottom."

Chapter Thirteen

Matthew eyed the costume in his valet's hands gravely. "I should have known," he said. "I am sure I told Darden a domino would suffice. I suppose he found it amusing to send over this monstrosity."

The monstrosity in question was an old-fashioned soldier's uniform with more gold braid on it than would be suitable for an entire regiment, some very tight-looking pantaloons, and high-shined hessians. There was a sword belt with a hilt, but when one pulled it out there was no actual sword. The mask itself was black, its back band embroidered with the words, *Much Ado*, should anybody be in doubt as to the nature of his costume.

"At least you are to go as a soldier," Marcus said.

"But Benedict from *Much Ado About Nothing*? Why? I am nothing at all like that fellow, always arguing and throwing round insults as if it were his career."

Marcus did not answer, and Matthew noticed he'd turned away rather quickly.

"What?" he asked. "I do not carry on so. Oh, I know of what you think—my scolding of the Bennington girls from time to time. That has not been for my own amusement, but a necessary duty. In any case. Darden does not make a joke of that. I am certain he is rather grateful for the help."

"I suspect Lord Darden did not give much thought at all to the costumes, but just took what he thought looked interesting."

"I do not suppose there is any way to get hold of a domino on such short notice?"

Marcus shook his head. "You leave in less than an hour."

Matthew sighed. "I did not even wish to go. However, Darden says Conbatten will certainly be there. He must be stopped, somehow."

"I wonder what the great duke will don as a costume?" Marcus said. "Whatever it is, the irritating Henri will no doubt brag of it."

"If I understand that duke at all," Matthew said, "Conbatten will come as Conbatten and everybody will think it's marvelous."

Marcus sniffed. "If the great Henri expects to wheedle a compliment out of me for *that*, he will be very much disappointed."

With that denunciation, Marcus began to dress him in an entirely ludicrous costume. How Conbatten would appear, and what exactly Matthew would do to keep him from Beatrice, he did not have the first idea.

⟫⟪

BEATRICE WAS DELIGHTED with her costume. It was a lovely dark green silk, cut in the old style with very full skirts and a lace fichu. The composer of the costume had been clever, because really it could have been taken as so many different things. On the back of the mask, *Much Ado* was embroidered to signal that she was Shakespeare's Beatrice.

Darden was going as Puck, the devilish sprite who caused so much trouble and confusion in *A Midsummer Night's Dream*. His spiky ears were rather marvelous and his cloak of green silk was stitched together in pointed layers to seem as leaves from a forest's tree.

Miss Mayton had decided to go in widow's weeds, in honor of all her dead gentlemen. Rather than a mask, she had draped a long black lace veil over her head. A *very* long veil—it nearly reached the floor.

Beatrice thought she looked rather otherworldly, like a ghost from the past who drifted through the halls at night.

The earl, vastly entertained by the costumes around him, went in a simple domino.

As their carriage set off, Beatrice saw Van Doren mount his horse to follow them behind. He was dressed as a dashing soldier of old, with enough braid for a general. Perhaps he was meant to be a general of some sort?

"Van Doren is looking very dashing," the earl said. "A soldier's uniform suits him. I must say, though, I am rather surprised that he comes. It is the sort of thing I would have imagined he'd find foolish."

"I think he has discovered that while in Town, it is perhaps not so wise to denounce things foolish," Darden said. "If Lady Bloomington wishes to have a masque, then her circle of acquaintances and anybody she deems worthy must go to a masque."

"I suppose Van Doren's admirers will be very charmed by him in that outfit," the earl said, laughing.

"He does seem changed by London," Darden said. "What do you think, Bea? Is Van Doren not improved?"

Beatrice found the question very uncomfortable. She did not know if Van Doren was changed or improved or if her view of him was changed and improved.

"He does not scold so much," she said vaguely, "which of course is an improvement."

"Did you notice that he seemed more interested in the one-eyed duke and his governess than he has in the past," Miss Mayton said from behind her lace veil. "I am sure I noted it last evening."

"Did you?" the earl said jovially. "I had not perceived it."

"Perhaps his interest was piqued by the one-eyed duke's murderous rampage through the village," Beatrice said. Her tone verged on petulant, though she did not know why it should be so.

"I think Van Doren is coming into his own," Darden said. "He is becoming the gentleman he was destined to be and we should all forget the scolder he once was."

With that bizarre notion, they proceeded to Lady Bloomington's masque.

They were not long on the journey as they only traveled to Mayfair. There was a fairly long line of carriages lined up on the road to Lady Bloomington's house, and so they would likely spend more time waiting than they had being driven.

Darden opened the carriage windows, claiming the night was so mild it would be a shame not to do so. The night *was* mild, but Beatrice thought her brother was far more interested in hailing other gentlemen he was acquainted with who arrived on horseback.

Beatrice had thought they would have Van Doren at the window, but he seemed to have disappeared behind them somewhere. Rather, Mr. Cahill and Lord Dunston came together, both atop their horses. Mr. Cahill was a vicar and Lord Dunston was Dick Turpin, though Beatrice had to inquire to be told he was the famed highwayman.

The two gentlemen were in high spirits and recounting the success of Lady Bloomington's last masque. Apparently, Lady Bloomington kept the champagne flowing and there were some who awoke the next day very glad they had been behind a mask.

"You see," Lord Jericho said, "it is not just in the refreshment room. There is a pause between every dance and footmen come round with it on trays."

"As well as food, though they are tiny little things," Mr. Cahill said.

Lord Jericho nodded. "Lady Bloomington has connections to France and she calls the little bites her entremets. As you take one, you are handed a linen napkin. A fresh one each time! The laundry must be astronomical."

"I was told," Mr. Cahill said, "that this abundance of carefully composed food and top-notch champagne is Lady Bloomington's answer to Almack's sour lemonade and dry bread, as she has never been issued an invitation."

"Well, she would not have been," Lord Jericho said with a laugh. "It is well known that she discomfited Lady Castlereagh by her opinions on Lord Castlereagh's politics."

Quite suddenly, Darden looked almost startled. Mr. Cahill and Lord Dunston slowly followed his eyes.

Goodness, it was Conbatten and all three gentlemen looked a bit faint. Beatrice really did feel they put the duke on a high pedestal he neither required nor asked for.

The duke wore a domino with the hood thrown back and maneuvered his horse round the carriages. He nodded to Lord Dunston and Mr. Cahill and they backed up their horses to give him room to approach the carriage.

"Darden, Lady Beatrice, Lord Westmont, and…is that you, Mrs. Mayton?" the duke asked.

"Yes, it is me, Your Grace. Though, it is *Miss* Mayton."

There was only a flicker of surprise across the duke's features. "Pardon the mistake, my good lady."

"Think nothing of it," Miss Mayton said with gracious condescension.

Beatrice suppressed a smile. She did not suppose the duke *would* think much of it.

"Now tell me, Lady Beatrice," the duke said, "what lady do you come as?"

"I am Lady Beatrice from *Much Ado about Nothing*," she said, turning her head so that he might see *Much Ado* written on the back band.

"Very clever," Conbatten said.

"Do you think so?" Darden asked. He sounded very much like a schoolboy looking for approval.

"As I have said," Conbatten said smoothly. "May I hope," he said to Beatrice, "that you fully intend to verbally joust your way through the evening in a Shakespearian fashion?"

Beatrice smiled. "Only if I am provoked, Duke."

"I will be careful not to provoke, then. Assuming I am allowed onto your card."

Beatrice nodded. The duke bowed and spurred on his horse.

"Did you see, father?" Darden asked. "Did you see what he is like?"

"I saw a tall man atop a horse," the earl said.

"My lord, he is more than tall!" Mr. Cahill cried, maneuvering his horse back toward their window.

"Indeed, my lord," Lord Jericho put in behind him. "So much more than tall."

Beatrice was rather amused by their awe of the gentleman. She suspected they had none of them ever spent a deal of time talking to Conbatten. He had a certain reserve to him, but beyond that he was genial enough, as far as she could see.

As she mused, Beatrice saw Van Doren come into view. She could not imagine where he'd been, he ought to have arrived directly behind them.

She could not deny her father's charge that he looked very well as a soldier.

Mr. Cahill and Lord Jericho acknowledged him but could not stop their reverence of Conbatten.

"What I find so striking," Mr. Cahill said, "is the way he wears only a domino and even that seems particularly well cut."

"I wonder if he had it tailored?" Lord Jericho asked.

"Van Doren," Darden said, "you have just missed Conbatten. He was very determined to stop and inquire if he would be permitted onto Beatrice's card."

"I would not say I *missed* him," Van Doren said.

"No, Lord Van Doren, but you did. He was just here," Lord Jericho said.

Beatrice bit her lip. She was so well-used to Van Doren's way of speaking that she knew precisely what he meant—he was not downcast over having come too late for the encounter.

"Lady Beatrice, Earl, Miss Mayton," Van Doren said. "You all look very well."

"I am a widow, Lord Van Doren," Miss Mayton said.

"Naturally," Van Doren said drily.

"What held you up?" the earl asked. "We thought you were just behind us."

Van Doren looked decidedly uncomfortable. "Lady Clara wished a word," he mumbled.

"Ah, the ladies are so clever about things like that!" Mr. Cahill said.

"Of course," Lord Jericho said, "Lady Beatrice has no need for such arts. We made are way over to her carriage quite of our own accord. We were determined to be certain we should be permitted onto Lady Beatrice's card. After all, Conbatten cannot take *all* the dances."

Beatrice had no idea why Lord Jericho was going on in such a fashion. Did he imagine her tortured gentleman was somewhere nearby and listening in on their conversation?

From the carriage just ahead, Beatrice heard a rather loud female voice say, "Ah, Lord Van Doren, I see you have spotted us!"

Van Doren's horse sidestepped, and he looked toward the voice in some surprise as he had certainly not spotted anybody.

It was Lady Mary, on the hunt already.

"She seems very keen," Darden said.

Beatrice could not make out what Van Doren thought of being hailed so. He only said, "Well, I will see you inside."

Beatrice casually leaned closer to the window to observe him stopping at Lady Mary's carriage.

The lady was practically hanging out the window! It was very brazen, she thought.

Did he not see it as such?

Beatrice attempted to parse what must be in Van Doren's mind, to be so pursued.

It occurred to her that he might be flattered. He might not even see the impropriety of it. Had it been Beatrice, herself, leaning out a carriage window in such a manner, he'd have no end of scolding to deliver.

And yet, he appeared quite unruffled.

Mr. Cahill leaned down in his saddle and said in a low voice, "Mark me if there is not an engagement before the season's end. At least, if Lady Mary has anything to do with it. I only say, if Lady Clara has any notion of securing Van Doren, she better step quick and look lively."

"Lord Van Doren has no need of an engagement!" Beatrice said. She'd said it quite suddenly, before her good sense had a moment to stop her. Why on earth should she have said such a thing? Out loud? It was stupid enough that she had, for a moment, *thought* such a thing.

"Every lord has need of an engagement," the earl said jovially. "The question is never that, it is only when he will get round to it."

"Lady Mary comes from an old family, has a sizable dowry, and is well-respected," Darden said.

"I do not see *you* chasing her around, Darden," Beatrice said.

This had the effect she thought it might. Darden was twenty-one and her father had not yet pressed him to find a wife, but that would not go on forever. This conversation was perhaps skating too close to another conversation Darden was definitely not ready to have.

Ahead, Van Doren turned his horse, and it appeared as if he would not linger at Lady Mary's side.

It was then that she saw it. On the back of his mask was embroidered, *Much Ado*.

It took her some seconds to understand how it could be. Then she saw precisely how it could be, it was another of her brother's jokes.

"Darden," she said, "did you happen to acquire Van Doren's costume for him?"

Darden leaned forward and looked out the window as Van Doren rode forward.

"Ah, I see the jig is up on that," he said with a smile.

"What is the jig?" the earl asked.

"It is only much ado about nothing, father—Beatrice is Beatrice and Van Doren is Benedict," Darden said.

The earl erupted in laughter. "Oh, that is very good! Because they argue so much!"

Beatrice narrowed her eyes. Her costume was supposed to hint to her tortured gentleman that she was both a wit and a devotee of Shakespeare. She supposed Darden had amused himself with the idea that he could accomplish that *and* play a joke.

Lord Jericho broke the silence. "What do you say, Cahill? Let us repair inside and see if one of us has the nerve to inquire of Conbatten whether he has a tailor do something with his domino."

With that, the two gentlemen bowed and moved their horses forward.

Finally, their own carriage moved forward too.

"Now that was a very pleasant interlude," the earl said.

Beatrice forced herself to smile, though her feelings were running in a not as pleasant direction.

<hr />

MATTHEW HAD ONLY just got inside the doors and he was already entirely irritated.

First, he was waylaid by Lady Clara on the street.

Then, he was informed that the great Conbatten had tracked down the earl's carriage and made a point to stop.

Then, he was roped in by Lady Mary, her carriage just ahead of the earl's. What had the lady been thinking of? He could not possibly have spotted her when he was not even looking!

She had called out to him, practically hanging out her window, and he'd no choice but to attend her. That had led to an introduction to her father, who he really had no wish to know.

Lord Covington had eyed him like horseflesh and Matthew dreaded to discover what the gentleman had been told about him. He also wondered if her coming as Catherine of Valois was meant to be some sort of hint that he might be her Henry the Fifth.

At least, she arrived as *Shakespeare's* version of that couple. If Lady Mary had read any history books, and he doubted she had, she would not think that marriage anything to emulate.

A footman came round with a tray of champagne. Matthew took one and downed it.

No sooner had he emptied his glass, but it was taken from him and another supplied. Along with that, there were very odd trays approaching with small bits of food on them, each one secured by a thin wood stick.

He took one and discovered it was a baked scallop topped with a circle of thin-sliced ham. It was not bad at all, though he shrugged at the strangeness of food arriving on sticks to people who were standing up.

Matthew supposed everything would be strange this night. People in all manner of dress swirled round him. There were milkmaids and vicars and nuns and Vikings. Mixed into all of this, were dominos everywhere. Precisely what he wished to be wearing himself.

He had no trouble spotting Conbatten. For one, his height gave it away. For another, who else would have so many fawning over him?

Well, at least Matthew could relieve his valet's feelings when he understood that Conbatten's valet, the insufferable Henri, could come up with nothing past a very usual domino.

Finally, he saw Beatrice come in with the earl, Darden, and Miss Mayton.

Miss Mayton looked more like a specter than a widow. Her short and stocky frame was entirely garbed in voluminous black taffeta, a black lace veil practically coming to her feet.

Beatrice was dressed as a lady of old. She might be a lady-in-waiting to a Renaissance noblewoman.

Beatrice made her curtsy to Lady Bloomington. She turned to somebody just coming in. Matthew squinted. There was some sort of writing on the band at the back of her mask.

Much Ado…

Much Ado? As his own mask said too.

The situation became clear enough in a moment. Darden. Another of Darden's jokes.

That scoundrel! How dare he set up him and Beatrice as Shakespeare's Beatrice and Benedict! It was absurd and embarrassing.

He took another glass of champagne from a passing tray.

Matthew had every intention of sipping, as he'd drunk the last two rather fast. However, it was a bit too much to see Conbatten leaving his admirers and heading over toward Beatrice.

He downed it, handed it to a passing footman, and hurried forward.

Matthew was not alone. Apparently, the YBC rogues had gathered to await her entrance. Lord Jericho, Mr. Cahill, Sir Matthew, and Lord Dunston were also swooping toward her.

He pushed past them and arrived at the earl's side. Conbatten had taken a sudden turn and strode toward the cloakroom so at least he was got rid of, but the YBC fellows were not so shaken off.

The earl looked bemused at the gentlemen now surrounding his party. "Well?" he said.

"Lord Westmont," Lord Dunston said, "we are all, of course, hoping to put ourselves down on Lady Beatrice's card.

"Yes, yes," the earl said. "I will only point out that a card not yet retrieved cannot be written upon."

All of the gentlemen looked toward the cloakroom.

Conbatten came forward. "Lady Beatrice, I have taken the liberty of retrieving your card."

He held it up.

Matthew snatched it from his hands and said, "A gentleman so recently met should perhaps not have taken such a liberty."

The YBC members shrank back. Matthew thought he might have phrased that differently. Or not actually torn the card from the duke's hand. He supposed he had three glasses of champagne to thank for his rashness. But it was done now.

Conbatten looked at him through hooded eyes and Matthew began to wonder if he were on the verge of being called to duel.

"Indeed," Conbatten said, in a tone so dry it could start a fire.

"Indeed," Matthew answered, having no possible rational answer. He wrote his name down for supper and handed the card to Beatrice. He hurried away before he was forced to examine her expression, or anybody else's, too closely.

That had been an unfortunate encounter. However, at least the great Conbatten would find himself foiled in his attempt to secure Beatrice's supper.

Further, he had not given Conbatten time to challenge him to a duel over the insult. Matthew had always vowed he would not duel until he had sons on the ground. He had no younger brother and it was the stupidest thing in the world to lose an estate to a distant cousin.

DARDEN THOUGHT HE must be satisfied that his plan to bring Van Doren and Beatrice together was moving along at a terrific pace. After all, had he not just watched Van Doren snatch Beatrice's card out of Conbatten's grip?

On the other hand, he had just watched Van Doren snatch Beatrice's card out of Conbatten's grip.

He could not have imagined that anybody would dare cross Conbatten. Now, Van Doren had done the unthinkable.

Conbatten watched Van Doren storm off. He turned to Lady Beatrice and said,

"Your friend seems very hotheaded."

Beatrice appeared at a loss for an answer, and as well she would be. The last thing Van Doren had ever been accused of was hotheadedness.

"Duke," the earl said, "Lord Van Doren is our neighbor. He and Beatrice have grown up together and so I suppose he must be given great latitude on account of it. He has always been very protective of my girls, there are five of them you see, and so I cannot fault him for that."

"He really is a good sort," Darden said. "When you become acquainted with him."

Darden noted Conbatten looking to Beatrice to discover what she would say.

"He is…" Beatrice began. "He is…well, he is Van Doren."

Conbatten nodded, as if that were all he needed to know. He glanced at Beatrice's card and said, "May I?"

Beatrice nodded and handed it over. Darden noticed none of his YBC members had the nerve to step ahead of Conbatten as Van Doren had just done.

Darden, peeking over at her card, noticed that Van Doren had put himself down for supper. Good show, old fellow!

Conbatten put himself down for the first, bowed, and retreated into the crowd. His YBC members did their duty in putting themselves down for various dances.

Further, they had done an excellent job of pointing out to Van Doren how many admirers Beatrice had. Conbatten had been the icing on the cake, though the duke could not know it.

Somehow, Van Doren had been unconscionably rude to the duke and walked away without earning himself a meeting at dawn.

All proceeded nicely, albeit hair-raisingly.

Chapter Fourteen

Beatrice found herself very grateful for the glass of champagne she was handed. What a scene she had just found herself in the middle of!

What had Van Doren been thinking? She watched him now, drinking his own glass as Lady Clara chattered on to him about something or other, and Lady Mary was swimming through the crowd in his direction.

Perhaps he'd had more than one glass already. She had never seen Van Doren in such a temper. Oh, he scolded often enough, and glowered when she and her sisters teased him.

But this was different. To personally assault a duke!

And then, what did he mean by taking her supper? On any other night, she might have supposed he wished to have the time to scold her on some matter. This night, she had done nothing at all and it was him that ought to be scolded.

Darden's friends had drifted off. Apparently, there was a lady dressed as a wood nymph they were all keen to speak to.

"The duke was very gracious, I thought," her aunt said from underneath her widow's weeds. "Though, what on earth has got into Lord Van Doren I cannot say."

The earl chuckled but did not reply.

"Nobody can say, Aunt," Beatrice said. "It was most unaccountable."

"I suggest that we all stop measuring Van Doren by the stick you are used to using at home," Darden said. "At home he was a scold, now he is Benedict. He is a different man."

Darden was naming some of her own thoughts a little too close for comfort. Van Doren *was* different, somehow.

And why was he always pushing into her thoughts? Why was she just now staring at him while he spoke to Lady Clara and Lady Mary, rather than wondering where her tortured gentleman was at this moment?

Perhaps it was only that Van Doren was there, right in front of her, while her mysterious gentleman remained anonymous.

That was likely the case. Though, she would not soon get out of her mind the picture of Van Doren forcefully taking her card from the duke's hand.

He could not have meant it to be a great compliment, as he rarely paid them, but had it been any other man…well, she would have received the action as highly passionate.

"My dear earl," her aunt said, "what do you think of the duke taking Beatrice's first dance?"

"I think somebody had to take it and he is as good as anybody else," the earl said.

"But he is a duke and pays her marked attention!" Miss Mayton said.

"So he is and so he does," the earl said. "Though, Beatrice's heart will go where it wishes with no regard for rank. Of that, I am certain."

Beatrice smiled, for of course he was right. Conbatten might be King of England and she would not consider him. Nor did she believe he had the slightest wish to be considered. Perhaps that was why they seemed to be becoming friends—neither of them had the smallest inclination for anything more.

The duke was perennially fawned over and attempts at seduction came at him from all sides. It must be a relief to the gentleman that she harbored no such designs on him.

"I suppose Van Doren does not see it quite that way," Darden said. "He most assuredly took Beatrice's supper to stop the duke from doing so."

"Why should Van Doren insert himself into my preferences?" Beatrice asked. "Had I a preference for the duke, which I do not, it must be nothing to Van Doren."

"And yet," the earl said, laughing merrily, "it did not seem as nothing. Ah, young gentlemen, they are vastly amusing."

Beatrice did not find anything amusing in the idea. In truth, she was rather shaken by it. What did her father and her brother hint of? That Van Doren had some sort of particular regard for her? That he was…jealous?

That could not be so.

But what if it were so?

Van Doren? Harboring feelings for her? Did he actually have feelings to harbor? Until tonight, when she thought his mask had slipped just a bit, he had kept them very much under wraps.

What if he had strong feelings and had been hiding them? How would she view it?

Her mind, generally so useful, seemed unable to consider the question. It was as if the very notion froze her thoughts and they would not go further.

Oh, it was all such a muddle.

The orchestra had been tuning for some minutes and now Lady Bloomington was led to the top of the ballroom. Conbatten came to collect Beatrice for the first dance. It was to be a quadrille.

They took their place just below Lady Bloomington's set, the duke always being afforded a good placement on the floor.

As they waited their turn, the duke said, "I am finding this evening very illuminating, Lady Beatrice."

Beatrice was certain he looked for some explanation regarding Van

Doren's bizarre behavior, beyond her father's noting that he was a longstanding neighbor.

"I will apologize on behalf of Lord Van Doren," she said, "though I cannot account for his behavior. I am hoping it can be blamed on too much champagne."

The duke looked at her critically. "Is that what you were hoping for?" he asked.

Beatrice was a bit baffled by the question. "I do not know what else I might hope for," she said.

"I see. Perhaps it is confusing to you to have so many gentlemen circling round, perhaps you hardly know where to look."

Now Beatrice was entirely confused. Did he make some comment on Darden's friends? Of course, he did not know of their real purpose in luring out the tortured gentleman and so would believe them to be suitors.

"Anybody with a pair of eyes can parse what is really happening around you. The fools can be easily enough stripped out of the scene to arrive at the truth of the situation."

Beatrice was becoming flustered and felt her cheeks get hot. It seemed the duke hinted that Darden's friends were not convincing.

Rather than answer directly, she said, "You speak in riddles, duke."

"And you would have me speak plainly?"

"I'm not certain," she said honestly.

"Lady Beatrice," he said, his tone containing a hint of exasperation, "a gentleman does not rip a card out of *my* hands for his own amusement. Not when he risks meeting me at dawn to answer the insult."

"You would not challenge him?" Beatrice said, her blood running cold in her veins. She could not know the duke's skill with pistols, but she could guess at them. Van Doren might be killed, and all over a fit of pique! She would never forgive herself. Never.

"Duke, please do say you will not," Beatrice said.

"I most certainly will not," the duke said. "Far be it for me to kill a fellow for being hopelessly blinded by love. And blind to his own intentions, I suspect."

Beatrice's relief at the duke's assurance that he would not call out Van Doren caused her to take some moments before comprehending the rest of what he'd said.

He thought Van Doren was in love with her. It was not true, of course. Neither she nor her sisters believed Van Doren could be in love with anybody. It was not in his nature.

But then, her father and her brother had hinted something along the same lines.

Lynette's words came back to her. Someday a lady would bring Van Doren to his knees.

It could not be her, though. She had seen no signs!

"Duke," she said slowly, chafing under his amusement, "I will hold you to your assurance that you will not demand a duel. However, I must also inform you that your guess could not be further from the truth."

"We'll see," the duke said, with a rare laugh.

MATTHEW HAD NOT escaped the various nets set out for him. Both Lady Mary and Lady Clara had placed themselves in such positions, cards dangling, that he'd no choice but to put his name down.

At least he had dodged their suppers, though he cringed at Lady Mary's petulance and Lady Clara's disappointment over it. They seemed particularly put out that he was to take Beatrice into supper.

He was beginning to think he ought to go home to his estate to escape these two ladies. He was beginning to think that both of them meant to trap him somehow.

But then, if he did go, he would be leaving Beatrice behind, unprotected from the duke.

Matthew thought he began to understand why the duke had not demanded he answer the insult of ripping her card from his hand. The fellow had not wished to discompose or displease Beatrice. Certainly, that could be the only reason for it.

Now, he led Lady Mary through the changes and they returned to their place.

"Lady Clara claims that you are forever hanging about Lady Beatrice Bennington," Lady Mary said, "though I assured her that you were a longstanding friend to that house, having neighboring estates."

What a thing to say. And what a fishing expedition. As if he was ever *hanging about* anybody! He was a viscount; he did not hang about anywhere.

And then, why was the lady repeating something she had most likely been told in confidence, *if* she had ever been told it at all. Did she wish to paint Lady Clara as unseemly jealous?

"The Bennington family and I are of long acquaintance," he said noncommittally.

"Of course," Lady Mary said. "And so quite natural that you would put yourself down for her supper."

"Indeed so."

"Although, there is some talk going round about a scuffle between you and Conbatten over Lady Beatrice's card?"

Matthew inwardly groaned. No doubt Darden's friends, always looking for an amusing piece of gossip, had gone round making it more significant than it was.

"There was no scuffle," he said.

"Ah well," Lady Mary said, looking very pleased to hear it, "you know the *ton*, always talking. They say there is a battle for Lady Beatrice's heart. Personally, I think they've got it all wrong. It is true the duke pays marked attention, but I have never seen anything but old family friendship on *your* side."

Matthew would very much like to know who *they* were who did all this talking. Of course, *they* might be only Lady Mary's imagination.

Then again, they might not. At least, not as far as the duke paying Beatrice marked attention. Anybody could see that.

"Perhaps the duke does pay marked attention," Matthew said stiffly. "He is not alone, as far as I can see."

"Oh no, he is not," Lady Mary said. "But nobody believes in Lord Darden's friends—they are only amusing themselves. Everybody knows their circumstances and, while all different, none of them are set to marry any time soon. Goodness, they just put that club together, the Young Bucks Club, I believe they call it."

This was outrageous…and all too believable. Matthew had thought there was something false in those idiots. They were toying with Beatrice for their own amusement! And Darden was allowing it to go on!

Did nobody in the world have any sense left?

Mercifully, no dance could go on forever. Though he had thought it exceedingly odd to have footmen running about, dispensing champagne on the ballroom floor, he was now rather glad of it.

He took a glass from a passing tray and fortified himself for his dance with Lady Clara. Hopefully, that lady would not have as much to say as Lady Mary had.

***

THE DANCE BEFORE the supper was approaching ever nearer, until suddenly it was time. Beatrice's thoughts had been racing this way and that, never stopping at any firm idea.

She could not know if other people's assumptions about Van Doren were true. It seemed so unlikely. It seemed so impossible. But what if it were not impossible?

Beatrice had a feeling very like she used to have all those years ago, as if her blood had run to champagne when she noted him riding out of the wood and toward the house.

Back then, she would be giddy and grab one of her dolls to leave in the drawing room and then act shocked to her shoes when he hid it. She would demand he retrieve it and he would demand she find it and it would be a merry hour of hunting round the house.

Was this odd returning feeling real though, or just a sort of nostalgia for a time gone by? Was it real, or just the fantasy she had built up back then, and long outgrown?

Beatrice had stolen glances at Van Doren all night and made herself a tedious dancing partner in the process, she was sure.

When she stepped back and viewed him, he was so handsome. So commanding, somehow. She watched his dance with Lady Mary and he did not look over-jolly and forcing amusement, as so many gentlemen were prone to do.

There was something thrilling in it. But, were she to allow her feelings to go any particular way in regard to Van Doren, could it be right? What of her tortured gentleman?

He, though she did not yet know his identity, was consumed by passion. While the idea Lynette had posited, that Van Doren would be brought to his knees, was a thrilling one, it was likely not true. In the end, he was too sensible and too constrained to be brought thus. It was only thrilling in its utter impossibility.

Beatrice began to notice that her requirements, those attributes she had composed so carefully before coming to Town, had not been thought of recently. Why was she not hoping for a gentleman tearing out his hair these days? There *was* a gentleman in such a condition, so why think of anybody else in any manner at all?

Could her father have been right all along? That she would throw her requirements out a window?

But if that was what she did, who did she throw them out for?

As much as she felt a pull toward Van Doren, it would not suit. He could not be what she needed. He was not passionate, and she could not live life without passion.

He was ever so handsome, but he did not have the temperament for a lady like herself.

And this was all assuming he harbored some feelings for her, which seemed too improbable to be true.

"Lady Beatrice," he said, coming to collect her.

Beatrice felt herself pink. The way he said *Lady* Beatrice, as if he had not always known her, sent a shiver down her back.

"Lord Van Doren," she said, resting her hand on his arm.

He looked at her quizzically. "You have taken to addressing me as lord?"

"Well, you *are* one, and you have taken to addressing me as lady," she said.

He did not answer and led her to the floor. As the first couples took their turn, he said, "I suppose you wish for an explanation regarding recent...events."

"If you mean ripping my card away from the duke, I have told the duke you had too much champagne. He assures me he will not challenge you."

"I am not afraid of a challenge," Van Doren said.

He said it a little heated, Beatrice thought. Who was this person, getting heated all the time?

"Nor do I require you to play my second with that duke," Van Doren said.

That duke? What did he mean by it?

"Van Doren," she said, getting a little heated herself, "you have spent all your life never putting a foot wrong and very happily being the scolder. Now, you are in a pique because you have put yourself in a position to be scolded. You do not like being in the wrong and take it very badly."

"Perhaps I am not convinced I *was* wrong," Van Doren said.

"And now you know how it is to be on the other end of the stick.

When you have time to consider it, you will certainly conclude that you were wrong." She paused, and then said, "I only give you that hint."

Beatrice did not have the first idea of why she was carrying on such an argument. She had not planned to.

He did not answer but looked a little red in the face to hear his own words come back to haunt him. They were silent as he led her through the changes, but he looked at her with an intensity she had never seen before.

It was really very discomposing.

They went on in that manner until the dance came to an end. He silently escorted her to a table in the dining room. They were served even more champagne, though Beatrice was convinced that was the last thing Van Doren needed. She did not know what else could account for his strange behavior this night.

He said, "I find myself in the uncomfortable position of having to inform you of something that I know will displease you and I fear may injure you."

Beatrice looked at him uncomprehendingly. Certainly, he was not going to attempt to scold her on some matter when *he* had so recently acted outrageous?

"These YBC fellows, Darden's friends, this circling round you they do, I pray none of them have been able to touch your feelings because it is all an act. Disreputable and ungentlemanly, but a farce."

Beatrice took in a breath. He had discovered Darden's ruse to draw out the tortured gentleman. How had he discovered it? Darden would not have said anything and she could always count on her sisters and her aunt to keep a thing quiet. Had he just concluded it on his own?

"So," she said slowly, "you have figured it out, or were told."

"You knew of it?" Van Doren asked, evidently in some surprise. "Why would you allow it to go on? Why would Darden allow it?"

Ah, so he had deduced it somehow, but he did not know the why of it. She must tell him something, though perhaps as little as possible.

"It is only a little game, meant to draw a certain gentleman out," she said.

"A game!"

"A ruse, if you will," Beatrice said.

"A ruse!" Van Doren said, downing his champagne and signaling the footman for another.

"Yes, just a ruse. We did not tell you as we were all certain you would not approve."

"All?" Van Doren asked. "Do you say your father is aware of this…ruse?"

"Father?" Beatrice said. "Well, no, of course not my father. He does not like to be troubled by such things."

"You did not tell him because he would not have approved."

"Perhaps not, but I really believe he will approve in the end," Beatrice said, attempting to keep the defensiveness from her voice.

Of course, they had all very happily concluded that the earl need not be told as there was no cause to trouble him. They had all perfectly well known that was a happy excuse for not telling him, as he likely would not approve.

"He ought to know," Van Doren said.

"Do not make that your business, my lord," Beatrice said.

"I see," Van Doren said. "So you are decided on this gentleman you wished to draw out, then?"

"I have decided nothing," Beatrice said. How could she have decided when she had not yet even met her tortured gentleman?

Van Doren was staring morosely at his champagne. He must not know that her tortured gentleman had not yet stepped forward.

Beatrice was beginning to wonder if that mystery gentleman ever would come forward. She was beginning to wonder how much she cared if he did or not. After all, how manly could he be if he were still hanging back? Should not a manly tortured gentleman be willing to overcome his torture? Or at least try?

As she considered the idea, she realized she was becoming rather fascinated by this new and temperamental Van Doren. She cautioned herself not to be carried away by it, though. Once he'd sobered himself, he'd likely be the same steady Van Doren she'd always known.

At least, she thought so.

Chapter Fifteen

Matthew waited to mount his horse until the Benningtons had got in their carriage. He'd informed the earl that he would escort them all home to protect them from thieves and other unsavory sorts who lurked in the streets late at night.

It was all nonsense, of course. The earl's coachman would be well armed, and they were not traveling far. In truth, he wished to ensure that Conbatten did not have the same idea of escorting the carriage home. The man might have the effrontery to try it, just as he'd given himself leave to collect Beatrice's card.

The duke, fortunately, was nowhere to be seen, and so they set off.

What an evening! His head hurt already; he should have never had so many glasses of champagne. He was grateful that the journey was to be short, rather than clear across London. He was very much looking forward to his bed.

The morrow would be soon enough to decide what to do about this ridiculous ruse Beatrice had involved herself in. They had all conspired to draw out a particular gentleman and though Beatrice had not owned it, he knew very well that the duke was their target. Anybody with eyes could see it.

It was astounding that Darden would have consented to such a scheme. If he understood his own sister at all, he would know Conbatten was not right for her. And what if the ruse was successful and prompted a proposal? Would not the duke eventually realize he'd been tricked? Would not Beatrice, should she wed him, pay the price for that? A marriage could not be built on trickery!

They made their way through the darkened streets, only the sound of horses' hooves clip-clopping and Miss Mayton's chattering in the carriage to accompany them home.

Matthew maneuvered his horse round a corner as they neared Portland Place and came upon a group of street urchins. They had cornered a dog and were pelting it with stones.

"Blast!" he said, reining his horse in and leaping down.

The Benningtons' carriage came to a stop and he heard Beatrice calling out the window. "Do make them stop, Van Doren!"

The Benningtons' coachman was climbing down from his box. "On my way, my lord."

The ruffians understood in a moment that they were to be entirely outmanned. Particularly since the coachman had decided to wave a pistol at them. They set off at a run, but for the smallest who had fallen on the cobblestones.

Matthew grabbed him by his shabby coat collar and hauled him up. "What do you mean by it, boy?"

The boy looked up at him with wide eyes. Whatever sort of gang of ruffians he was part of, he did not look old enough or streetwise enough to manage it. Matthew presumed being able to run without falling down was a rudimentary requirement for such activities.

"Where do you live?" Matthew said.

"Nowhere," the boy squeaked out.

"Where are your parents?"

"I don't got none," the boy sobbed.

Matthew was not certain if the boy was lying or not. He suspected not. Or, if he was, his parents certainly did not keep very good track of him.

The dog, a small creature of undetermined parentage with a light and matted coat and an alarmingly pronounced underbite, shook himself and wagged his tail.

"I never did throw one stone!" the boy cried. He pointed at the dog and said, "He knows it! I only pretended for the others!"

Matthew's feeling that this particular boy was not up to a life of criminal activity was further confirmed.

"Oh Papa," Beatrice said from the carriage, "it seems he is an orphan. We ought to take him on."

Matthew turned toward the carriage, still holding the boy by the collar. "You cannot take in every crying boy you encounter, there is the dog too, and you've just installed another boy and a pile of cats into the house."

"Now that is true, Beatrice," the earl said.

"We cannot leave them alone on these streets to starve," Beatrice said.

"What you cannot do is save everybody," Matthew said.

"Perhaps not," Beatrice said, "but fate has put these two in our way and we cannot abandon them."

Matthew sighed. The boy looked up at him, hopeful. The dog wagged its tail.

"I'll take them," he said.

"You'll take them?" Beatrice said, the surprise in her voice evident. "Really?"

"Really," he said.

"But what shall you do with them, Lord Van Doren?" Miss Mayton asked.

The question of the hour. "I have no idea," he said.

He picked up the boy and put him in the saddle. Then, he approached the dog. "If you bite me, it will only be the cap-off to an all-round ridiculous evening."

Matthew scooped up the dog, who did not bite him but rather attempted to lick his face. "You," he said to the boy, "carry the dog."

"What if he bites *me*," the boy whispered.

"He would have every right and you'll say nothing about it," Matthew said, depositing the dog into the boy's stiff arms.

Then, he grabbed the horse's reins and led him down the street. If there were one firm opinion he could leave this cursed night with, it was he would never again attend a masque.

He had insulted a duke, discovered that Darden's friends had been enacting a ruse to make Conbatten feel pressed over having competition, understood that Beatrice was considering that gentleman seriously, been scolded by her, hunted by Lady Mary and Lady Clara, and ended it all by adding a street urchin and flea-ridden dog to his household.

Evenings like this did not happen in the countryside. The countryside would never dare try it.

BEATRICE FOUND ALL of her sisters asleep in her bedchamber. They had certainly meant to wait up but had drifted off one by one.

As they had fallen asleep, they awoke one by one as Lynette brushed out her hair.

"Oh, Bea, we could not bear to wait until morning," Juliet said, yawning. Her youngest sister was the last to wake and had struggled up in Beatrice's bed. "Did your tortured gentleman make himself known?"

"He did not," Beatrice said.

Just then, Miss Mayton poked her head in the door. "I thought I heard talking. I ought to scold you all off to bed, but of course I will not. You could not help it."

"We did not even stay up too late, Aunt," Cordelia said, "we just slept in here so we could find out right away. But, it seems the mysterious gentleman is still mysterious."

"So he is," Miss Mayton said, bustling into the room. "I am beginning to wonder what he waits for."

"As am I," Beatrice said. "Just this evening, I thought, well if he were very brave he would have come forward and if he is not very brave, could he really be my one true love?"

"Indeed, you did think of Henry the Fifth's bravery as a requirement. Well, it is a very fine muddle we find ourselves in," Miss Mayton said. "Goodness, what an evening! I suppose you told the girls all about Lord Van Doren?"

"Van Doren?" Rosalind asked. "Has he been making himself popular again? It seems so unlikely."

"He remains popular, particularly to two ladies who seem to wish for his company very much," Miss Mayton said. "But that is nothing compared to what he did."

The sisters all leaned forward. "What?" Viola whispered.

"The duke, Conbatten you understand," Miss Mayton said in a lowered voice, "was so good as to retrieve Beatrice's card at the beginning of the evening. Just at the moment he approached with it, Lord Van Doren ripped it right out of his hands."

"No," Rosalind said.

"He never did," Juliet said.

"He did," Beatrice said.

"Why?" Viola asked.

"Nobody knows," Miss Mayton said.

"Has he gone mad, do you think?" Juliet asked, her tone a little hopeful that it might be the case.

"I do not know what has happened to him," Beatrice said. "On the way home, we came upon boys throwing stones at a dog. Van Doren chased them off, but for one who was too small to get away. He's taken the boy *and* the dog home."

"No," Viola said, perfectly expressing all the sisters' disbelief.

Beatrice nodded. "He did, we saw it."

"Do you suppose," Rosalind said, "that there is something in the

London air that is affecting him?"

"That might be it," Viola said. "If one were to examine the facts, Van Doren was one way in the country and now he is going entirely another way."

Beatrice agreed with that wholeheartedly. She was a little relieved that it was not just her imagination in thinking it. Everybody saw it—Van Doren was suddenly…different.

"He ought to be careful with this new way of going on," Rosalind said. "He is probably lucky that the duke did not demand satisfaction for the insult."

"Conbatten promised me he would not go so far," Beatrice said. She did not say, however, why Conbatten would not challenge Van Doren. Though, his words still rang in her ears. *Far be it for me to kill a fellow for being hopelessly blinded by love. And blind to his own intentions, I suspect.*

No, she would never repeat that. Not to anybody. She also did not tell her sisters that Van Doren had guessed at Darden's scheme and knew the YBC gentlemen's attentions were only meant to draw out another gentleman.

Beatrice sighed. At least Van Doren did not seem to know which gentleman, any more than she did herself.

"Van Doren used to be so predictable," Rosalind said.

"Now, one wonders what he will do next," Cordelia said.

Yes, indeed, Beatrice thought. One did wonder.

❯❯❯❮❮❮

MATTHEW WOKE TO blinding sunlight coming in the windows. He was certain Marcus had very purposefully failed to close the curtains to express his unhappiness over having to give both a dog and a boy a bath in the middle of the night.

It had been completely necessary—both of them were filthy and he would not countenance his house becoming infested with fleas.

Based on the barking he'd heard coming from below stairs, the boy had taken it better than the dog had.

Before he'd sent him on his way to a tub, Matthew had discovered the boy's name was Shrimps, as he'd always been on the small side. Matthew was certain there was a proper name on a birth record somewhere, but Shrimps did not know what it was.

He'd been in the workhouse with his mother, who had since died. He'd escaped to take his chances on the street and been pulled into a gang run by a couple of men operating out of Rats' Castle. The boy was lucky to be alive, as many who had walked those dirty, claustrophobic streets did not do so for long.

Both the boy and the dog were to go to the stable. He did not imagine his coachman would thank him for the dog, in particular, but there was nowhere else suitable for the animal.

He rang the bell and was hoping for his butler, rather than his valet, but it was Marcus who came through the door.

"Close those curtains, if you please," he said.

"Goodness! Did I leave them open?" Marcus said, hurrying across the room to do as he was bid.

"I know very well you purposefully left them open to take your revenge regarding the boy and the dog."

Marcus pursed his lips, a sure sign that he'd not got over his pique. "My lord, you do not know the half of what has gone on. Nobody knows what to do about it."

Matthew sighed. "Order me breakfast and then tell me all about it."

"Breakfast has been ordered, I did it as soon as I heard the bell and Cook was frying eggs as I made my way up. James will bring it up in a tick, as Genroy is far too taken up with managing the chaos below stairs."

There was a soft knock on the door and Matthew was grateful to hear it. He expected he would need several cups of coffee to fortify himself against his valet's soon to be delivered complaints.

Marcus took the tray, sent James on his way, and brought it to the bedside. Matthew took his coffee and said, "Well? Talk away."

"It is just this," Marcus said, "I got them both into the bath, as you ordered, which was no mean feat." He held up his hand for examination and Matthew could see red bite marks. At least the skin was not broken.

"The boy or the dog?" he asked, regarding the marks.

"How should I know?" Marcus said. "They were both like wild animals! Shrimps, that is what he calls himself, was convinced I meant to drown him. As for that dog, well, I only say…"

"So it was a trying evening," Matthew said.

Marcus laughed. It was the particular laugh he used when he meant to indicate his astonishment and derision at another's naiveté.

"That was only the beginning!" he cried.

"There is more."

"So much more," Marcus said.

For the next half hour, Matthew listened to all that had transpired below stairs.

After the bath in which all parties were nearly drowned, both the boy and the dog were dried off by the kitchen fire and fed. Then, Genroy attempted to escort them out to the stables, but the boy became hysterical, the dog howled, and they would not be moved.

Shrimps claimed he was terrified of horses and would die of fright in a stable.

"He is no such thing," Matthew said. "I threw him on the back of my own horse last night and he didn't complain at all. He was more afraid of the dog than the horse."

"I do not doubt it," Marcus said. "We are all convinced he is lying, but what can we do? The dog, who he has named Oyster because of the color of his coat, appears to fear anything that Shrimps pretends to fear. When the boy cries, the dog howls. It is ear shattering."

Marcus further relayed that Shrimps, cheeky little thing that he was, insisted that he must stay in the kitchens. He was determined to be a cook someday. It was his lifelong dream, he said.

Matthew found that rather rich, as his life had only gone on for seven or eight years so far.

Marcus explained that Genroy questioned Shrimps rather close about this lifelong dream of his, and it seemed his reasons were twofold: one, a cook was always nearby food, and two, a cook was always nearby a fire.

"So here we are," Marcus said, "Cook has got a boy and a dog in the kitchens and he does not have the first idea what to do with them."

"Not the first idea?" Matthew said. "Put the boy to work."

"And *Oyster*, as that uncouth canine is now called?"

"If the dog is content to sleep by the fire and be fed on scraps and gets in nobody's way, it may stay. If not, it must go. Tell Shrimps to keep him in line or they're both out. That should put the fear of God in him."

Marcus nodded and gave a little sniff, no doubt disappointed that Shrimps and Oyster were not on their way out this very minute.

His valet picked up the rumpled coat that had been part of his ridiculous soldier's uniform from the evening before.

Matthew said, "I will cheer you up, Marcus. Conbatten's valet could only manage a domino last evening. The annoying Henri will have nothing to brag of."

This did, to Matthew's amusement, appear to cheer his valet quite a bit.

"I knew it," he said victoriously.

"Conbatten had the effrontery to collect Lady Beatrice's card," Matthew went on, "which I snatched right out of his hand."

Marcus was nearly transported by this piece of news. "Snatched. I only wonder what the insufferable and puffed-up Henri will say to that!"

"I expect he will say nothing, as the duke will not be in a mood to brag of it."

"And I suppose the great Conbatten did not have the nerve to make you answer for the insult," Marcus said, looking very pleased. "All show, just as I thought."

"He did not challenge me because Lady Beatrice implored him not to, though I informed her that I needed no such assistance."

"Did she step in like that?" Marcus said, sounding a little wistful.

"You know Lady Beatrice, she is not afraid to step in anywhere. The further problem is, she is seriously considering that fop who lounges in a bath half the day."

"Lady Beatrice and Conbatten? Does she know about Henri, though?" Marcus asked. "Have you told her what sort of French blowhard that fellow is?"

"I have not," Matthew said, as always confounded by why his valet seemed to believe that Beatrice would give a toss for anybody else's valet.

"I've got to warn the duke off," he said. "Somehow."

"Perhaps you could do it at the YBC masque on the morrow?"

Matthew put his coffee down and sat up. "Another masque? I just swore I would never attend another of those ridiculous things."

"But it is Lord Darden's event," Marcus said. "You did say you would go. The Benningtons might be very put out if you did not attend, and then who knows what the duke would be up to, left to his own devices."

Matthew groaned. "At least get me a domino," he said.

"My lord, it is Lord Darden's masque. Remember, one must come as something ridiculous."

Matthew eyed the crumpled soldier's uniform. "So I am to be stuck in that again."

"I do not believe so," Marcus said. "Lord Darden said he would arrange a costume."

"Well, isn't that wonderful news. He is so trustworthy; I am sure he will choose something suitable."

"Lord Darden?" Marcus asked, failing to hear the sarcasm.

"Never mind," he said. "You'd best go below and check that Shrimps hasn't burned down the kitchens."

Just then, there was the clatter of hoofbeats, three or four horses it sounded like, coming to a stop out of doors.

"Oh God," Marcus said, clutching his throat. "He's changed his mind. Conbatten has sent his seconds."

Matthew felt a chill in the warm room. He took in a breath. If it were to be so, then let it be so. He would not refuse a challenge.

Marcus ran to the window. Peering out, he turned and sank down with relief onto the cushioned alcove.

"It is not him, my lord. It is only Lord Darden's friends from that club of theirs, coming to call on the Benningtons."

"Coming to call on Lady Beatrice," Matthew said. "They are largely to blame for why Conbatten moves as quickly as he does. They have made him believe they are in competition for the lady's heart. I will put a stop to this nonsense. Get my clothes!"

Chapter Sixteen

Beatrice was in the drawing room with Miss Mayton and her sisters as they opened acceptances for her ball. So far, only the Megthorns had bowed out, as they had sickness in the house.

Tattleton opened the drawing room doors and said, "Lord Jericho, Lord Dunston, Sir William, and Mr. Cahill."

The men all came in looking very well after such a late night. Beatrice perfectly understood why they were there. Darden had said he had it on good authority that the mysterious gentleman was practically haunting Portland Place these days. He was to see the faux suitors arrive.

But would he do anything about it? Or would he just continue to watch and be tortured? It was becoming a bit tiresome, really.

"Gentlemen," Miss Mayton said, "we are just going through the acceptances for Beatrice's ball—it looks to be very well attended."

"We will all be there, naturally," Sir William said.

"And perhaps some other mysterious gentleman too," Lord Dunston said.

"Indeed," Lord Jericho said. "Darden says that when he composed the invitation list, he cast a wide net on the single gentlemen side of things. He is certain that whoever this fellow is, he's got an invitation."

Beatrice was a little startled to hear it. Somehow, she had not thought of the tortured gentleman as ever stepping through the door into her own house.

"I wonder what he does just now?" Cordelia said.

"Perhaps he stares at the invitation, tortured," Rosalind said.

"Or perhaps he is somewhere right outside," Sir William said. "Darden said he'd been told that the gentleman is often in the vicinity of Portland Place."

The footmen opened the doors and brought in a tea service. Tattleton followed behind them and said, "Lord Van Doren."

Beatrice felt as if a cold draft had come into the room.

"Van Doren, what do you do here?" Juliet asked.

"What does anybody do here?" he asked tersely.

"Van Doren, the man of the hour," Sir William said.

"Indeed, the tongues are wagging all over London I'll reckon," Lord Jericho said.

"I do not know why they should," Van Doren said.

"Come now, Van Doren," Mr. Cahill said. "Nobody gets in Conbatten's way. They just do not do it. So, of course it must be interesting to see it done."

"The *ton* does love a story to tell," Lord Dunston said.

"Perhaps the *ton* would like to discuss how a certain four gentlemen have conspired to pose as suitors to draw another gentleman forward," Van Doren said.

Beatrice should have known Van Doren would not drop the matter. Though, she still could not understand why he seemed so furious over it.

The four gentlemen so recently accused glanced at each other. Juliet nearly shouted, "Who told him? Who told Van Doren about the ruse?"

"Nobody told him," Beatrice said. "He guessed at it."

"Now he's getting *smarter* too?" Viola said. "What is happening?"

"Well now, it is only a little ruse, after all," Lord Jericho said.

"It is a lie," Van Doren said. "It is underhanded, and it is trickery."

Sir William waved his hands as if Van Doren had it all wrong, which he most certainly did. "You see, Van Doren, it is all kindly done. We only wish to help two people to find each other."

"The fellow needs help being found, does he?" Van Doren said sharply.

"Yes, indeed he does," Mr. Cahill said.

Just then, the earl came in. "What ho? I did not know we had visitors, and Van Doren too."

Beatrice fairly held her breath. The gentlemen made their greetings to the earl, though they all looked suddenly pale. It was clear enough that nobody knew if Van Doren was on the verge of acquainting her father with Darden's scheme.

"I see my timing is not ideal," the earl said. "It is so strange, but I find myself on tenterhooks to know how the one-eyed duke and his governess get on. Perhaps we might hear after dinner, Miss Mayton."

Miss Mayton, a bit wide-eyed, said, "Oh, but why not now? I have already told these gentlemen of where we are so far. They were most interested in it."

It was a clever bid to change the subject, though the earl looked not very convinced. "Really?" he asked.

"Oh yes," Lord Jericho said.

"We're on tenterhooks ourselves," Sir William said, nodding enthusiastically.

"Tied up in knots over it," Mr. Cahill said.

"On the edge of our seats," Lord Dunston said.

All of them studiously avoided Van Doren's eye, as did everybody else in the room but for the earl.

"Well now, Van Doren, could you stand for another chapter?"

Van Doren forced a smile. "Why ever not?"

Miss Mayton hurried to her sewing basket and retrieved her book. Beatrice could not help noting how relieved everybody in the room appeared. Except her father, of course, who only looked well pleased, and Van Doren, who scowled.

She felt a twinge of guilt over keeping her father in the dark about what had been going on and why Darden's friends had been following her about like a pack of puppies.

But then, the earl really did not like to be troubled over things.

"Now, as we know," Miss Mayton said, "the duke has been on a rampage in the village to avenge whoever attacked his gentle governess."

She trotted back to her seat. "Of course, we also know she was not attacked, but rather fell off the roof while attempting to view the duke in his bath."

As Beatrice knew perfectly well that the lords Dunston and Jericho, Sir William, and Mr. Cahill were not at all acquainted with the story, she pressed her lips together to stop from laughing. They all looked almost…frightened. She could not blame them—it did sound rather odd to hear it summed up like that.

Miss Mayton began to read.

"*Please, Duke, no more murders!*" *the gentle governess cried.*

"*I will not stop until I avenge you, no matter how many men must mistakenly die!*" *the duke shouted.*

"*Duke, truly, I fell off the roof. I was attempting to see you in the bath.*"

"*See me in the bath? No governess tries to see a duke in a bath!*"

"*But you see, I was hoping I might view…your missing eye.*"

"*But how? It is missing!*"

"*Well, I wished to see if I could live with it missing.*"

"*I see! At least, I see out of one eye! Did you view it, my gentle governess?*"

"*Um no, you were facing the wrong way.*"

"*The wrong way? So you would have only viewed my…*"

"*Yes, I did view that. And then fell into the bushes from the shock of it.*"

"*You must view my missing eye now. It is very terrible, but I must show you and then you will know!*" *the duke cried.*

"I am ready."

The duke slowly removed his eye patch. The gentle governess braced herself for the horror she was to view.

Surprisingly, the only thing the gentle governess saw was a perfectly good eye blinking back at her.

"But Duke! It is just an eye!"

"No, the eye is gone!"

"To the looking glass, Duke, it is not gone."

The duke raced to a looking glass. "My eye. How did I all along think it was gone?"

"You are not missing an eye. Duke, you are mad!"

"Mad? I suppose I am! Gentle governess, can you live with a madman?"

Miss Mayton closed the book. "So now the question is, can the gentle governess live with a madman?"

"He had his eye all along," Cordelia said happily. "Well, I am pleased."

"The poor gentle governess was thinking so much about the missing eye that she did not notice the duke was mad," Viola said.

"I really am on tenterhooks about how the whole thing will turn out—so many twists and turns," the earl said.

Beatrice thought Lord Dunston, Lord Jericho, Mr. Cahill, and Sir William looked less on tenterhooks and more stunned. Van Doren only sat shaking his head.

"That certainly was a twist and turn," Mr. Cahill said. "A mad duke…"

"Dukes are no more exempt from the malady than anybody else, I suppose," Van Doren said.

"Yes, but for him to imagine he'd lost an eye when it was there all along?" Sir William asked.

Van Doren stared at him and said, "Perhaps he was led astray somehow. He was led to believe a thing that never was."

Beatrice could feel them all growing uncomfortable in the idea that Van Doren was hinting about their ruse to draw out the tortured gentleman.

Juliet jumped from her seat. "I've written a new ode, Papa, if you would like to hear it."

"Of course I would, my dear, but perhaps it is better saved for when it is just the family and Van Doren."

"Do not say so, Earl!" Lord Dunston said, seeming just as enthusiastic to get Van Doren off the subject of the ruse. "We have had the privilege of hearing one of Lady Juliet's odes already and are all quite eager to hear another."

"Seconded!" Lord Jericho said.

Juliet pulled a scrap of paper from her reticule. "Now mind you, this is written in honor of Conbatten."

Beatrice pressed her lips together. She could not fathom why Juliet had written an ode to Conbatten. Nor could she fathom what Conbatten would think of it.

"Ah, the duke!" Sir William said, his voice filled with reverence.

"It is called *Ode to a Duke Retrieving a Lady's Card.*"

Beatrice silently groaned. Perhaps this was not the right moment to poke at Van Doren's behavior at the masque. Not while he was outraged at their ruse to draw the tortured gentleman out, her father sat right there, and he was so convinced the earl ought to know about it.

Juliet plowed on.

The duke does a favor, kindly meant,
Then is punished by a hot-tempered gent.
What could possibly transpire in that deranged mind,
But perhaps it has been lost, which would be about time.

Juliet curtsied. The earl roared with laughter. "Oh, that is very good, very good indeed. You see, Van Doren, she has heard of your taking Beatrice's card from the duke."

"I gathered that," Van Doren said, his jaw muscles looking very tight.

"Say, that reminds me, Van Doren," the earl continued, "how did you get on with the boy and the dog?"

Before Van Doren could answer, the earl said to the other gentlemen, "You see, last evening we came upon a group of boys pelting a dog with stones. Van Doren took the smallest boy and the dog home with him."

"Now that is charitable, Van Doren," Lord Dunston said. "But, what would you do with such creatures? I do not suppose the dog can hunt?"

"Only for its dinner in the kitchens, I imagine," Van Doren said. To the earl, he said, "The boy does not know his name and has always been called Shrimps. He's since named the dog Oyster. I planned to send them to the stables, but they are both wily creatures and remain in the kitchens."

"Ah yes," the earl said. "I suppose a young lad like that would prefer to stay close by food and fire."

"That was precisely his reasoning," Van Doren said drily.

Thinking to divert the conversation away from anything that had to do with last evening, Beatrice said, "My brother's ball is on the morrow, my lords. In what ridiculous costume do you come?"

"That is a very great secret, Lady Beatrice," Mr. Cahill said. "Darden has worked tirelessly to get us kitted out. We will surprise you with our ridiculousness."

"Van Doren," the earl said, "what will you wear?"

"I haven't the faintest idea," Van Doren said. "Darden was to sort something out."

"Whatever it is," Lord Dunston said, "it is sure to amuse."

"Amuse who?" Van Doren said.

Beatrice could not make him out. Van Doren was, just at this moment, sounding very like his old self. And yet, when he had arrived, he'd been more the new and temperamental Van Doren. Who was this back-and-forth person?

"I am to once again go in my widow's weeds," Miss Mayton said. "Lord Darden believes that, as I was never formally married, coming as a widow would pass muster at the door."

"Our aunt was so close to the altar, though," Viola said. "Several times."

Beatrice could see very well that none of the gentlemen knew how to respond to that statement, as they did not know the circumstances.

Sir William shook his head sadly. "War," he said softly.

"Oh no, Sir William," Miss Mayton said, "it was far more terrible than that."

The gentleman appeared alarmed to hear it.

"Aunt," Cordelia said, "do tell the gentlemen about poor Count Tulerstein. And then, if they are willing, I will act out Desdemona."

Beatrice smiled her approval at Cordelia. Her sister had expertly steered the conversation away from any talk of the events of last evening or any ruses that might have been guessed at.

⇶⇷

TATTLETON WATCHED IN some despair as one of the cats gnawed on the lock to the tea chest like any housebreaker.

Oh, those felines had been very manageable when they'd arrived. Young and underfed, they had spent most of their time in a basket. But now! Now, everywhere he looked there was a cat.

Hanging from curtains and attempting to jump onto counters, and he'd even discovered one in his bed! He was certain there had only been four of them arriving, but now it seemed like there were ten. They were under siege!

It was very hard to work under such conditions. Poor Mr. James had all but given up the ghost—he'd spy a cat licking at a haunch of beef he'd just brought in from the cold cellar and collapse in a chair.

What none of those creatures had managed to do was catch a mouse. The young ladies had sworn the kitchens would not have a mouse dare enter under threat of so many cats, but it turned out they were quite useless at the activity.

At least Charlie, the young fellow who'd come along with those feline wretches, was turning out very good. He was small, but he worked like the devil himself and Tattleton often sent him to bed, lest he not send himself to bed.

Charlie was about the only good news in his sphere just now. As if below stairs were not hectic enough, above stairs was not much better.

Lord Van Doren had dropped some heavy hints in the drawing room this afternoon and it was clear he knew of the scheme Lord Darden had enacted.

But poor Lord Van Doren! Most obviously, he did not know *he* was the intended target! Nor did Lady Beatrice know it. Nor did Miss Mayton or any of the sisters know it.

Lady Beatrice was always staring out of windows, attempting to spot her mystery gentleman. Her sisters were endlessly speculating on who he was and what he was doing at any given moment. Lady Juliet had gone so far as to write an ode as a wedding present.

Lady Beatrice was pining for a gentleman who did not exist and Lord Van Doren was pining for nobody at all!

What would happen when all was known? Tattleton was very afraid it would create a rift between the family and their neighbor. And all of this going on under the earl's nose!

Mrs. Huffson bustled into the servants' dining hall. "Goodness, Mr. Tattleton, you do seem so on edge these days."

"I have much weighing heavy on my mind, Mrs. Huffson."

The housekeeper glanced at one of the cats hanging from a curtain rod, that feline appearing to think over whether it ought to hold on or drop.

"Well now," she said, "they won't be kittens forever. They'll settle in six months or so."

Tattleton fairly shivered at the thought of where the family would stand six months from now.

>>>><<<<

MATTHEW HAD GONE over to the Benningtons' to make Darden's friends aware that he knew of their ridiculous ruse to drive Conbatten forward in his attentions to Beatrice. If Darden would not put a stop to it, then he would.

He had done it, though they had not looked half as ashamed as they ought to.

Perhaps the only recourse was to tell the duke that he'd been the subject of some trickery.

It was a delicate matter. For one, the duke did not like him. For another, might the fellow not demand an answer on the green from the actual perpetrators?

Darden would not thank him to have four of his friends challenged by a duke.

Still, the man had a right to know. Once he knew, he would rethink his interest in Beatrice, which would be well for her. Though she might not comprehend that at this very moment.

She had no doubt been swept away by the idea of being pursued and becoming a duchess. She would see, over time, that it could never have made her happy. She would see she would have spent her life toe-tapping, waiting for the duke to emerge from his endless bath, and then been miserable when he spent more time admiring himself than his wife.

The earl had invited him to dine the evening before, but he had chosen to take his leave with the other gentlemen. He had considered that he would do well to enjoy a night of peace and quiet with no odes, one-eyed dukes, Desdemonas, or Count Tulersteins to put up with.

Cahill, Dunston, Sir William, and Jericho had been all most perplexed to hear of Count Tulerstein throwing himself off the side of an alpine cliff.

Lord Dunston had even gone so far as to say, "Did they send out mountaineers for a search party to recover him, dead or alive?"

Matthew had cleared his throat and said, "Lord Dunston, once one of Miss Mayton's suitors has decided to kill himself, there is no turning back."

This earned him one of Miss Mayton's indignant sniffs, and dagger eyes from her charges.

Not to be put off, Cordelia was determined to enact her version of Desdemona. Candles were naturally knocked over, though fortunately they were not lit.

The gentlemen had taken their leave shortly thereafter and he was not surprised. Those fellows may have been eager to accommodate Darden in his unfortunate ruse but holding up under the Benningtons' habits was another matter.

Though Matthew had sought a quiet evening, he had not got one. Oyster seemed to consider the entire house his new territory and insisted on sneaking above stairs whenever he got the chance.

Once there, he went from doors to windows, barking menacingly at anything that might be out there and trying to get in.

Shrimps had made a leash from some twine and he would pull at Oyster, the dog would growl, Shrimps would cry, Oyster would howl, and then they would be friends again.

The footmen had been run off their feet trying to track them down by the sounds of crying and howls and then corral them back downstairs again.

Now, he sat in a bath before he must attend Darden's ball. Unlike the great Conbatten, it was nowhere near ninety-eight degrees. It was decidedly chilly and he was certain it was purposefully done by Marcus to continue to express his displeasure over Shrimps and Oyster.

So many people imagined their servants had no power, but he knew better. They could make life decidedly uncomfortable when they were in a temper. Further, a servants' hall was its own carefully formed society. Whenever a new being was introduced into it, there was a shake-up before a settling down. Introduce a wily boy and a troublesome dog and, well, it was bound to be chaotic.

Matthew could not dwell on his own household, though. More pressing matters were at hand. He had not yet decided what to do about the duke, but something must be done. He'd begun to lean toward telling the duke there was a game afoot regarding Lady Beatrice, but not who was involved in the scheme. Conbatten might guess at Darden's friends, but if he could not be certain, it must head off any danger of a duel.

It was a risky strategy and he had not entirely concluded it was the right one.

Marcus hurried in with a large box. "My lord, you are not going to like it."

"Let me guess, Oyster has once again gone mad over intruders who are not there and Shrimps is wailing over it."

"That, yes, but that particular circumstance is becoming so usual one hardly notices."

"Then what?"

"This," Marcus said, laying the box down. "Lord Darden has just dropped it off, your costume for the ball."

"What is it," Matthew said with a long sigh. "What ridiculous costume am I to appear in?"

"A pigeon, my lord," Marcus said. Then he hunched up his shoulders and squinted to prepare himself for the oncoming wrath.

"Do not be absurd. Even Darden could not have sent such a thing."

"He has though, and he says it is in the spirit of the thing and the earl is going as a squid."

"I will not dress as a pigeon. It is out of the question."

"But my lord, if the earl is prepared to appear as a squid…"

That idea did give him pause. He was surprised to hear it, of course. But then, if even the earl was prepared to make himself ridiculous… Though, he so disliked making himself ridiculous!

On the other hand, he would also make himself ridiculous if he were thought a poor sport by showing himself in a pique and refusing to attend.

"How bad is it?" Matthew asked. "I presume you looked before bringing it up."

"It is not as bad as you would imagine. Assuming you have an exceedingly vivid imagination," Marcus said.

From below, Matthew heard Oyster howling and Shrimps weeping over some new upset.

He'd like to howl and weep himself.

CHAPTER SEVENTEEN

LYNETTE FUSSED WITH the various accoutrements of Beatrice's costume. Darden had promised he would help her dress for his tomfoolery ball, and he had. She was to be Anne Bonney—fearless lady pirate and excellent swordswoman.

Personally, she did not see what was so ridiculous about a lady pirate and found herself well-pleased with the choice. Darden had attempted to dress her father as a squid, so she felt herself very lucky to end up a pirate.

Her sisters were crowded into her room, in part thrilled with the costume and in part dejected that they had not one of their own.

Beatrice was already dressed in a very roomy linen blouse, a voluminous lace fichu tied in a gentleman's knot at her neck, and a skirt of sturdy kersey.

"Oh look," Viola said, pulling the hilt of the cutlass from its scabbard, "there is no blade."

"It looks ever so menacing, though," Juliet said.

Lynette looked critically at the silk sash and the broad leather belt. "I reckon the sash goes under the belt to keep it secure?"

"Yes, I believe the pistol is hidden in the sash with just the butt showing, and then there is the leather pouch that will be my reticule for the evening," Beatrice said. "I believe the belt goes through the loop on the pouch."

"Goodness," Rosalind said, "you will be well-armed."

Beatrice laughed at the notion. "As I have no blade and the pistol is only painted wood, I shall only *look* well-armed."

Lynette made the arrangements. "Now, there is only the hat," she said.

The hat in question was a jaunty brown felt with a deep brim and a brown plume.

"Do set it at a dashing angle, Lynette," Cordelia said. "She is a pirate, after all."

"Yes, yes," Lynette muttered, never very enthusiastic about receiving directions from five different people, though she ought to be well-used to it.

"Beatrice," Viola said, "what shall you do if your mysterious gentleman keeps hiding himself away? Shall you end the season with no engagement?"

"I hardly know what to think," Beatrice said, "nor what to do. It seems he really should step forward and if he is not able…"

"If he is not able, then he is no Henry the Fifth," Cordelia said.

Beatrice nodded. She did not say that her feelings had started to turn against the mysterious gentleman. Or that she thought of him less and less.

"I wonder what Darden has planned for Van Doren," Rosalind said. "I do hope he does not come as a pirate too."

Beatrice understood what her sister alluded to. She said, "I believe Darden understands that I was not amused to find our neighbor coming as Benedict to Lady Bloomington's masque and will not try another such joke."

"Our brother is so very amusing, though," Juliet said.

"Our dear brother," Cordelia said. "Just think, Beatrice, you will be one of the honored guests—it is Darden's club, after all."

"I cannot imagine what he's planned for the evening's festivities," Viola said.

"Whatever it is, let us all hope Van Doren does not throw cold water on it," Juliet said.

"Indeed," Viola said, "let us hope he is not ripping your card from a gentleman's hand."

Beatrice felt a flutter at the mention of that circumstance. It really had been so bold.

"Darden has finally resigned himself that Papa will not go. Our dear father said he would not be dressed as a squid for even the king," Cordelia said.

"Father is rather well-pleased that he will go to Lord Camden's house for cards instead," Beatrice said. "We cannot fault him for it, he says that lord keeps excellent port."

Miss Mayton drifted in; a haunting specter dressed in her widow's weeds. She moved quickly across the floor, and it must be presumed her feet marched forward, but she was so completely covered from head to toe it did appear as if she glided rather than walked.

"Aunt, if I encountered you in a dark corridor late at night, I should be very frightened," Juliet said.

"Miss Mayton bobbed her head under her black lace veil. "A widow must always be found haunting, having suffered a great loss. Naturally, as I have suffered so many different losses, it must be particularly striking."

"Do you suppose Beatrice's tortured gentleman will finally step forward this evening?" Rosalind asked.

"Hmm, I cannot be certain. Though, there is every chance of it. Perhaps when he sees Beatrice as a bold pirate, he may think to be bold too."

Beatrice did not answer that idea. But really, she would prefer a gentleman who did not need to be coaxed into declaring his passion.

⇶⇷

DARDEN LOOKED ABOUT his club with a satisfied eye. He patted his well-padded stomach and shifted his crown. He was dressed as Henry the Eighth, with his intimates dressed as his six wives. Cahill and Jericho, Anne Boleyn and Katherine Howard respectively, had tall collars with just peepholes for eyes and carried platters with plaster heads on them. It was entirely absurd, and he had no idea what they would do when it came time to dance.

"Gentlemen," Darden said to the members of the YBC who had gathered round him, "you will recall the scheme I designed to bring Lady Beatrice and Lord Van Doren together. Jericho, Dunston, Sir William, and Cahill have done a masterful job at assisting me. Now, I need you all. What I ask is that you put yourself onto my sister's card as fast as possible. I wish for her card to be filled before Van Doren has a chance at it."

"Ah, you mean to force him to recognize his own feelings at being left out of it," Lord Dunston said.

"Indeed," Darden said. "This may be the final push. At least, I hope it is. I am running out of ideas on what to do with that fellow and my sister."

"Have you seen any promising signs?" Lord Harveston asked, his tall and lanky frame draped on a windowsill.

All the men involved in the scheme nodded vigorously. "Surely you heard about Van Doren tearing Lady Beatrice's card from Conbatten's hands?" Sir William asked.

"From *Conbatten's* hand, you understand," Lord Jericho said.

"I had not heard the report; I just got back into Town," the baron answered, examining his medieval plague mask.

"It is not only us that Van Doren takes for suitors, he also seems to believe Conbatten is a suitor too."

"Conbatten," some of the members murmured.

"Did we invite the duke to the ball?" Lord Harveston asked.

Darden shifted uncomfortably. "In the end, we did not."

"We were afraid he would decline the invitation," Lord Dunston said.

"Or that he would accept it," Lord Jericho said, nodding.

"Aside from that always prickly question," Darden said, "we are to have a smashing time and we are to continue our progress on *Campaign Shenanigans*. Beatrice and Van Doren must be made to see the truth of things."

"He must be well on his way," Lord Dunston said, "we have seen how he acts when we call on Lady Beatrice at the house. He practically flies across the road."

"Surely, they must come to their senses," Sir William said.

"I am hopeful of it," Darden said. "As a final touch, I have arranged for bunches and bunches of red roses to be delivered to Beatrice two days from now, from a secret admirer. That will accomplish two things, I hope—Van Doren will go mad wondering who they are from, and they will serve as nice decoration at Beatrice's ball. You see? My father had already given over a nice budget for flowers so why should they not serve a dual purpose?"

"And *this*, Darden," Lord Jericho said, with a flourishing bow, "is why you lead us."

Darden slapped his friend on the back. "Tonight, our battalion rides to the breech and prays for a swift victory."

⋙⋘

MATTHEW HAD GONE back and forth on whether he ought to go to Darden's ridiculous masque. For one, the costume. A pigeon. Was it some sort of insult? For another, he had firmly decided that masques were irritating and foolish.

However, the earl was going and it was his own son's event. Further, Conbatten would no doubt be there. Matthew was determined to speak to the duke and set him straight.

Finally, at Marcus' coaxing, he'd donned his ludicrous costume. It was comprised of a very long coat of grey feathers, a hat formed into the face of a pigeon with a very sharp beak, and a grey velvet mask for his eyes.

He could not bear to look at it, but if the earl were willing to go as a squid, he supposed he must just gird his loins and forgo complaint.

Matthew left the house well ahead of the Benningtons. He did not wish to ride beside their carriage and be teased all the way to St. James Street. He would make his way quickly, in the dark. The strangers he passed might be amused, but they would not know who he was.

Getting out of the house was more difficult than he had imagined. Oyster had gone positively mad at the sight of him cloaked in feathers, then Shrimps had come running and screamed as if he encountered some otherworldly creature.

Genroy had led them both away, Shrimps weeping and Oyster's underbite chattering.

Matthew supposed a boy brought up in a workhouse had not had a prior opportunity to see a gentleman on his way to a masque. Nor, apparently, had a dog who'd lived on the streets had that opportunity. For all that, though, the two of them were exceedingly high-strung!

The Young Bucks Club, located at a fashionable address on St. James Street, had a lime mortar front with ostentatious Greek columns at its entrance. The footmen at the doors were all dressed as bucks—their heads sprouting ridiculous antlers and their cloaks of deer hide.

Darden claimed his club was devoted to shenanigans and tomfoolery, so Matthew did not know what else he'd expected.

The footmen made a great show of examining his costume to deem it appropriately ridiculous, which of course it was, and then the doors were opened and he went inside.

One of the things he disliked so much about masques, aside from his own embarrassing costume, was that it was very hard to recognize anybody. A sea of absurdity was in his view, and it was difficult to know who he looked at.

Though, he could make some guesses. Henry the Eighth was certainly Darden, and only his friends would be strange enough to put on dresses in what he presumed were meant to be that unfortunate king's even more unfortunate queens. It must be so, as two of them carried round plaster heads on platters.

Then, amongst the crowd, he spotted who he really sought this night.

Conbatten.

If there were others difficult to recognize, it was not so with Conbatten. His tall and lanky frame stood out among the crowd. He wore a medieval plague mask, its pointed beak even more ridiculous than his own pigeon's beak.

This was the moment. Beatrice had not yet arrived and he must straighten the fellow out before she got here.

He marched over to the duke and tapped him on the shoulder. "A word, if you please."

Conbatten turned to him and Matthew could not see his expression, hidden as he was behind his plague mask.

"I feel it is my duty to point out that all thought of pursuing Lady Beatrice must be put aside. I know that you have felt the pressure of believing that other gentlemen seek her out, but they are only amusing themselves, they are not serious."

Conbatten did not reply, but only stared at him.

"Most importantly, though," Matthew continued, "you are not at all suited. Lady Beatrice requires a gentleman who will put his attention on admiring her. You, Your Grace, cannot be that man. Everybody knows you spend far too much time on your person to be capable of it. I do not mean to be harsh, but I only give you that hint."

Matthew had tried to keep his voice low, but was now cognizant that he had attracted the attention of some who were nearby. He must conclude the conversation.

"I just say, I have known Lady Beatrice since childhood, you and she are not at all suited," he whispered hotly.

"What on earth are you talking about?"

Conbatten had finally replied…but it was not Conbatten. Matthew did not know who it was, but it was not the duke.

He'd been certain it was the duke! Who else was so tall?

"Might I have your name, sir?" this man who was not Conbatten asked.

"No need, do excuse, a bit of a mix-up, never mind, and forget all about it," Matthew said.

He could not ignore the titters he heard round him. What had he just done?

Matthew spun on his heel to get away from the situation, his feathers flapping in all directions.

He hurried away, only to find Beatrice had just come through the doors and was entirely surrounded by gentlemen. Naturally, some of them were Henry the Eighth's wives—otherwise known as Darden's friends who liked to stir up trouble.

Matthew would very much like to feel that their little game was at an end. That he had just informed the duke that it was to go nowhere.

That was not to be. He had informed *somebody*, he just did not know who.

His hope was that the who in question did not know him either. Though, that was not likely to last long. If the man made enough inquiries, it would come out.

Perhaps the onlookers who had overheard bits and pieces had not heard enough to put anything together. That could very well be.

Matthew took in a breath. Yes, it would probably all come to nothing. In the end.

He strode toward Beatrice, or rather the crowd of gentlemen surrounding her. He finally pushed his way through.

Beatrice peered at him. "Van Doren?" she asked.

He nodded and she laughed merrily. "Goodness," she said,

"Darden has done very well by you in the ridiculous department."

"Indeed," he said through gritted teeth. "And you are?"

"Anne Bonney, lady pirate. As you can see," she said, patting her scabbard and the butt of a pistol, "I come well-armed."

"May I?" he said, reaching for her card.

"Oh dear, it is quite filled up, I'm afraid."

"Really," Matthew said, glancing at the fellows who were all now avoiding his eye and drifting away. "I am surprised you did not save a spot for the great Conbatten."

Beatrice looked at him from under the brim of her hat and said, "Darden did not invite the duke. It was the usual problem—they were afraid he either would not come or would come."

"Ridiculous," Matthew muttered. "Who are all these men on your card?"

"Darden's friends, mostly. Should I inquire," Beatrice said, eyeing his feathers, "are you…a pigeon?"

"So I am told," Matthew said. "I only agreed to it as I understood the earl was to come far worse and I did not wish him to do so alone."

"Ah, the squid costume," Beatrice said, laughing. "Papa said not even the king could force him into such a thing. He's gone off to play cards and drink excellent port at Lord Camden's."

There were times when the Benningtons made Matthew feel as if his head might explode into a thousand bits. There had been no need for him to come at all! The earl was not here, Conbatten was not here, and Beatrice's card was filled.

"Lord Van Doren!" a voice sounded behind him. It was a voice he had grown to know all too well. Lady Mary.

He turned as Lady Mary said, "And Lady Beatrice, too."

Lady Mary was dressed as a mermaid, doused in blue and green sequins, and dragging a tail by way of a train behind her.

Matthew bowed and would have forced out some sort of pleasantry had he been given a moment.

"Lord Van Doren," Lady Mary plowed on, "you have chosen to come as a pigeon."

"It was not that I chose—"

Lady Mary waved a sequined fan at him and said, "Everybody knows that the pigeon mates for life."

"I hardly think my brother intended to send such a message," Beatrice said. "Lord Darden chose the costume for our neighbor."

Lady Mary's eyes narrowed just a little bit. "I see," she said. "Well, in any case…"

Now Lady Mary was fairly dangling her card in front of him. He really had no choice. "May I?" he asked, reaching for it.

Lady Mary smiled graciously. "Of course, Lord Van Doren."

As Matthew filled his name in, he was consumed by a desire to be back in his own house. He would not mind Oyster barking his head off or Shrimps weeping in despair or Marcus huffily complaining. At this point, he would delight in it.

Over Beatrice's shoulder, he spotted Lady Clara coming through the door. He bowed to Lady Mary and quickly took himself off in the other direction.

⇒⇒⇒⇐⇐⇐

BEATRICE HAD FOUND herself initially amused and then a little nonplussed by Van Doren. That he came as a pigeon, well, she would have never imagined Darden could get him into such a costume. Though, she could very well see how he might have felt pressed if he believed her father was to come as a squid. He was very loyal to the earl.

But then, he had inquired why she had not saved a spot on her card for Conbatten. The *great* Conbatten, he'd said. He'd practically spit the words out. He'd seemed to be in no better of a temper when he asked who had put their names down on her card.

The entire exchange had given Beatrice a giddy feeling. He seemed to have gone to the new Van Doren this evening. The one with feelings about things.

Beatrice watched Van Doren cross the room with Lady Clara in pursuit. Lady Mary, who Beatrice had been hardly cognizant was still standing next to her, said, "It must be gratifying to you, Lady Beatrice, that your neighbor is so admired everywhere he goes."

"Van Doren?" she asked absentmindedly. Lady Clara had caught up to him on the far side of the room.

"Naturally, Lord Van Doren," Lady Mary said. "Of course, there has been speculation that perhaps there is to be a match between you, but I have had the pleasure of dancing with the lord several times and so, rest assured, I know the truth of it."

"The truth of it?" Beatrice asked, turning away from Lady Clara and Van Doren to attend Lady Mary.

"Lord Van Doren has gone out of his way to hint to me that there is nothing but neighborly friendliness between you. He was very keen that I understand that point. *Very* keen, if you understand me."

"I am afraid I do not, Lady Mary," Beatrice said warily.

Lady Mary laughed behind her fan. Then in a low voice, she said, "He wished me to understand that his interest lay in another direction entirely." She glanced at Lady Clara and whispered, "And it is not in *that* direction."

"Indeed," Beatrice said, her mind racing to parse what the lady was telling her.

"Well," Lady Mary said, "it will all be spoken of in good time, I expect."

She smiled and moved away.

What would be spoken of? Did she mean to say that Van Doren had hinted at an engagement? To Lady Mary? It was impossible! No, not to Lady Mary.

Beatrice paused. Was it impossible, though? Van Doren would

need a wife, he was practical, she was suitable. She was also determined.

And then, why had he made such an effort to explain his *neighborly* feelings?

Miss Mayton glided up beside her. "My dear," she said, "I have just been to the refreshments room and you must see it. Each thing put out is ridiculous in its own way. I just ate a strawberry dipped in gravy. It was melted chocolate, of course, but it is in a gravy boat. Too amusing."

"Aunt," Beatrice said, "do you think it is at all possible that Van Doren might propose to Lady Mary?"

Miss Mayton turned, and Beatrice presumed she was looking at Van Doren across the room, though she could not be certain what happened under that veil. How her aunt had got a strawberry under there, she really did not know.

"It is possible," her aunt said. "She seems to come with the right attributes—family, money, and such. He is such a no-nonsense sort of person, he might not factor affection into it. Who knows where the pigeon will land to roost in the end."

Beatrice felt her insides go cold and she shivered. It could not be. He could not wed Lady Mary. He must not marry anybody; she had always thought so.

As skilled as she was at ignoring any thoughts that were inconvenient, there were occasions when her mind would not be denied. Her mind would be so determined to catch her attention that it would not give up until she listened to some unpleasant idea.

It did so now, and what it wanted to say was very terrible. He should not marry anybody because…well, because he was Van Doren! He was meant to stay just as he was, following her round wherever she went.

Beatrice felt positively sick. She could not bear him going away because she wished him by her side. She was jealous of him. Jealous of his attention. Van Doren! How had it happened? She had long left behind any feelings she'd had for him.

She had convinced herself that the only reason she found it startling that Van Doren would dance at a ball, or be admired by other ladies, or wed someday, was because she was just used to him being about.

It was more than that, though.

Now, she began to feel just as she had all those years ago. That plaguey feeling of bubbles in her blood was back. It was not as Miss Mayton described—she did not feel as if her hair had been struck by lightning, or that she was drowning but had air, or that her heart had sped forward. She just felt sick.

This…whatever it was she felt, had been tiptoeing back ever since they'd come to Town. Ever since she'd stepped back and viewed him as others did. It had crept in so softly that she'd not perceived it until Lady Mary had threatened to steal him away.

It was a disaster. He did not love her and he would not follow her round forever. Had he ever done when she was a girl, and she thought he might have, he did not now. What had been between them had not tiptoed back for him. She was only a duty.

Oh, Conbatten and even her father had hinted that Van Doren had some regard for her, but she knew how far it went. He did not have *that* sort of affection for her. There were simply not the signs of passion. And, if he did not feel anything now, he never would.

Beatrice felt something though. She would not name it, though she was very afraid she knew its name.

If her mysterious tortured gentleman were to step forward now, what use? She could not wed the man while always looking back at Van Doren.

Beatrice was terrified of what the future might hold for her. She must step aside and allow Rosalind her chance at finding true love next season. She would grow older and eventually become a Miss Mayton.

One of her sisters would have a passel of children and she would guide them as best she could and tell them of her tragedy in love. When she visited Darden, she would make herself pleasant to his new neighbor—Lady Mary, Viscountess Van Doren.

"Aunt," she said gravely, "I have just realized I will never marry."

"Of course you will, my dear."

"No, I do not believe so. Just as you have been so unlucky, I have been too."

"I have faith that your mysterious gentleman must step forward sooner or later," Miss Mayton said.

Beatrice shook her head. It did not matter. The only gentleman who should step forward would never step forward.

The orchestra had tuned and Mr. Cahill approached for the first. Beatrice forced herself to smile. She would make herself pleasant all evening. It was her life now—pretending to be satisfied with her circumstances.

To think, of all the directions her life might have taken it had gone this way. It was not at all what she had imagined.

Beatrice thought how ironic it was that she had begun the evening as Anne Bonney but would end it as the future Miss Mayton.

She would not have a string of tragedies to reflect upon as Miss Mayton had. She would just have the one.

It felt as if that would be quite enough.

Chapter Eighteen

Matthew had no engagements for the three days leading up to Beatrice's ball. There were invitations, to be sure, and even one for a dinner at Lady Mary's house issued by her mother, but he had declined them as "prior engaged." As for Lady Mary's invitation, he had to restrain himself from writing "prior engaged forever no matter what day you pick."

It was a relief to live quiet, or as quiet as one could be with the likes of Shrimps and Oyster in the house.

Darden's masque had been harrowing. Aside from his misstep of approaching Conbatten who was not Conbatten, there was no longer doubt in his mind that Lady Mary wished to hear him speak of marriage. Had any lady in the history of mankind ever stomped round a subject so thoroughly?

He was to know her views on the management of servants. After hearing them, he did not think she would very much approve of his current circumstances. One howling dog and one weeping orphan continued to sow chaos below stairs.

He was to understand her views on children, which were not very like his own ideas. As far as he could gather, once a child was produced, one need not look upon them until they were sixteen and could talk sensibly at a dining table.

He was to know how much she preferred Somerset to any other county, as if he would believe she'd done extensive exploring throughout England to come to that conclusion.

Most outrageously, he was to know that it was said that there was madness in Lady Clara's family, and one could never be sure how that would be passed down through the generations.

Lady Clara had been a deal more circumspect in their time together, though he felt there was danger there too.

After he'd silently condemned Lady Mary's behavior, there was his own to reflect on. He'd lectured a fellow who he'd assumed was Conbatten but was not. He'd been so determined to inform the duke that the match was ill-favored that he'd rushed to the first tall man he'd seen. Then, once he'd spoken the words it seemed…inappropriate to say the least.

What if it *had* been Conbatten and he'd been successful in driving him off? Would Beatrice thank him for it? What had he been thinking, presuming he knew what was best for her? Or what she preferred? He'd been very highhanded and poking his nose in where it did not belong.

Beatrice was to make her own decisions and create her own life with no management from him. It felt as if…as if she were slipping from his grasp. A grasp he had no right to in the first place.

Still, she should not marry Conbatten. Beatrice was too good for him, duke though he might be. She deserved someone who would be very careful of her, not some careless duke.

On the first day of nothing to do, he had answered a letter from his steward and various other correspondences and had read all evening. Now it was the second day, and he began to feel restless.

He crossed the street to the Benningtons, as perhaps there would be some entertainment there, even if it were as ludicrous as hearing of the deranged one-eyed duke and his rather bizarre lady love. Did that governess really imagine she could cure madness? If she could, she would do well to share that information with the world.

Tattleton led him into the drawing room. "Lord Van Doren," he intoned.

Matthew looked about the room, but he did not see Beatrice. Only her sisters and Miss Mayton. Oddly, Miss Mayton was once more dressed in her widow's weeds, only missing the absurd black veil.

"Lord Van Doren," Miss Mayton said.

"I thought you were going round as a pigeon these days," Rosalind said, laughing at her own supposed wit.

"Because he thought Papa would actually go as a squid," Juliet said with a snort.

"Very funny," Matthew said, taking a seat. "Miss Mayton, I am surprised to see you still dressed in black. Were you intending to carry on so indefinitely?"

"I do not see why not, Lord Van Doren. I have suffered as any widow has."

"Terribly suffered. As you well know," Cordelia said.

Matthew decided there was no point in pursuing why the lady who never married was to dress herself as a widow forevermore. "Where is Beatrice? I mean, Lady Beatrice?"

"She is under the weather with a headache," Miss Mayton said. "I told her she had better rest, as her ball is the day after tomorrow."

"Did she invite you to the ball, Van Doren?" Viola said, keeping her expression grave.

"Of course I received an invitation."

"Now my dear," Miss Mayton said to Viola, "do not forget your father's hint about Lord Van Doren."

"That our neighbor could have been worse," Cordelia said with a shrug.

"We are all agreed on that point, Aunt," Juliet said. "But he is still Van Doren."

"Is it really true that you have grown very popular and that two ladies are chasing you round the town?" Rosalind asked.

"What nonsense," Matthew said.

"That's what *we* thought, how could it be?" Juliet said.

"But Beatrice and our aunt both say it is true," Viola said.

"Miss Mayton," Matthew said, "I would thank you not to put about such fables."

Miss Mayton smiled and said, "Come now, Lord Van Doren. A widow may speak plainly. If you mean to deny that Lady Mary hunts you like a king after a stag while Lady Clara hangs back just a little to appear more modest, then, well really."

"First," Matthew said, "a widow is under the same conversational constraints as anybody else. Second, I do not think my interactions out in society have any place being discussed in this drawing room."

"Then why did you come?" Juliet asked. "You know perfectly well that we discuss everything between us."

Matthew rose. He could not answer the question; he did not know why he'd come.

"Please tell Beatrice that I hope she feels well soon. I bid you good day."

BEATRICE HAD SEEN Van Doren cross the road to the house from her bedchamber window. Oh how differently she looked at him now! He was so handsome, so smartly dressed, he walked with such purpose. He was of good character through and through—why had she always taken all of that for granted?

She had gone down to breakfast early and then retired to her room with a headache. It was not particularly a lie; her head did hurt. Everything hurt. She felt as if she had tumbled down a hill and bruised herself all over.

Beatrice had been locked away alone ever since. She could not hide in her room forever, she knew that. But just one day. One day to stay quiet and resign herself to what would be her gray and lifeless future.

When Van Doren had been let in, she crept to the top of the stairs. She could not face him yet. She would master herself and be able to do it, but not today. Not so soon after being assaulted by her own feelings.

After Tattleton had led him into the drawing room, the butler had been fetched urgently by one of the footmen. There was an emergency in the kitchens, something to do with cats and the larder and Cook with his head in his hands.

As the butler had been called away so swiftly, the drawing room doors had been left open. Beatrice lingered at the top of the stairs to hear what was said.

She rather wished she had not.

There was the usual teasing from her sisters, and how could there not be when they all knew he'd gone to Darden's masque as a pigeon?

But then had come the question of ladies admiring Van Doren. Miss Mayton had put it in the plainest terms and Van Doren had not denied it. He'd only ordered them all to stop talking about it.

Beatrice suspected Lady Mary knew her business. There would be an engagement coming soon.

It would not be a passionate match, but then Van Doren did not look for that.

How would it be when she went home? She supposed he would not visit half so much and when he did, he would bring his lady.

Was there any polite way to say that she wished Lady Mary to never darken her doors? Probably not. No, of course not. She had already vowed to herself that she would make herself pleasant to the new viscountess. She must just get used to it.

Beatrice rubbed her temples. She wished she had never come to Town. She wished she was back in the country with her sisters, only imagining what coming to Town would be like and being scolded by Van Doren.

Beatrice took a deep breath and straightened her skirts. She must just keep walking forward. She must get through her ball. The season would go on and then it would end and then she could retire to the country. It would be time enough then to tell her father that she would never marry.

She was not so certain she would tell him why, though. She was not certain she would ever tell anybody that.

※

Tattleton regarded Mr. James with his head in his hands in the corner of the kitchen. Charlie, the helpful little mite, was patting the cook's shoulder sympathetically.

There were trails of sugar icing leading out of the larder and all round the kitchen. There were also four cats who appeared as if they were stepping on hot coals—they leapt and twirled in the air and had wild looks on their faces. Tattleton could not tell if they were enjoying themselves or dying.

"You see what's happened, Mr. Tattleton," Mrs. Huffson whispered. "The kittens have got into Mr. James' sugar icing for the cake meant for Lady Beatrice's ball."

The cats sprang and hissed and swatted at the air.

"Have they been poisoned by it?" Mr. Tattleton asked, nearly hoping the answer was yes.

"Oh no, nothing so bad as that," Mrs. Huffson assured him. "I believe the sugar has given them…an extra spring in their step."

"That is the last thing they needed!" Tattleton said.

"Aye, I am aware. Take heart, it won't last forever. Just like children, in an hour or so they'll run down like clocks and be sleeping peacefully in a corner."

"An hour?" Mr. James cried from his corner.

Tattleton was at his wit's end. There was nowhere in the house where peace was to be found.

The preparations for the ball had him run off his feet, Lady Beatrice was ill though the ball was the day after tomorrow, Miss Mayton had taken to dressing herself as a widow, it seemed Lord Van Doren was on the verge of a proposal to a certain Lady Mary while poor Lady Beatrice pined for a nonexistent man who they all speculated would come to the ball though he did not exist, and now Mr. James' sugar icing was just a distant memory.

"I think you'd better sit down, Mr. Tattleton," Mrs. Huffson said. "You look a bit unsteady. I'll fetch you a cup of tea and that shall put things right."

Mrs. Huffson was a dear lady and so Tattleton did not inform her that it would take far more than a cup of tea to set things right in this house.

BEATRICE HAD WOKEN and got out of bed, determined that she should take up her regular habits. Her ball was on the morrow, and she could not hide from the world longer.

Over the breakfast table, her sisters had been all excitement for the upcoming ball. They would not be able to attend, but the earl had taken pity on them and said they might view the ballroom from the balustrades above stairs that overlooked it.

They were to keep the corridor dark so they were not seen spying and the earl had particularly looked at Cordelia when he forbid lit candles.

They were perfectly amenable to staying in the dark and had already planned to pack a picnic basket full of things that could be eaten by just feeling what they were. As far as Beatrice could gather, this was mostly biscuits.

Beatrice had done her level best to appear happy and enthusiastic and she thought she had done a good job of it. None of her sisters seemed to suspect anything was amiss and if she could fool *them*, she could fool everybody.

She could never tell them how she felt. It was so odd—she had always told her sisters and Miss Mayton any thought that popped into her head. She would not tell them her changed feelings about Van Doren, though. Not that they'd ever believe it.

Now, they were all together in the drawing room, staying out of Tattleton's way. He was just now in the ballroom supervising the artist come to chalk the floor while the footmen managed vendors of all sorts coming in and out of the servants' entrance with goods that had been ordered.

Apparently, a cake had been ordered along with everything else, as the naughty kittens had got into Mr. James' sugar icing and the cook had been too shaken by it to begin again.

Tattleton suddenly arrived at the drawing room doors. "Miss Mayton, Lady Beatrice, well I hardly, I do not know, you see…"

"What has happened, Tattleton?" Beatrice asked, alarmed by the confusion on his features.

"Flowers," he said.

Beatrice wrinkled her brow. She could only suppose that what had been delivered was not what Darden had ordered.

"Are they so terribly bad?" she asked.

"They are roses. *Red*. Addressed to Lady Beatrice!" Tattleton cried, as if announcing the house was under attack by enemy forces.

"Red roses for Beatrice," Viola said, clapping her hands together.

"Finally, the tortured gentleman makes a move," Juliet said.

"Goodness, it does seem promising," Miss Mayton said. "You'd best bring them in and we will peruse the note."

"All of them?" Tattleton asked.

"I would say so, I do not see the value in bringing in only some of them," Miss Mayton said complacently.

Tattleton nodded, turned, and signaled to the footmen.

Beatrice was surprised that there were two arrangements rather than one. And then further surprised when the footmen went and came back in three more times. What on earth?

Her aunt bustled over to Tattleton and took the note, hurrying back to Beatrice. "Let us see who is so generous by sending this abundance of flowers. You open it and I will read it over your shoulder."

"As will all of us," Juliet said, leaping from her chair.

The sisters all gathered round Beatrice as she opened the card. All it said was—*For Lady Beatrice on the occasion of her ball. An Admirer.*

"Mysterious," Cordelia said.

"Who else would send mysterious flowers but your mysterious and tortured gentleman," Rosalind said.

"Indeed, it must be so," Miss Mayton said. "These are the first words he speaks to you but there will be more. Depend upon it."

Beatrice thought they must be right. It was too extravagant to be from anybody who was *not* tortured over her. It was also exceedingly regrettable. The tortured gentleman was set to reveal himself, only to discover he'd come too late. Her feelings had drifted somewhere else.

Much to her surprise, Tattleton returned. Surely, there could not be more flowers?

"Lady Jersey," he announced, his eyes wide as saucers.

Beatrice leapt to her feet, as did Miss Mayton and her sisters. They all curtsied low at the lady's approach. "Lady Beatrice, Miss Mayton," Lady Jersey said, looking round the drawing room. "I presume these are younger sisters?"

"Yes, Lady Jersey," Beatrice said, rather wondering at the lady's sudden appearance in the house.

"You may send them away," Lady Jersey said. "I wish to speak to you on a matter."

Juliet looked poised to speak, but Rosalind squeezed her shoulder and she thought better of it. She, Juliet, Viola, and Cordelia curtsied and filed out of the room, just as Tattleton hurried in with a tea service.

"I see your house readies for your ball," Lady Jersey said.

"Indeed, my lady," Beatrice said.

Lady Jersey turned to Tattleton. "I suspect you are run off your feet. Do carry on, sir, we will be quite all right fending for ourselves."

Tattleton bowed deeply and Beatrice knew him well enough to know he was suitably struck by the sentiment. Perhaps it would make up for the kittens' foray into the sugar icing.

After the door closed behind him, Beatrice poured the tea. She did not know why Lady Jersey had come, nor why her sisters must be sent away, but she worked hard not to be overawed.

Lady Jersey suddenly appeared cognizant of Miss Mayton's current mode of dress. "Dear lady, I fear you have suffered a recent tragedy. My condolences."

"Oh it is not recent, I'm afraid," Miss Mayton said.

"I see," Lady Jersey said, puzzled. "At Almack's, I did not recall you dressed in—"

"It is rather complicated," Beatrice said quickly.

Lady Jersey, astute woman that she was, gathered that whatever the circumstance, it was probably best left unexplored.

She gazed round the room at the vases of red roses. "I presume for the ball? I would not have had them delivered so early, but with the proper care I dare say they will be all right."

Beatrice nodded, as it seemed impossible to explain that they'd been sent by a tortured gentleman whose identity remained a mystery.

"Lady Beatrice, I am so fond of your father that I felt I must come here directly after hearing the most shocking report."

Beatrice paled. Whatever it was, it sounded very bad. What could it be, though? She could not think of anything she'd done…unless Darden's scheme to draw out the tortured gentleman had somehow come to light.

"My lady?" she asked.

"It seems that Lord Van Doren, who I personally vouched for on Darden's recommendation, has made a spectacle of himself and dragged you into it."

"Lord Van Doren? A spectacle?" Beatrice said. Could Lady Jersey refer to Van Doren taking her card from Conbatten? Certainly, that had not been a spectacle. Ill-advised, but not a spectacle.

"You see, Lady Jersey," Miss Mayton said, "Beatrice is confused because Lord Van Doren does not have the sort of feelings that would lead to an actual *spectacle*." She leaned forward and said, "Confidentially, he does not seem to have much in the way of feelings at all."

Lady Jersey sipped her tea and set it down. "Is it correct that Lord Van Doren attended Lord Darden's club ball as a bird of some sort?"

"A pigeon, yes," Beatrice said. "It was as ridiculous as it was meant to be, and I do not think he appreciated it."

"A pigeon, yes, that is what I was told. Whether or not he was delighted with it is rather beside the point. A gentleman dressed as a pigeon approached Lord Harveston, one of the club members. As everyone was masked and the baron is of similar build, meaning he is unusually tall, that gentleman was taken for Conbatten."

Goodness. Did Van Doren say something wrong to the duke? Or rather, Lord Harveston who had been taken for the duke?

Beatrice remembered Van Doren's words—the *great* Conbatten, said so scathingly.

"Lord Van Doren proceeded to lecture the gentleman that he was not at all suitable for you as he took far too long with his toilette," Lady Jersey said.

"But why should he say anything of the sort?" Beatrice said, her mind racing. It was not a question Lady Jersey had any hope of answering, but it was the only question on her mind. Why would Van Doren go out of his way to be so outrageous and attempt to drive off

Conbatten?

She understood what she hoped the answer might be. That he might have some sort of feeling for her. Though, she also knew how highhanded he could be. Just because he wished for another to step away did not mean he wished to step in.

"Lady Beatrice," Lady Jersey said, "I do not have the faintest idea why Lord Van Doren might say or do anything as I do not particularly know him. Do I take it, from your reaction, that there is nothing between you and the duke?"

"Nothing at all, my lady," Beatrice said.

"Ah, that is a shame," she said. "It would be a brilliant match."

"Fortunately, my lady," Miss Mayton said, "Beatrice is not at all swayed by money and title."

"Is that fortunate?" Lady Jersey said, clearly not seeing the appeal of such an opinion. She turned to Beatrice and said, "If Lord Van Doren wishes to keep his voucher to Almack's, he'd best rein in his unusual behavior. Otherwise, I will be forced to rescind and that always looks very bad."

"But I am not sure that *I* can advise him," Beatrice said, wondering how in the world to broach such a conversation.

"Well somebody must!" Lady Jersey said imperiously. "In the meantime, I will speak to Conbatten to make him aware of the situation. I will suggest he bow out of your ball to tamp down the talk. He will agree that if he does not turn up, he cannot be considered a suitor. That is what we must always do at such moments—tamp down."

"Is it really so very much talked of?" Beatrice asked.

"Of course it is. Every mama in London has designs on Conbatten, making him perennially interesting. Every member of the *ton* delights in being the first to pass some tidbit along. They have nothing to do but talk, and so talk they do. Sometimes, I rattle on about absolutely nothing so they can't get a word in. It amuses me."

Lady Jersey rose. "I will see myself out. If your butler at all resembles mine on the eve of a ball, he is on the razor's edge of a nervous collapse."

Lady Jersey sailed from the room and out the front doors, closing them behind herself.

"Well my goodness," Miss Mayton said, appearing perfectly satisfied, "Lord Van Doren has put a foot out of place. He ought to be lectured about it, just as he has so delighted in doing all these years."

Beatrice nodded absentmindedly, though she had no intention of lecturing Van Doren on the subject.

"You might end whatever scathing words you put together with *I only give you that hint*." Miss Mayton said with a snort. "That is amusing, is it not?"

Beatrice forced a smile. "Ever so," she said. Though, she was less amused and more burning with curiosity. What had been his purpose? Did he know he'd approached the wrong man?

Her sisters all filed back into the room and Miss Mayton speedily apprised them of the cause of Lady Jersey's visit.

The great lady herself might not have been so determined to send them away, had she known how quickly they would return and that nothing would be kept from them.

"Hah!" Juliet cried. "Van Doren has gone mad. I knew it should happen sooner or later—one cannot be coiled up tight like a spring without eventually popping loose."

"Is that it, though?" Rosalind asked. "Or is he just sticking his nose in like always? It would be just like Van Doren to believe he had some right to direct who you ought to pay attention to, Bea. Even if *we* know Conbatten is not your true love, *he* does not know it."

"I think he just likes to boss people about," Viola said.

"Also, he has always thought he is the most important person living," Cordelia said. "I see how he looks down upon my Desdemona. Perhaps he could not stand being outranked by a duke, so he sought to put him down."

"I only wonder at his becoming so intemperate," Miss Mayton said. "It is not at all what he has been."

It *was* rather intemperate for Van Doren to speak to the duke regarding her, and outrageous to mention the duke's toilette. Why had he done it? Why had he been intemperate?

Beatrice's rational mind told her to put it aside. Rationality, though, never stood much of a chance on a battlefield when hope was poised for combat on the other side.

Hope was determined not to be vanquished.

It was the stupidest thing in the world, but she had the tiniest shred of hope and found herself very loath to part with it.

Perhaps she would hint to her father that Van Doren ought to be asked for dinner. It was to be a quiet family night in, as the ball was on the morrow. Perhaps he might say something about why he'd approached the duke who was not the duke.

Chapter Nineteen

Matthew had been surprised that the earl had sent a note over, asking him to come for dinner. He'd have thought the house would already have its hands full on the eve of Beatrice's ball.

Still, he found himself grateful for it. Three days of nothing to do had sounded welcome at the beginning of it, but he'd found himself exceedingly restless. In the country, there would be no end of things to do around the estate. Not so here, though.

He'd become reluctant to even take his horse out to the park, as the first time he'd done so he'd encountered Lady Mary and her mother in their carriage. He'd got the distinct impression that they'd been looking out for him.

That was rather confirmed when he'd spotted her carriage twice passing his house, only to turn around at the end of the street and go back out again.

As far as he could tell, Lady Mary's mother had no more circumspection than her daughter.

It was to be an early dinner and Tattleton had opened the door to him with a look that was not his usual steady composure. He was rather wild-eyed, his suit rumpled, and if Matthew were not mistaken, there was a deal of cat hair on it.

"I'll show myself in, Tattleton," he said. "I am certain you have a hundred matters to arrange."

Tattleton nodded and hurried down the corridor to whatever it was that made him look like he'd seen a ghost.

Matthew entered the drawing room to find them all gathered.

"Van Doren," the earl said, "good of you to come. Now, I probably should have explained in my note that we are to have a buffet and serve ourselves. Tattleton has more than enough to do, we shan't wish him to be standing round supervising our dinner. I hope that does not disappoint?"

"Certainly not," Matthew said. He turned to Beatrice. "Have you recovered from your headache?"

"Oh yes, thank you," she said rather quietly. Matthew was not so certain it was entirely true. She was more subdued than would be usual.

"Is Darden joining us?" Matthew asked, already guessing that he was not. The fellow was sure to be at his club as he always seemed to be.

"He is at his club," the earl said. "Some sort of meeting or other he's heading up. I cannot hold it against him—he's made absolutely all of the arrangements for Beatrice's ball. I have not had to lift a finger other than to hand over bank notes."

"He's been very good about it," Cordelia said.

"He is the best of brothers," Viola confirmed.

"Darden is a prince among brothers. But, if nobody else is going to say it, I will," Juliet said. "Van Doren, we have all heard how you accosted Lord Harveston believing him to be Conbatten."

Matthew stared at Juliet. How on earth would she have heard of it?

"What's this?" the earl asked.

"I accosted nobody," Matthew said. Though, he rather *had* accosted the fellow who he now knew as Lord Harveston.

"Lady Jersey was here today, Papa, to tell Beatrice all about it," Rosalind said. "It has gone all round the town."

"Yes, because Van Doren was trying to warn off Conbatten from Beatrice," Cordelia said.

"He said the duke takes too long with his toilette to be of any use," Viola said.

The earl roared with laughter. "Yes, everybody has heard of that—strictly ninety-eight degrees and champagne. Oh, that is too good."

"I am sure that it must have been some sort of misunderstanding," Beatrice said, looking at him strangely.

What did it mean? Did it mean she was all in for Conbatten?

"There is no misunderstanding that fellow's habits," Matthew said in a brusque tone.

"There is some misunderstanding about yours though," Rosalind said. "Why have you become so intemperate in London?"

"I am not intemperate!" Matthew said. Rather, he'd almost shouted it, which did sound rather intemperate.

"Now then, let us not tease Van Doren more or he'll not even stay for dinner," the earl said. "We would not wish that, as we have a special treat for afterwards. Miss Mayton is going to read the conclusion of our story of the one-eyed duke and his governess. Gracious, I'm on tenterhooks about it."

Matthew could not say he was also on tenterhooks about it. As a usual thing, he would not care to hear any more of that drivel. However, this particular night, he welcomed anything that would get them all off the subject of his outrageous behavior at Darden's masque.

A harried footman entered and said, "My lord, the buffet has been set up."

The earl nodded and rose. "Shall we go in, then? We shall be like an army on the move, foraging the forest and taking sustenance where we can find it."

Matthew did not think soldiers could expect a spread laid out on silver platters on a sideboard were they to be out foraging in a forest, but then he did not say so. The less attention he drew upon himself this night, the better.

He had hoped his mistake at Darden's masque would not be known widely, but apparently it was. Had Conbatten heard of it? What would he do about it?

Beatrice's ball was on the morrow and of course the fellow would turn up. Would Conbatten seek him out and say something of it then?

Or worse, would he say something to Beatrice? Something that had nothing to do with Viscount Van Doren and everything to do with the rest of her life? Something that could not be undone and would set the course of her life in what he knew to be the wrong direction.

If only he had handled things better.

He had not the first idea how that would have been, but certainly he had overlooked some sensible thing he might have done.

As it was, he'd only made a fool of himself and accomplished nothing but gossip.

BEATRICE ADORED HER father, but she had been bursting with frustration when he'd stopped her sisters from teasing Van Doren. He'd not been forced to explain why he'd tried to warn off the duke and it remained as much a mystery as ever.

They'd gone into dinner, or the buffet as it was, and things had gone along merrily enough, though both she and Van Doren were rather quiet throughout.

Her sisters were delighted with the buffet and Viola got up no end of times to take a little more of this or that from the sideboard as if the fun were in the getting up.

Beatrice hoped Viola did not get a stomachache, as she had on their trip to Town when she'd been too enthusiastic about the ham slices.

There was much talk of the ball, and then Matthew said, "The roses look very well. I am surprised they were delivered so early, though."

"Goodness, I hadn't even noticed," the earl said. "Mrs. Huffson always has so many flowers about the place that I do not even see them anymore."

"There are vases upon vases of red roses," Matthew said. "Certainly, they must be for the ball."

"Yes, I suppose they must," the earl said.

"Actually," Miss Mayton said, "those arrived today from an admirer. We do not know who, as it was unsigned."

"All of them from the same fellow?" the earl asked. "And then he does not even sign the note? That's a lot of money spent to forgo claiming credit for it. Young gentlemen really are so amusing."

Van Doren did not look as amused. He looked dark as thunder.

"I did not think to trouble you over it, Earl, for just that reason," Miss Mayton said. "I imagine that whoever the gentleman is who has been so generous will reveal himself at Beatrice's ball. *Then* we can see what we think of it."

"Indeed," the earl said. "Well, my girl, whoever your admirer is, he is certainly well-heeled."

"You know I do not care for any of that, Papa," Beatrice said. It seemed the most appropriate thing to say, though what she would really say if she were to speak her thoughts was—*The flowers are from the tortured gentleman, and it no longer matters who he is.*

"Ah, but as your father," the earl said, "I do care for the practical side of things. Bring who you like to my notice, as long as he can care for you in a suitable manner. No penniless poets, if you please."

"Oh Papa!" Juliet cried. "You must not hold it against a poet to be penniless! I would happily live in a garret if my true love was a poet."

The earl laughed heartily. "I can assure you, Juliet, that if you lived in a garret, it would not be happily. You are far too fond of your comforts."

"But it would be enough if he were a real poet," Juliet said. "I am a poetess and so we would live gloriously on words."

Beatrice saw all eyes drifting toward Van Doren. This was just the sort of moment when he would say Juliet was being ridiculous.

For some reason, he said nothing at all and was wholly concentrated on his beef.

"What say you, Van Doren?" the earl said jovially.

Van Doren looked up and shrugged. "I dare say Juliet knows her own mind."

What did he mean by it? He was meant to be explaining to Juliet that she was completely wrongheaded.

"Sisters," Juliet said, "did I not say Van Doren has gone mad?"

"I think you may be right," Viola said, nodding. "He is not at all what he was."

"To think," Rosalind said, "he is to allow Juliet to live in a garret."

"He would have been so against the idea a month ago," Cordelia said nodding.

"I am here. And can hear you," Van Doren said. "I am not in the least mad."

Perhaps he was not mad, Beatrice thought. But Viola was right, Van Doren was not at all who he had been. He had become rather mysterious.

In the end, it had been *he* that was her mysterious gentleman. It was only a shame he was not tortured over her and never would be.

"Enough talk of garrets, I think," the earl said. "I cannot wait longer, I must know what will transpire in Montclair Castle with that rascally duke and his gentle governess. The terrible goings-on have been riveting so far."

⋙⋘

MATTHEW STARED AT the roses propped on every available surface in the drawing room. They'd all pretended they did not know who sent them.

He knew well enough. It was Conbatten. Who else had such means? Who else would dare it?

Then, that fellow would turn up tomorrow night and collect the credit for his gesture and he would ask Beatrice the momentous question.

The only thing that gave Matthew pause about his assumptions was that Beatrice did not seem particularly bowled over by the gesture. He would have thought she would be. It was just the sort of grand posing and posturing she'd been looking for.

"Now, as we know," Miss Mayton said, book in hand, "the duke has realized he killed three innocent villagers by mistake, he is not missing an eye after all, and is only suffering from madness. Now our governess must discover if she can live with a madman."

Matthew suppressed a sigh. He was feeling like a bit of a madman himself these days.

The duke collapsed into a chair. "My sweet governess, can you love a madman who has only one leg?"

"One leg?" the governess said, staring at both of his legs.

"I cannot recall exactly how I lost it, was I in a war, do you suppose?" the duke said, staring at the same two legs the governess was looking at.

"My dear duke, you are not missing a leg, it is only your mind playing tricks!"

"No, it cannot be! I can see with my own two eyes, one of those eyes I just found out I still have!"

The governess raced over to his chair and grabbed at both his legs. "Can you feel my touch on both your legs?" she asked.

"I can! I have two legs! Now, sweet governess, will you kiss me, assuming I have two lips?"

The governess leaned forward and kissed the duke. It was a magical kiss sending shooting stars throughout the heavens and the angels sang through their tears of joy.

For all the angels singing, though, the governess was determined to confirm a particular matter. She said, "I will only kiss you again if we are to marry. I will not become a mistress."

"My mistress! You adorable little fool! No bald man can attract a mistress!"

"You are not bald, my dear darling," the governess whispered.

"No? Then we shall marry even though I am NOT bald and COULD attract a mistress!" the duke cried.

And so, they did marry. The villagers were exceedingly surprised by this turn of events, but grateful too. The gentle governess who was now the duchess had assured them that there would be no more mistaken murders. She did not think.

The duke loved his duchess so well that when she said he did have all his fingers and he did still have a nose on his face, he chose to believe her and turn his mind to what else might be missing from his person.

The duke and duchess had many children between them and while all of them were eccentric, not a one of them was totally mad. The castle turned into a very lively place, what with all the children about and the duchess often heard crying, "Do not fear, Duke, I can see your arm with my own eyes." Or, "Believe me, my love, you are not turning into an octopus." Or the oft heard, "I swear to you that your body has not disappeared completely."

They lived happily ever after.

The End.

Miss Mayton sighed contentedly and closed the book.

"I had a feeling they should work it out between them," the earl said.

"What did you think of it, Van Doren?" Juliet said, clearly attempting to bait him into saying something uncivil.

If he were to give his real opinion, he might express his wonder at an author who had composed such absolute drivel, the publisher who had taken it on, and Miss Mayton who had paid money for it. But then, the earl had for some reason been taken with the story and he would not for the world insult the earl.

"I am glad it all resolved happily, I suppose," he said.

"You cannot be glad," Viola said.

"I will not believe you are glad for a moment," Cordelia said.

Matthew rose. "I will be off," he said. "I should not like to keep the servants up longer than necessary on the night before a ball."

"We will see you on the morrow, then," the earl said.

Matthew bowed and let himself out.

What an evening. He'd been exposed as a foolish gentleman and caused gossip that had reached the house. Conbatten had not exposed himself, but rather filled the house with red roses.

What he thought of the fictional duke and his sweet governess was of no matter. There was a real duke to contend with and Matthew was certain all would come to a head tomorrow night.

DARDEN LOUNGED WITH his sisters in the drawing room. As a usual thing, he ought to be off to his club, but this evening was Beatrice's ball and he must stay on hand in the house. He could not say why there were always last-minute emergencies leading up to a large gathering, but there always were. He'd told his father he'd steer the ship for the ball, and he would.

A footman brought in a note for Beatrice and she opened it. "Conbatten sends his regrets," she said.

"Lady Jersey knows her business," Darden said. He was, naturally, disappointed that Conbatten was not coming to his house. However, the cause of it was one to rejoice in. Van Doren had made himself an absolute fool by attempting to drive the duke away from Beatrice and ending by lecturing Harveston instead.

"We still cannot work out why Van Doren did it," Cordelia said.

"I say he's gone mad," Juliet said. "He's even said I might live in a garret with a poet."

"Really?" Darden asked. "What else did he have to say for himself last evening?"

"He was glad everything ended happily between the duke and his gentle governess in Miss Mayton's book," Viola said. "You will never convince me he was glad."

"I do not think he liked the red roses at all," Rosalind said. "Though, that was at least very usual for him. He does not appreciate a grand gesture."

"We think he's become intemperate," Miss Mayton said. "That seems to be how London has affected him, though we cannot think why."

"Perhaps it is because he finds himself pursued by Lady Mary and Lady Clara," Darden said, hoping to elicit some response from Beatrice. She had so far been silent on the subject of Van Doren.

"Maybe that is it," Miss Mayton said. "Beatrice, you did wonder if Lord Van Doren was thinking of proposing to Lady Mary."

"*She* says he is," Beatrice said sullenly.

"Does she go that far?" Darden said. He supposed he should not be surprised. Lady Mary was a determined little minx and had clear enough set her cap in that direction. He'd found the circumstance rather useful in engendering some sort of jealousy or feeling in Beatrice.

"*She* says he's made it a point to hint that he's looking in her direction," Beatrice said.

"I don't believe it," Darden said, lest his sister believe it a little too well. "Lady Mary is not at all suited to Van Doren."

"We will get to see with our own eyes this evening," Rosalind said. "Papa is allowing us to watch from the little balustrade above the ballroom."

"In the dark," Juliet added.

"No candles whatsoever," Cordelia said. "There are the silk curtains there and they do go up rather fast in a flame."

"It will be very funny, do not you think?" Viola said. "To see Van Doren going round a ball like any other gentleman and having ladies admire him. I cannot even imagine it; I'm going to have to see it with my own eyes."

"I can assure you," Darden said, "Van Doren cleans up rather well."

"Is this Lady Mary to attend?" Viola asked. "I should like to get to the bottom of that situation. I should like to have a look at her if she is really to become our new neighbor."

"I am certain she will come," Darden said. "She and her mother both accepted the invitation. I do not believe, however, that you will ever welcome Lady Mary as the new viscountess."

"How do you know, though?" Beatrice asked.

Finally, he detected some interest. He said, "Because as intelligent as Van Doren is, he will take some time to become acquainted with his own heart. Lady Mary will not be found there."

"Oh really?" Juliet said, all skepticism. "Now Van Doren has a heart? What is to happen next, I wonder?"

Chapter Twenty

Matthew had spent the morning pacing the house. He felt he needed exercise but was loath to take out his horse and somehow encounter Lady Mary. Twice in the past days, he'd spotted the lady and her mother going up and down Portland Place without stopping to actually call on anybody. They could be lying in wait anywhere.

He'd taken to walking back and forth along the first-floor corridors and making circles round empty bedchambers.

Matthew had started the morning downstairs in the drawing room, watching the vendors carts come fast and furious to the Benningtons'. The ball was only hours away and the last-minute arrangements were going full speed.

He'd even seen Darden outside directing this or that person. Apparently, the admired older brother had at least decided to forgo his club on this day.

What was to be done about the approaching events that he knew were all too certain? Eight vases of red roses portended something significant. Conbatten was planning to make his move this very night.

Matthew was torn over what his place was in this fiasco. For all he knew, Beatrice was set on Conbatten and determined to become a duchess. That would be, after all, her purview. She had a right to choose her own future and what she preferred.

On the other hand, if that was what she thought, she did not know what was best for her! She would have failed to know herself and what she required, despite having made a list of requirements. She would always be second fiddle to a man like Conbatten. Beatrice needed to be first fiddle.

Was he to stand back and allow the disaster to unfold before his eyes? Or was he to interfere in some way, though he did not have any right to do it?

Perhaps he ought to go to the earl and attempt to convince him of the impending catastrophe? Though, as a father, perhaps the earl would not be so opposed to seeing his daughter a duchess.

It would be hopeless to approach Darden. All the YBC appeared to worship Conbatten—Darden would be delighted with the match. He would be delighted to be related through marriage to the duke.

But could they not all see it was wrong?

Marcus interrupted his pacing and his thoughts. His valet had fairly flown up the stairs and was nearly out of breath.

"My lord," he said, gasping and holding onto a doorframe, "Genroy has just informed me that, that—"

"That what?" Matthew said, beginning to wonder if the house was on fire. Or worse, Lady Mary had arrived.

"Conbatten," Marcus said. "Genroy has just put him in the drawing room."

"Conbatten? Here?"

"Yes, here," Marcus said. "If he's come to issue you a challenge, do not accept it. He's said to be a crack shot. At least, so says his insufferable valet. We can fly to the continent until things settle. The point is, stay alive!"

Matthew felt as if his blood had run cold. Slowly, he said, "If he issues such a challenge, I will accept. I will have no choice in the matter. In any case, I'm a crack shot too."

Marcus had gone very pale. He could not guess if it were fear for Matthew's person or fear that Marcus would soon be out of a job due to his viscount lying dead on a green somewhere.

Another thought occurred to him. "It would be strange, though, that he'd not sent a second, or even brought one."

"Is that strange? Good! Maybe I am wrong, then!" Marcus whispered.

"Whether you are right or wrong, I'd best go find it out," Matthew said. He straightened his coat and hurried down the stairs.

Genroy was just coming out of the drawing room. Softly, he said, "He does not want tea or anything else."

Matthew did not know if that were ominous or not. However, there was no use in delaying. He must face whatever was to be faced.

He strode through the drawing room doors.

Conbatten was looking his usual carefully dressed and slightly bored self, lounging on a window seat and watching the hive of activity at the Benningtons' house.

"Lord Van Doren," the duke said, "I hope I do not disturb."

"Not at all, though I am surprised to see you here," Matthew said.

"As am I, rather," Conbatten said, removing a stray pale hair from his sleeve that had no doubt been left behind by Oyster. "However, Lady Jersey found it convenient to call on me yesterday to acquaint me with some facts I had not been aware of."

"My unfortunate words to Lord Harveston, I suppose," Matthew said.

"The very ones," the duke said. "I am to know that you have warned me off Lady Beatrice. That the YBC gentlemen only amuse themselves in an attempt to drive me forward in my pursuit. Oh, and I take too much time on my toilette, though I cannot fathom how anybody would know anything about my personal habits or why they might have formed an opinion about them."

Matthew felt faced with a crossroads. Should he attempt to minimize what he'd said, or should he go forward and explain to this duke exactly where matters stood?

He knew what he must do. It might end in offense. Even a duel. But he must put Beatrice's long-term happiness first.

"Your Grace," he said, "I did say all those things, and I will say more to avert a disaster. There has been a plot going on to draw you out and drive you forward. They refer to you as the mysterious tortured gentleman, but they all know it is you."

"Do they?" the duke said, looking amused.

"Indeed they do," Matthew said, not having the first idea why the man looked amused. "They know perfectly well that the pile of red roses is from you."

"They know that, do they?"

"Of course they do. Their plan has been all too successful, but it is not right. Not just for Beatrice's happiness, but for your own! She is not right for you, she would always be second fiddle and she cannot be happy unless she is first fiddle."

"I see," the duke said. "So, I have been drawn out and driven forward, I am the mysterious tortured gentleman that they all know the identity of, I've sent heaps of red roses and what next? Do I presume I am to propose at her ball?"

Matthew could not understand why the duke was taking all of this so casually. But then, he supposed that was Conbatten's nature—another reason he would not suit Beatrice.

"Well, yes, that is where we are. Now, I know Beatrice has many attractions, but you must be convinced that it is not the right match for either of you."

"Consider me convinced," the duke said drily.

"What?" Matthew asked. What sort of game was this fellow playing at?

"Your aim was to convince me—I am entirely convinced."

"I see, well I had not imagined you would…" Matthew trailed off, hardly knowing what to say.

"You had not imagined I would give up so easily," the duke finished for him. Conbatten rose and straightened his cuffs. "I am beginning to find the two of you a bit tiresome, Lord Van Doren."

"The two of us?"

"You and Lady Beatrice. It is as if you need to be clubbed over the head to understand a point."

Matthew stiffened. "And what point would that be, Your Grace?"

The duke looked at him under hooded eyes. "*You* are the mysterious tortured gentleman. *You* are the one to be drawn out and driven forward. I suspect nobody in that house knows it but for Darden. How they could not have guessed it, I know not. For myself, I wrangled the information from Mr. Cahill, who seemed entirely sheepish when I left him."

That was the last thing Matthew had expected to hear. It could not be true. Why on earth would Cahill say such a thing? The man was a troublemaker, but this would really be a step too far. It made no sense whatsoever.

"I see you have been struck dumb," the duke went on. "Let us hope the condition does not last through the evening lest you fail to communicate this fact to Lady Beatrice. As for myself, I do not attend this night, as you have been so good as to send gossip flying round the town. I will assure you, though, that had I attended there would be nothing for anybody to speculate on, both on my side and her own."

"But, I do not understand…"

"Apparently not," the duke said. "Never were two people less aware of their own inclinations, it seems."

The duke made his way to the door. In parting words, he said, "If you intend on winning Lady Beatrice, I suggest you meet her requirements. I really do not see how it could be more straightforward. And, by the by, I did not send roses of any sort. I will assume that was Darden's doing."

With that, the duke left his house, and left Matthew standing in the drawing room attempting to understand what had just happened.

His feet began to move, though he did not really notice it. Matthew climbed the stairs feeling as if he *had* been hit over the head with the club Conbatten had just mentioned.

Before he knew where he was going, he was back in his bedchamber.

Marcus stood wide-eyed. "Is there to be a dawn meeting? Tell me quickly, lest I die of dread just thinking about it."

"There is not," Matthew said, wandering to the chair by the window.

"Excellent!" Marcus fairly cried. "The duke has been turned from his purpose and all is well."

"A duel was never his purpose," Matthew said.

"What did he want with you, then?" Marcus asked, being unable to control his curiosity.

"This ruse that Beatrice and Darden's friends have been engaged in, this plan to draw out a mysterious gentleman," Matthew said, "the duke claims *I* am the mysterious gentleman."

Marcus staggered and clutched at the top of a chest of drawers to steady himself. "I am all agog," he whispered.

"As am I," Matthew said. "It cannot be true, I do not think. I suspect Cahill was only amusing himself in telling the duke such a story."

Marcus suddenly got a faraway look in his eyes. "It might be true."

"How so?"

"First, those YBC fellows are all in awe of Conbatten, I doubt any of them would toy with the gentleman. Second, days after we arrived to Town, you sent James across the road with a note for the earl. Tattleton did not answer the door, it was one of the footmen, who said to take the note to the lord's library. James expected to find the earl there but just as he was poised to knock, he heard Lord Darden talking to Tattleton about making sure the drawing room curtains were open when there were callers so you would see it, and then something about delivering Lady Beatrice any notes or flowers when you were there."

"Why have you not spoken of this before?"

"Because it did not mean anything at the time. James told the story at the servants' table, and we all took it to be more of the Benningtons' teasing. We all know how they tease and harass you."

"Still, I…"

"And was it not Darden who dressed *you* as Benedict to Lady Beatrice's Beatrice?" Marcus said.

"Well, yes—"

"And has it not been all of Darden's friends, save for Conbatten, who have surrounded Lady Beatrice. You told me yourself how ridiculous they were about it and how it was not real."

"Of course, I understood there was a plot afoot, but I can hardly think *I* was the target of it."

"It makes sense though," Marcus said. "Darden trusts you, who better to trust with his sister?"

It was impossible to fathom. He and Beatrice?

It was not that he…at least over the years he'd wondered…but then she'd turned away from him so firmly, making her disdain so well known… She could never…

But what if she could?

Could she?

Matthew was forced to face that his feelings were not much changed from what they had ever been. When Beatrice had begun to outgrow whatever feelings she'd had on her side, it had been a blow. A terrible blow, actually.

A blow he'd not seen coming.

The scenes of how it happened came rushing back to him. He had refused to even think of the circumstances for years, but now they came in a flood.

Beatrice had long put away her dolls and he, Beatrice, and Rosalind were deemed old enough to attend small neighborhood parties. The events were always silly affairs, held early and generally hosted by one of a handful of families. They were expressly meant to give the young people experience at socializing and dancing.

He had been in the habit of leading Beatrice to the floor when there was dancing, but then Rothcraft's cousin, a seventeen-year-old baron from Suffolk had come to stay. That fellow had led Beatrice to the floor before Matthew even knew what was happening. He'd been left behind and stuck with Rosalind.

Later that evening, feeling very opposed to this invading cousin of Rothcraft's, he'd counseled Beatrice that she ought not flutter her lashes at the fellow as he would not be in the neighborhood long. Once he was gone, he'd forget all about her.

She'd looked at him with absolute contempt and said, "Do not suppose you can direct my thoughts on any matter, Van Doren."

Beatrice had spent the rest of the evening making herself as pleasant as possible to the baron.

That had been the beginning, but it had not been the end. After that night, she'd made it perfectly clear that she no longer admired him or cared to consider his opinions.

He'd buried the blow under a storm of lectures and strongly worded hints. He'd known when he was doing it that it was only driving her further away, but what else could he do? He was not going to moon over a lady who held him in contempt.

What if she did not, though? She was always so very contrary, perhaps she harbored some kind of feeling for him and simply would not show it.

It seemed dangerous to attempt to find it out though. She might laugh in his face and then have the advantage of knowing she'd conquered him while she remained unscathed. He could not live with that.

But then, apparently he could not live with her marrying somebody else either. He'd acted irresponsibly when he'd thought a proposal from Conbatten was in the works. He'd become intemperate and they'd all noticed it. He'd stirred up gossip. And why? All to stop Beatrice from getting married.

"What are you going to do?" Marcus said softly.

"I have no idea."

"But you must do something!" Marcus cried.

Matthew really thought he ought to rein in his valet. He was certain that other lords' valets did not attempt to direct their actions. Further, if he were to do something, he ought to have done it years ago. It was far too late now. He imagined.

But what if he were mistaken? It was not as if he'd been in the habit of getting things right recently.

"Conbatten said I should meet her requirements."

Marcus scrunched up his face with worry. "Her requirements? There are so many of them!"

"Indeed," Matthew said. "Though they all seem to boil down to the same thing. Beatrice Bennington has only ever been interested in a lovesick lunatic."

Marcus rubbed his hands together. "You could manage it. I'm sure you could. Easily," he said encouragingly.

Matthew thought it should probably give him some pause that his valet thought he could easily manage acting the lunatic.

"It might be your only chance," Marcus said, urging him on. "Conbatten may not have designs on Lady Beatrice, but somebody will. Maybe even more than one—this town is filled with rogues on the lookout for a dowry."

"Rogues," Matthew muttered, feeling a great wish to hunt them all down. His valet was right, they were everywhere, hiding round every corner. If not Conbatten, then somebody else would pop up. And then another and another, like so many foxes poking their heads from their dens.

He could not keep them all at bay. Not unless…

Not unless he was prepared to risk his pride and dignity, knowing he might very well find himself on the losing end of the stick.

Still, was not the risk worth something? If he did not risk, he knew the outcome—a lifetime of regret. This was, at least, a chance. Even if it were slim.

He must just take it.

"Right!" he said loudly. "Lunatic it is, then."

Marcus nodded with enthusiasm. "The dark blue coat, I think. And perhaps we can leave your hair mussed, as if you've been tearing at it."

"I'll threaten to do a violence to myself," Matthew said. "Really, at this point, I just might."

He had always been so rational and even-tempered. Now, he found he would not have to take too many more steps to arrive at lunatic. That girl had driven him to the edge of madness.

Matthew could not predict what the end of it might be, but for now he would shut his eyes to the dire consequences lurking at the edges of his thoughts. He would barrel forward just as any man in battle must do, refusing to consider that the going forward might end in disaster.

Beatrice's ballgown was positively lovely. The softest silk in a cream color with cream rosettes around the bodice. Oh, how she would have been in raptures had her future not suddenly fallen to pieces.

She at least did not have to pretend at gaiety to her sisters just now, as they'd all hurried off to arrange their picnic basket and the various pillows and blankets that would be required to make their perch behind the balustrades comfortable.

Miss Mayton remained in her widow's weeds, though she'd added a small tiara the earl had given to her last Christmas.

Lynette fussed with Beatrice's hair, making last minute adjustments.

"Well, my dear," her aunt said, "I am all but certain we will discover the identity of the tortured gentleman this evening."

"I am sorry to say that I no longer care, Aunt," Beatrice said.

Miss Mayton fussed with her tiara, which seemed not all that steady on her head. The lace of her ghostly veil was not suitable for a good grip. "Oh dear," she said, "he has waited too long and worn out your patience."

"Something like it," Beatrice said.

"But perhaps your mind will change when all is revealed. After all, we do not have the first idea what he is like. All we know is that he has held back because he has been afraid you would die, as did his mother and sister."

Beatrice nodded. That had all sounded wonderfully romantic when she'd first heard it. Now, she began to think it was rather stupid. Any gentleman must fear for his wife dying in childbirth, as it was not an uncommon occurrence. Her own mother had died so. It was the ultimate risk of being a woman, and everybody knew it.

Really, if *she* were not afraid to face it, she did not see why her mysterious gentleman should be wringing his hands over it.

Lynette finished with her hair and stood back pleased with the result. She had every right to be, it was soft and elegant.

What a night this would be if it were not for…if it were not for Van Doren. If it were not for what was not there for her and would never be.

"It is time for us to go down, I think," Miss Mayton said.

Beatrice nodded and they left the room. As she got to the top of the stairs and saw the hive of activity below, she had the urge to turn around and run back to the peace of her bedchamber.

What a thing, to be wishing oneself away from one's own ball.

She could not though. All of this effort was on her behalf. Piles of her father's money had been spent on it. She would never disrespect him with ungratefulness. She must smile and appear happy.

The earl met her at the bottom of the stairs. "You look lovely, Beatrice," he said.

Her father handed over her dance card and she slipped the pale blue ribbon round her wrist. How long ago it seemed that she had given her preference for the color of the ribbon to be used at her ball.

She forced herself to smile and said, "You are looking very elegant yourself, Papa."

Darden came striding in from the ballroom. "The chandeliers are lit, flowers everywhere, champagne on ice, supper cooking below, cats corralled in Mrs. Huffson's sitting room so that Cook does not keel over in apoplexy, musicians set up, and four sisters are giggling behind the balustrade over our heads. We are ready."

"Splendid job of it, Darden," the earl said. "And with a good fifteen minutes to spare before the carriages begin rolling down Portland Place."

"One wonders what sort of gentlemen we will see here tonight," Miss Mayton said.

"Do we wonder?" the earl said. "I presumed Darden was well acquainted with anybody on the list."

"Of course, yes," Miss Mayton said hurriedly. "I was more wondering about what attitude they might bring and what they might say."

"I wonder that myself," Darden said softly.

"Ah, I see your meaning," the earl said. "Who sent the flowers? Shall the fellow step forward and claim it? In truth, if he does not, I shall think him a very stupid fellow."

Beatrice suppressed a sigh. Everybody was talking, in one way or another, of the mysterious tortured gentleman. They did not understand that he had become entirely beside the point. A man saying nothing eventually became nothing. Especially when one's thoughts cleared and one could finally understand one's own heart.

One's own very, very stupid heart.

There was a sudden loud banging on the front doors. They all looked at one another. Miss Mayton's tiara slipped off her veil and clattered to the floor. Darden quickly swept it up and deposited it back in her hands.

Tattleton had not even gone to the front doors yet, ready to receive guests. Who would come so early and bang so hard?

Tattleton passed them by in a run, looking as if he were chased by a murderer. He reached the doors, straightened his tie, and threw them open.

Beatrice was startled to see the picture before her. It was Van Doren and it looked as if he were in the midst of some sort of dire emergency. He was dressed for the ball, but his hair looked as if he'd been through a windstorm. His eyes had a wild look to him. She peered over his shoulders and into the night, expecting to see flames at his windows or some other disaster unfolding.

She saw nothing of the sort. Had somebody been taken very ill then?

He strode in and nearly shouted, "I demand to speak to Lady Beatrice alone. At once."

"What?" she asked.

"You heard me," he said gruffly.

Miss Mayton attempted to step forward, but the earl took her arm and said, "We will be in the drawing room."

A crushing weight of an idea swept into Beatrice's thoughts. She knew why he had come. He'd come to tell her…he wished to tell her first—he had engaged himself to Lady Mary.

Her father, Darden, and Miss Mayton retreated, the drawing room door closing behind them.

Why had they left her alone to hear this dreadful news?

"Hand over your card this instant, Beatrice," Van Doren said sternly.

"My card?"

Beatrice did not know what else to do but comply, though now she was confused. If he wished to wed Lady Mary, why did he ask for her card?

Why did he look as if he'd lost his wits? Which seemed both frightening and…rather attractive. Why had he come into the house in such a manner? What was he doing?

She handed over her card and he began to pencil his name in. And then pencil it in again. And then again until every spot was taken.

"Now you see, Beatrice, I have filled out your dance card for every set and shall do something outrageous if you challenge that idea for even a moment."

"Would you really?" Beatrice said, feeling a little faint.

"Of course I would, you dear girl," he said, his voice going softer. "*I'm* the mysterious tortured gentleman."

"You?"

"Cannot you tell?"

"Well, no, I could not," Beatrice said, looking at him in wonder.

"Did you wish me to be?"

"Just recently…"

Van Doren swept her up in his arms. "You have made me a lunatic, Beatrice Bennington."

Beatrice drooped in his arms, and she wondered if her legs had decided they were tired of holding her up. Was this real? It did not seem as if it could be.

How had she come to be in Van Doren's arms? And him seeming so…intemperate.

"I was thinking tonight of when Rothcraft's cousin came to visit," he said, holding her close against his chest and whispering in her ear. "That insufferable baron who danced with you. Do you remember?"

She nodded, wrapping her arms tight around his neck. Of course, Beatrice did remember. It had been the first moment that she'd chafed under Van Doren's directives. He'd said the baron would leave the neighborhood and forget all about her, which of course he had. She'd been so stung by it.

"That was the beginning of the coolness between us," Van Doren said softly. "I ought to have fixed it right then and there and I am determined to do so now."

"Oh, I am glad."

Van Doren pulled away ever so slightly and looked down at her upturned face.

"I hoped you might be," he said, leaning down to her lips.

He kissed her rather more passionately than she had imagined a staid gentleman like Van Doren might. He seemed more a pirate or highwayman than a viscount and it took her breath away.

He paused and looked into her eyes.

"Do that again," Beatrice said.

Van Doren smiled, and then he did do it again.

What the past few moments had wrought! She would not need to be a spinster after all. That was, assuming…

He'd moved down and was doing wonderful things to her neck with his lips. She whispered, "Do you mean to marry me, then?"

"Of course I mean to marry you," he whispered into her hair. "Why else would I have railed against Rothcraft's cousin, or spent half my life at your house, or spent this ungodly season driving every other gentleman off? I'll not have you marry anybody else." He paused and then whispered, "And that is my final hint."

She traced her finger along his lips, those lips she'd been looking at all her life. "Do you suppose you might do a violence to yourself were I to refuse?" Beatrice asked. She did not have the least intention of refusing, but she was interested to know how it would be if she did.

"Entirely likely," Van Doren said, nuzzling her neck.

"And your hair, it almost seems as if you've been tearing at it?"

"Terribly. It's a miracle I have any left."

"And I suppose if you could not drive suitors off, you might have demanded a duel?"

"I would line them up and dispatch them one by one."

"Well, then," Beatrice whispered, "I say I will."

"Dearest Beatrice, the girl I have loved all along, even when I convinced myself otherwise."

"I have been just the same," Beatrice said.

She heard the soft whine of the hinges of the drawing room door and then Miss Mayton cried out, "Beatrice!"

"It is all right, Aunt," she said, entangled in Van Doren's arms. "I'm going to marry him so he doesn't do a violence to himself."

"Van Doren?" Miss Mayton said, as if she had not heard correctly.

"Indeed, Van Doren," Beatrice said laughing.

The earl pushed the doors all the way open and strode out to the hall. "Well done, my boy! Though, perhaps unhand my daughter until you are actually married."

Beatrice blushed over the idea. Van Doren only reluctantly let her go.

Darden slapped Van Doren on the back. "About time, old fellow. I knew you'd see it in the end. And you too, sister."

"What do you mean by it, Darden? That you thought it all along?" Beatrice asked.

"Naturally," Darden said. "Who better than Van Doren for Beatrice?"

"My lord," Van Doren said to the earl, "I may have been precipitous in asking Beatrice before speaking with you, but it had to be done."

"Yes, yes, never mind that. I've been hoping for this match for years."

"Father!" Beatrice said.

"Did I not say you'd throw all your requirements out a window?" the earl said, laughing. "Who on earth did you think I was talking about?"

Van Doren cleared his throat. "As to Beatrice's requirements, I have already threatened to do a violence to myself, done quite a bit of tearing of hair, and will shoot at any suitors who will not be driven away otherwise."

"Yes, you see, Papa, Van Doren has met my requirements perfectly."

"I am staggered," Miss Mayton said. "Of everything I have ever thought possible, Lord Van Doren threatening to do a violence to himself never presented itself to me. Be careful, my lord, these things can get out of hand rather quickly, as I know from my own experience."

"Do not fear anything, Aunt," Beatrice said merrily, "if you will recall, I have only ever wished for threats. I am not unreasonable."

Van Doren looked at her from narrowed eyes. Of course he would look at her so, as she had been entirely unreasonable. But what matter? He loved her anyway, and he always had.

Poor Tattleton had been standing by the door ever since he'd opened it. The earl said, "Tattleton, perhaps call Lynette to touch up Beatrice's hair, as it's been mussed. We have only minutes to spare, I think."

Tattleton nodded. Fortunately, Benny and Johnny came to take up their duties and the earl sent Benny instead. Benny could accomplish it at a run and Tattleton looked as if he might fall over just now.

Lynette arrived in a hurry, carrying a comb and pins. At least, Beatrice supposed she'd come quickly. She and Van Doren had spent the time staring at each other.

It was not many more minutes before carriages began to arrive to the house.

MATTHEW HAD STEPPED back and allowed the family to line up to greet their guests.

He would marry Beatrice Bennington. There was a wonder to it. There was a further wonder that he'd come into the house as he had—like a veritable lunatic.

She *had* driven him mad though. All her life she'd done it. He'd almost convinced himself to forget all about her. He'd thought he'd done just that.

But then seeing her in Town, with all those irritating men circling round, well, something had to be done.

She was all grace just now, looking marvelous in her cream silk gown and acting the hostess.

What had he ever been thinking of with his list of facts to be discovered in a lady before moving forward to a proposal? Why had he ever been obsessed with how the lady would be at managing household accounts?

He did not care if Beatrice was incapable of adding up two farthings together.

He supposed all that nonsense of claiming he was logical and practical had been conjured up to protect himself, as he had not ever thought he would have her.

Matthew smiled at her and she smiled at him. As gracious as she looked while the guests filed in one after another, she was not paying particular attention to them.

Finally, enough of them were through the door and the rest could be managed by Tattleton. He stepped forward and led Beatrice into the ballroom.

Darden had done a very credible job. The ballroom glittered under the crystal chandeliers.

"Shall I really keep this card you've filled up?" Beatrice said of her dance card. "People will find it exceedingly shocking."

"Do you care?" he asked.

"Not a bit," she said laughing.

Lord Jericho approached. "Lady Beatrice, may I?" he asked, glancing at her card.

"Lady Beatrice's engagements are full," Matthew said gruffly.

"So soon?"

"So soon," Matthew said darkly.

Lord Jericho stepped back at his tone, appearing thoroughly confused. He hurriedly bowed and moved off.

"I believe you've frightened Lord Jericho with that growly tone. You are growing very intemperate, Van Doren," Beatrice said.

"Do you mind it?"

"I adore it," Beatrice said.

Benny and Johnny walked round with trays of champagne, a thing Darden had adopted from Lady Bloomington's habit of it. Though, Matthew understood it would not be arriving between every single set as Lady Bloomington's footmen had done. That was probably for the best, considering how so much champagne had affected him last time.

Matthew handed Beatrice a glass. At that moment, the earl dinged a spoon he'd got from somewhere against his own crystal glass to call his guests to attention.

As the room quieted, the earl said, "Welcome my esteemed guests, I am afraid I have brought you here under false pretenses."

There were various murmurs in the crowd, as everybody was always intrigued by something mysterious.

"This was meant to be my daughter Beatrice's ball to celebrate her entry into society," the earl continued. "It has turned out to be a celebration of her engagement to Viscount Van Doren."

There was a small yelp near the doors, and Beatrice turned to see Lady Mary being hushed by her mother.

From overhead, Juliet's rather clearer voice rang out. *"Van Doren?"*

Beatrice bit her lip. Matthew looked up to the darkened balustrade and called, "That's right, Juliet. I'm to be your brother-in-law. You may commence rejoicing at any time."

Beatrice leaned close to his ear and said, "It will be a shock to them, of course."

"Don't I know it," Matthew said.

"My entire family," the earl went on loudly, "does rejoice in this match." He glanced over his head and said, "The *entire* family."

There were soft groans heard from above as Beatrice's sisters got the message that there were to be no complaints. None made this night, at any rate. Matthew could only imagine what they'd have to say for themselves on the morrow.

"Well now, let us celebrate and open this engagement ball," the earl said.

Matthew thought the earl was rather beaming.

"Now," he said to Beatrice, taking her hand, "we will dance all night long together, as I have driven the rest of them off."

And so they did. Perhaps they were noticed missing at supper, but nobody thought to look in the library and Matthew was to later understand that the earl's search for them was entirely lackadaisical.

After the guests left the house, the library door was finally knocked softly upon and it was found that Beatrice had somehow mussed her hair again.

Matthew suspected her hair often would be mussed from now on.

⇾⇾⇾⇽⇽⇽

BEATRICE HAD TRIPPED up the stairs, leaving her father and Van Doren in the library to discuss the arrangements for a marriage contract. She did not give a toss what those arrangements were, as Van Doren had said he didn't care if she came with not a farthing, as long as she came.

She fairly danced into her room to find four sisters on her bed, staring at her intently.

"You will wonder at it, I know," Beatrice said.

"*Wonder* at it?" Juliet said. "Miss Mayton was so overcome that Lynette had to wave a vinaigrette under her nose and escort her to bed."

"It is just that, Beatrice," Rosalind said, "we have spent all our lives trying to get Van Doren out of our house. Are you really going to live in *his* house, never to escape him?"

"How are you to stand up against the speeches and hints and sermons, day in and day out, every minute?" Viola asked.

"Not to mention what he will say when he sees how wretched you are at adding up household accounts," Cordelia pointed out.

"Or planning menus. Remember that time you did it for practice? We still call that *never-ending pork week,*" Rosalind said.

"And you shall be terrible at managing servants as they will do what they like and you will never put your foot down," Viola said.

"We just do not see why you wish to live being lectured all the time," Juliet said.

"Oh, I do not think he will lecture me further," Beatrice said, laughing.

"So, we are to believe he is really done scolding us?" Viola asked.

"Goodness, I doubt it," Beatrice said. "He may be done lecturing *me*, but I imagine he'll still have plenty to say to you."

Below, Beatrice heard the front doors close. She ran to the window and her sisters followed her.

"Now," she said, "there he is, striding across the road. Look at him as I have done. Step back and see him as any other gentleman."

"We have always admitted he is handsome in his way," Cordelia said. "It is only when he starts talking."

"Yes, the talking," Viola confirmed.

"He has so much to say for himself," Rosalind said.

"Such a lot," Juliet said, nodding.

"Well, you are to know that he had such a lot to say tonight," Beatrice said, "and I could not tell you half of it without blushing a thousand shades of red."

Cordelia peered out the window. "Van Doren?"

"Indeed, Van Doren. He is more mysterious and tortured than you would imagine," Beatrice said. "He stormed into the house and threatened to do a violence to himself if he could not have me, tore at his hair – though, thank goodness he did not pull any of it out – put himself down for every dance on my card, and said he would meet any rival suitor at dawn. He was terrifically intemperate about driving off any other gentleman who thought to put himself on my card. Then he stole me away at supper, which was very wrong."

"Van Doren?" Viola said.

"Yes, Van Doren," Beatrice said, laughing. "It turns out he does have a heart after all, and it beats rather passionately."

The four sisters were silent for some moments, no doubt all attempting to reconcile the Van Doren they had always known to the Van Doren Beatrice described.

"Beatrice," Rosalind asked, "when did you realize that you loved Van Doren? It must have been a very great shock."

"A few days ago, when I thought he might propose to Lady Mary. And it was a shock indeed."

"That moment that you knew, was it as Miss Mayton has described?" Cordelia asked. "As if your hair had been hit with lightning, and you were drowning but had air, and your heart going too fast but feeling well?"

"Mostly, I felt sick," Beatrice admitted. "But I am well now. Very well."

⋙⋘

THE LAST GUESTS had been got into their carriages and Tattleton was finally at his leisure. He'd gone down to the servants' hall, leaving the earl and Lord Van Doren with port in the library.

The rest of the servants had been sent to bed, there would be time to clean up the mess made from the ball on the morrow. Only Mrs. Huffson had waited up. And the wretched cats, who had since been let out of her sitting room.

As that pack of diabolical felines prowled around pretending to look for mice they were never going to catch, the housekeeper poured him a brandy, and one for herself too.

"What a night this has been, Mr. Tattleton. I never saw an engagement coming between Lady Beatrice and Lord Van Doren. I never did see it coming a mile away."

"Nor I, Mrs. Huffson," he said. It was the truth, even though he had been an unwilling conspirator to Lord Darden's scheme to make it so. He'd thought the whole idea preposterous and Lord Darden completely out of his wits to imagine it possible.

"It's entirely befuddling," Mrs. Huffson went on. "They don't seem to have a lick in common. Miss Mayton was so overcome that Lynette had to apply a vinaigrette. What do you suppose drew them together?"

"I cannot say for certain, Mrs. Huffson, but I have been shocked to my shoes by some of the things I have observed this night."

Mrs. Huffson leaned forward and Tattleton was well aware that she would not sleep well unless she were informed as to why she might be equally shocked to her shoes.

Quietly, he said, "They were alone for hours in the library, the earl said not to look for them there, they entirely missed supper and did not even stand at the door when the guests departed. Then, what do you think I found when I was finally let into that room?"

"What?" Mrs. Huffson said, rather breathless.

"There were *several* hairpins on the carpet."

"Several!"

"Several," Tattleton confirmed. "I saw them with my own eyes. And Lady Beatrice's gown was rumpled."

"Rumpled?"

"Decidedly so," Tattleton said, nodding meaningfully.

"Well then," Mrs. Huffson said, "it seems they *do* have something in common."

THE BANNS HAD been read, the church had been got to, and the wedding breakfast commenced. It was a small affair, as both Beatrice and Van Doren agreed that outsiders had interfered enough in their affairs.

Of course, they also agreed that had those outsiders not interfered, they probably would have got nowhere.

Darden's plan to bring them together had been fully revealed and Beatrice was rather admiring of its many layers. Van Doren deemed it insane, despite having worked.

Though, he'd privately admitted to Beatrice that he also found himself relieved to know the reason why he'd never been invited to put himself forward for the YBC. Darden and his cronies could not have conspired about him if he were forever hanging about.

The days that had followed the ball had gone by on a regular schedule. Van Doren would make his way across the road at the earliest possible moment.

Rosalind, Viola, Cordelia, and Juliet would peer at him and question him and then step back and examine him again.

Beatrice would finally steal him off to her father's library, or they would ride out to the park, or they would visit Lackington & Allen and get lost in the winding corridors of books.

More than several hairpins were somehow lost during these activities.

They even encountered Conbatten one day in the park, they in a barouche and he atop his horse.

"I have heard congratulations are in order," the duke said to Van

Doren.

"Thank you, Your Grace. And as to anything that…was said, or hinted at…well…"

"Let us not revisit any odd conversations that may have occurred between us. Or between you and Lord Harveston."

"You are very kind, Duke," Beatrice said.

The duke laughed and said, "Oh, I am not sure it is kindness. The Benningtons have been endlessly entertaining this season. As I understand there is a whole line of sisters behind you, Lady Beatrice, I anticipate more amusements to come."

"I am afraid you may be disappointed. My sisters will be far more sensible than I have been."

"I will pray you are mistaken," the duke said, tipping his hat and riding off.

Now, the wedding breakfast had been laid and Beatrice watched as Juliet rose with a framed paper in hand.

"I composed this ode specially for Beatrice's wedding breakfast," Juliet said, "considering what I knew at the time. It's called Ode to the Mysterious Gentleman."

Tortured man, you have arrived!
I knew it from my gentle sighs!
Take heart my love, I will not die
Our life together is terribly nigh!

Juliet handed the frame to Beatrice. "It's less good now that I know who it's about."

"I thought it was pretty good," Van Doren said.

"You thought no such thing," Viola said.

"I'll never believe you thought it was good," Juliet said.

"I can think it was good if I want to," Van Doren said. "I have a mind to hang it in the drawing room in Faversham Hall."

"You never will," Rosalind said.

"I am determined to do so," Van Doren said.

Beatrice suppressed her laughter. Van Doren had taken to positively confounding her sisters by constantly taking unpredictable tacks.

In truth, he was far more unpredictable than she'd ever imagined. After all his lecturing over the years, it turned out he did not give a toss for how bad she was at managing household accounts. She had further apprised him of her less than stellar menu planning and that she could never be counted on to keep the servants going in the right direction. He didn't care about any of it.

"I have begun to believe that we can no longer predict what Lord Van Doren will do or say next," Miss Mayton said.

Tattleton had filled everyone's champagne coupe, though Juliet's and Cordelia's with only a half glass.

"Van Doren has surprised us all," Darden said. "Except, possibly, me."

"Now brother," Rosalind asked, "you must tell me outright if the YBC is to set about attempting to manage my season as you have done for Beatrice."

"I have not the least intention of it," Darden said. "There is no Van Doren in your life that needs a prodding forward."

"I should hope not," Juliet said.

"That would be rather a lot," Cordelia said.

"There cannot be two of them," Viola said, her tone hinting that she was rather fearful that there might be.

"I am here. And can hear you," Van Doren said.

Darden raised his glass. "To Beatrice and Van Doren."

The breakfast went on merrily for over an hour. Much discussion was had regarding the wedding trip. They were to stay across the road overnight, and then set off for Venice as Beatrice understood it was the most romantic city on earth.

Van Doren declared if he did not at least once stand up in a gondola, tearing at his hair and threatening to send himself over the side and into the murky waters of the canal he would not be worthy of the trip.

Miss Mayton did, of course, point out how often those sorts of gambits could go terribly, and permanently, awry.

Finally, the looks exchanged between husband and wife could not fail to be understood by everybody.

The family walked the couple to the front doors, the earl kissed his daughter, and they were off. They ran across the wide avenue of Portland Place, dodging a carriage as they went.

Genroy had been on the lookout for the viscount and his bride, and had the doors open at their approach.

"Lady Van Doren," he said, "welcome."

Beatrice thrilled at the address. Lady Van Doren.

"Come, Viscountess," her lord said, and they ran up the stairs together, scandalizing the servants.

Of course, once the bedchamber doors closed, Beatrice was rather scandalized herself.

What a man he was, with his shirt off. She'd thrown no end of handkerchiefs in the pond over the years to see if he would take it off and dive in, though he never had.

He had her in her arms. "I do not like to crease your dress," he whispered.

"There's nothing to be done about it," Beatrice said, not caring a jot for her dress.

"Oh yes there is," he said.

And so, Viscountess Van Doren discovered just how interesting it could be to have a dress off, rather than on.

CHAPTER TWENTY-ONE

ON THE NIGHT of his wedding, Matthew supposed he ought to have been stern with his servants and inform them that they were to stop their smirking at once.

He did not do it, though. They were all so clearly delighted with Lady Van Doren and tiptoeing around that first night so as not to disturb.

They had left the wedding breakfast to go just across the road and then scandalized the household by not even stopping to properly introduce the new viscountess to the servants before they ran up the stairs.

It could not have been helped, of course.

They had stayed up there for hours, only coming down when they really thought they must and not looking very well put together at that.

Lynette was to come on the wedding trip to dress Beatrice, but she would not arrive to the house until morning and so Matthew had done his best with the array of buttons involved in his lady's gown.

Finally, and disheveled, they had come down for dinner. The staff were all red-faced and he supposed he was too.

Shrimps and Oyster had at least provided a distraction from it. The dog escaped the kitchens and bounded up the stairs to discover what might be on the dining table. Shrimps was shortly behind, wailing in anticipation of being thrown to the road on account of it.

The boy and the dog were speedily whisked away in what was becoming a routine in the household.

He and Beatrice had not stayed downstairs for long, just enough time to eat and take a bottle of wine back up with them.

Now, they were in Venice, lazing the days away and lingering over dinner.

They had composed all sorts of ambitious plans for their wedding trip to the city, and absolutely none of it had been attained. They had not gone to the theater or gambled or shopped for art. They had not toured the museums, or even got themselves on a gondola to see the sights.

Rather, they lounged in their rented palazzo on the Grand Canal, breakfasting on a terrace and watching the boats glide by and then attempting to go out but never getting there.

It was as if a lifetime of tension and attraction had burst forth between them and they were both helpless in the face of it.

Lynette and Marcus did their very best to ignore what was in front of them. As they had both come on the trip to dress the viscount and his viscountess, they found they had far more time on their hands than they would have anticipated.

Beatrice had not the first idea of how they were to account for themselves when they returned home. What should they say of Venice? *Oh, Venice? Did I mention we had a lovely set of rooms?*

It was one such sunny morning in the city, with the warm breezes blowing Beatrice's already mussed hair even more so. The housekeeper looking after them had laid out a coffee service and a plate of pastries brought in from Caffè Florian on the terrace's small mosaic table. The poor lady seemed well aware of their habits and looking very much as if she'd rather *not* be aware of them.

"Rosalind's season is next year," Beatrice said, pouring the strong coffee into small cups. "I am very much hoping Conbatten is disappointed, and it all goes very smoothly."

"We shall see," Matthew said, his bare foot rubbing her leg beneath her dressing gown. "It might very well depend on whether or not Rosalind still believes in Count Tulerstein, Gregorio, and the Transylvanian fellow, among others."

Beatrice smiled. "Perhaps my aunt has exaggerated some facts about her romantic encounters on the continent, but certainly most of it must be true."

"Must it?" Matthew asked.

"I hope so," Beatrice said, laughing. "Miss Mayton has put romance in my heart and you will not get it out again."

"Nor do I wish to," he said, taking Beatrice's hand. "Somehow, it's been put into mine too."

"It is a nice thought, is it not?" Beatrice asked. "That we can go forward as romantic lunatics forevermore?"

"Oddly, it is."

Beatrice raised her cup of coffee. "Here is to my aunt, and all her dead gentlemen."

Matthew raised his own. "To Miss Mayton, the spinster in widow's weeds. Now, we ought to finish our breakfast and go out."

"Oh, yes, we really ought to go out."

"Though, I doubt we will go out."

"I believe you may be right."

⁂

UNBEKNOWNST TO ANY of the Benningtons, their three-day caravan to London had left an impression on at least one person outside of their own entourage. Miss Jane Austen had written an account of their meeting to her sister Cassandra shortly after it had occurred at The Angel in Basingstoke.

What an amusing evening we had two nights past. A lady named Miss Mayton told us a harrowing story, all of which I am certain was invented and all of which I will relay when next we meet. I will only say this, while it was poor Gregorio accused of pride, I rather think the moniker better suited to a particular Lord Van Doren at the table, who appeared to be at once disdainful of, and in love with, Lady Beatrice Bennington.

In any case, Gregorio's ridiculous story (and I cannot believe it to be true) has inspired me to some changes to First Impressions and so I must at least thank the Benningtons for that. I can never, I admit, thank them for Ode to a Farmer's Fence or The Terrible Goings-On of Montclair Castle. Though, on second thought, the terrible goings-on in that castle may prove instructive to my own efforts at novel writing, by way of what not to do.

What a delightfully absurd family the Benningtons are, I do wonder how they will make out in London. I am ashamed to admit that I will never know, as they did offer to correspond, but I claimed I was emigrating to America.

Now, I have frittered away much paper in avoiding why I have really written. I must acquaint you with a more serious matter, or perhaps not so serious once I have distance from it. I did a rather ghastly thing. I accepted Mr. Bigg-Wither and then cried all night and called it off the following morning. That, as you can imagine, is prompting my early departure from this house. I accepted him out of sense and then rejected him out of sensibility and so now you know your sister is an unreliable and flighty creature.

While Miss Austen's sister no doubt looked forward to hearing of the Benningtons and the unlucky Gregorio, and perhaps shuddered to hear of Mr. Bigg-Wither, Beatrice and Matthew made their way back to Somerset.

Beatrice did feel some trepidation upon taking on the mantle of mistress and managing a household. It was one thing for Van Doren to claim that he did not care if she could add up two farthings together, and another for him to see the result of it.

Fortunately, Faversham Hall's housekeeper, Mrs. Wells, had been thoroughly briefed by the viscount on what she might expect. Mrs. Wells was fully prepared to allow Beatrice to take the reins as much or as little as she liked.

It would turn out that this was never a very steady thing. There were times Beatrice found the household practicalities a bore and Mrs. Wells ran the place on her own. There were other times, though, when Beatrice threw herself into it.

Each time she was with child, her mind turned inward to the house and its doings—the outside world became nothing to her. Van Doren claimed she was a dove feathering her nest and that was precisely how she felt at such moments.

The nursery must be repainted, new curtains hung, rugs hauled outside and beaten, floors scrubbed, and perfectly clean linen laundered once more.

Beatrice had always been competent enough at embroidery but had thought of it as just something to pass the time. When there was a baby on the way though, she was rarely seen without her sewing basket. Things must be made and drawers must be filled.

Her sisters had of course been amazed to hear of Van Doren tearing at his hair and threatening a violence to himself at Beatrice's ball. They had been in full agreement that this sort of passionate intemperance could not last. Not with Van Doren.

It did last, though.

Beatrice sometimes thought of Van Doren as a dam whose walls had been breached. Once the flood came, there was little hope of damming it up again and she was glad of it.

There was no care too small to take for the viscountess and he got wonderfully growly if Beatrice were somehow inconvenienced. She had once caught the footmen laughing as they viewed him out a window being terrifically stern on the drive with the farmer's wife who supplied them with strawberry jam. It was Beatrice's favorite and apparently there had been some mutterings from the kitchens that they were running low.

As Van Doren paced and lectured that he would pay the woman double to take all of her jam next season, and the poor woman did her best to control her own laughter, the footmen snorted at the sight of it.

Genroy had finally discovered them and chased them away, but Beatrice thought she detected a smirk on the butler's lips too.

The servants were equally amused one day to catch sight of their master carrying a very heavily pregnant viscountess up the drive.

All that had actually happened was their carriage wheel had broken a mile back and though Beatrice was perfectly capable of walking, Van Doren would not hear of it.

The coachman suggested they stay with the carriage and he would go for the second carriage but Van Doren would not hear of that either. The heat would be far too much for Lady Van Doren.

Beatrice had been convinced he would expire before they ever got to the house, as with a baby so close to arriving, she was not exactly a feather.

He'd got her home, though, and she'd not walked one step of it.

That was Van Doren all over. Once he determined to do a thing, he did it.

He'd made the firm decision to be a lovesick lunatic and he would not be turned from his purpose.

Her father and Darden seemed to have believed Van Doren had a passionate heart in him all along and adjusted to this new way of going on far faster than any of her sisters did.

Beatrice and her viscount would ride to Westmont House for dinner of an evening, going through the small wood and following the trail Van Doren had worn in over the years.

The earl would sit comfortably in the drawing room and say something like, "Rosalind, do move that fire screen so that Beatrice is not chilled. You know how Van Doren gets about these things."

The viscount would nod gravely at his father-in-law and then watch closely to see that it was done.

Darden, on one of his rare visits, might say, "Van Doren, what's this I hear about you lecturing Mrs. Ramfeld on the amount of strawberry jam you require and how last season's delivery had fallen short of the mark?"

Van Doren would be wonderfully gruff and say, "Beatrice prefers it to all others."

Her sisters were mystified over this new Van Doren. Beatrice was not, though. The truth was, it had nothing to do with jam. He preferred *her* to all others, and she him.

While Van Doren never bothered to lecture her more on any subject, that did not stop him from delivering sage advice to Rosalind, Viola, Cordelia, and Juliet.

Beatrice had lost count of how many odes Juliet had written about Lord Scoldy-Breeches.

Scold them he might, but the sisters still had Miss Mayton and her tragic past on their side. That lady had not been at all put off by the unforeseen events of the season.

Miss Mayton continued in her widow's weeds, filled her time with reminiscing about all her many lost loves, and prepared Rosalind for her own romantic adventure.

Both Rosalind and Miss Mayton were firmly agreed that it was to be nothing like Beatrice's own. How could it be when she'd gone and married Van Doren of all people?

Rosalind had not been blind to how Beatrice had made out, and as she did consider herself a very practical person, she had made some firm decisions.

The most important revelation she'd had was that Beatrice's list of requirements had been much too extensive. Rosalind had thought long and hard about the single quality that would be absolutely required from her one true love and she'd settled on it.

He must be courageous. Her gentleman was to embody bravery in every possible manner. He must be physically strong and daring. He must be always scanning the horizon, lest there be any danger approaching his one true love, which would be her.

Preferably, he would wear his courageous heart on his sleeve so all might behold his devotion.

Whether that courageous fellow had any idea of what was to be required of him remains to be seen.

The End

About the Author

By the time I was eleven, my Irish Nana and I had formed a book club of sorts. On a timetable only known to herself, Nana would grab her blackthorn walking stick and steam down to the local Woolworth's. There, she would buy the latest Barbara Cartland romance, hurry home to read it accompanied by viciously strong wine, (Wild Irish Rose, if you're wondering) and then pass the book on to me. Though I was not particularly interested in real boys yet, I was *very* interested in the gentlemen in those stories—daring, bold, and often enraging and unaccountable. After my Barbara Cartland phase, I went on to Georgette Heyer, Jane Austen and so many other gifted authors blessed with the ability to bring the Georgian and Regency eras to life.

I would like nothing more than to time travel back to the Regency (and time travel back to my twenties as long as we're going somewhere) to take my chances at a ball. Who would take the first? Who would escort me into supper? What sort of meaningful looks would be exchanged? I would hope, having made the trip, to encounter a gentleman who would give me a very hard time. He ought to be vexatious in the extreme, and *worth* every vexation, to make the journey worthwhile.

I most likely won't be able to work out the time travel gambit, so I will content myself with writing stories of adventure and romance in my beloved time period. There are lives to be created, marvelous gowns to wear, jewels to don, instant attractions that inevitably come with a difficulty, and hearts to break before putting them back together again. In traditional Regency fashion, my stories are clean—the action happens in a drawing room, rather than a bedroom.

As I muse over what will happen next to my H and h, and wish I were there with them, I will occasionally remind myself that it's also nice to have a microwave, Netflix, cheese popcorn, and steaming hot showers.

Come see me on Facebook! @KateArcherAuthor

Printed in Great Britain
by Amazon